Also by Gae Polisner

THE PULL OF GRAVITY
THE SUMMER OF LETTING GO
THE MEMORY OF THINGS

GAE POLISNER

In Sight of Stars

WEDNESDAY BOOKS
NEW YORK

IN SIGHT OF STARS. Copyright © 2018 by Gae Polisner. All rights
reserved. Printed in the United States of America. For information,
address St. Martin's Press, 175 Fifth Avenue, New York, N.Y. 10010.

www.wednesdaybooks.com
www.stmartins.com

Designed by Anna Gorovoy

The Library of Congress Cataloging-in-Publication Data is available
upon request.

ISBN 978-1-250-14383-9 (hardcover)
ISBN 978-1-250-14385-3 (ebook)

Our books may be purchased in bulk for promotional, educational,
or business use. Please contact your local bookseller or the Macmillan
Corporate and Premium Sales Department at 1-800-221-7945, extension
5442, or by email at MacmillanSpecialMarkets@macmillan.com.

First Edition: March 2018

10 9 8 7 6 5 4 3 2 1

For Annmarie, who read chapter by chapter, draft by draft.
Because Klee was always your favorite.

And, for all who suffer and can't see the stars through the dark.

For my part I know nothing with any certainty.
but the sight of the stars makes me dream.

—VINCENT VAN GOGH

a splash quite unnoticed
this was
Icarus drowning

—WILLIAM CARLOS WILLIAMS,
"LANDSCAPE WITH THE FALL OF ICARUS"

Even before I push the fucking door open, I know.

Sarah is in there, moving in slow motion.

I head toward her, desperate to tell her, to reach out. To hear her tell me it will all be okay.

But, something's not right.

The silhouette of her body.

The cadence of arms and limbs

The pain is swift and excruciating.

I cry out, but no sound comes. I back up and turn to go.

I knew she couldn't help me.

She told me she isn't the one.

Someone—not Sarah—calls my name, says something obnoxious, and I freeze.

That douchebag Abbott.

I should hurt him, but no.

I don't give a shit. Screw him. Screw all of them.

I'm done with this place. Done with my mother. With Sarah. With Northhollow.

I jam my hands in my pockets and move fast toward the door, but Sarah yells to Abbott and he follows me.

My fingers strike metal in my pocket.

"Hey, man . . ."

Leave me alone!

I don't know why I do it. Pull it out. Brandish it in front of me.

I won't use it. At least not on him.

Show her. Show her how bad you hurt.

I reach up and slash.

The air grows cold and dizzying.

"Holy fuck! What the hell, Alden?"

I lie down on the cool tile floor.

This pain will make that pain stop.

"Alden, what . . . ?" Sarah stands over me, eyes filled with fear. I close mine against hers, as footsteps rush down the hall.

"What did you do? What did you do?" she whispers. Warm liquid runs down my neck to the floor.

Everything grows spotty.

Sirens drift in, soft, then screaming, pulsing red behind my closed lids. The ceiling grows farther away.

The door opens, and air rushes in.

Chatter, laughter.

(Someone is fucking laughing at me.)

More lights. A girl's voice. Not Sarah's.

"Jesus Christ. It's so not funny, man."

The sounds and faces swirl, blue and yellow, obfuscating, suffocating my brain.

Things come out of sequence. More footsteps. More voices. A bright, intense white in my eyes.

"Turn off that fucking light, asshole!"

Time slips.

It's not even now.

Someone says, "Look here. Look at me, son."

Someone says, "What the fuck happened here?"

Someone says, "Get away. He wasn't doing nothing. Leave him alone!"

The light flashes through both my eyes again.

"Turn it off! Please . . ."

Darker. *Better.*

I didn't expect so much blood.

Quiet.

Nothing.

"Klee?"

My mother's voice.

I close my eyes, blocking her out.

I didn't mean to do this. I'm not like him . . .

"You rest. I'll come back in the morning."

The tap of heels disappearing down a corridor.

Doors open and close.

I try to sleep, but strange voices wail and moan.

Wheels squeak on a linoleum floor.

A shade opens. *Daylight.*

A nurse smiles at me, eyes crinkled, half her face hidden in the flood of sunshine.

"How you feeling, hon?"

I shake my head. "*I didn't mean . . .*" but my words fail, crumbs stuck in cotton, buried under stone.

But I didn't . . . I wasn't trying to . . . It's something I need them to know.

"We've got you covered, hon," the nurse says, that one eye winking. Then another sharp stick, and the colors swirl some more.

Dusk. Heavy lidded. A toxic viridian green.

I'm in a dim, dusty studio. I squint in the low, filtered light.

Is this real or a dream?

"No matter. Come here. It needs a touch of Veronese?"

A man stands before me at an easel. Red beard, straw hat The canvas is covered in sunflowers. But the colors are wrong, and his beaker overflows. He dips his brush and swirls it till the water turns cloudy and crimson.

I reach out, knock it away, spilling the liquid to the floor. Violent red splatters across a shower door.

I cry out and a nurse appears. I feel the pinprick stick, swallow pills down, and the water runs clear again.

"Klee, it's me. Are you feeling any better?" My mother's voice, high and false, drifts in again.

I roll my head away, stare out a dirty window. The man from the studio is outside. His brush moves methodically over a canvas.

Wheat fields arise, vast and swirling. Oceans of golden waves. The sky lightens, electrifies blue mountains that hum beneath the glow of a yellow orb sun.

The man strolls, head down, straw hat shadowing his beard. Scythe in hand, he slices his way through the tall stalks.

On the sill: a crow lands. One, then another, and another. Beyond the sill, the field fills with them: black crows watching, waiting. A noise startles, setting off a frenetic flapping of wings. Dissonant static in my ears.

"Klee, sweetheart. Are you okay?" My mother again, concerned. "I'd like to get you out of here . . ."

A nurse: "Excuse me, Mrs. Alden. Best if I get in there. There you go, kiddo—"

Sarah.

Flashes of light.

A goddamned knife in my hand . . .

"Hold steady, son. Atta boy. Much better. You'll see. We're going to move you now."

Sun rises on morning. Starlings whistle and trill. The red-bearded man strolls through a manicured garden. A black cat scampers in figure eights around his legs.

A woman appears in the doorway of a white house with a blue roof. She calls for him. A crow watches from the roof, but the man doesn't answer, and the cat disappears.

The crow shrieks and takes off, and the sky shifts to a brilliant shade of madder red.

The man sits. The yard is peaceful and still.

He lays his hat in the grass and raises a pistol to his head.

Day ?—Morning?

"Klee?"

Dad and I are walking through SoHo. The day is bright and brisk. Our breath puffs out in front of us like steam from the street vents.

"Klee?" *Not my mother's voice. The wrong pronunciation.* I turn my head back to my dad.

We pass the familiar streets of the village—Broome, Spring, Prince—and head north on West Broadway. Clouds rush overhead, and the sky turns stormy and overcast.

Sarah is with me now, snow falling. Snowflakes catch in her black hair, white stars that shimmer and melt away.

She twirls toward me, smiling. Dad laughs and Sarah takes my hand.

Except, no. That's not right.

We're not in SoHo, or uptown.

There's no snow.

No Sarah.

And, Dad is gone.

"Klee? Are you here with me?"

Just me and this woman, in this room.

I scratch at my ear.

"Try not to do that," she says. I look up at the mottled ceiling tiles. "Can you talk a bit now, Klee?"

My name. She keeps saying it wrong. Phonetically, with the long-*e* sound.

I look up at her and drop my hand.

The woman is middle aged, familiar, with her bright cheeks and dark frizzy hair. Slightly overweight. She's told me her name before.

Andersen.

No. Wrong.

Alvarez.

Dr. Alvarez.

"Are you able to tell me anything?" she asks.

About what?

"About Sarah, Klee. About what happened?"

Right. That's why I'm here. Because of Sarah. Because of what I did. I shake my head. I don't want to think about that now.

"About you, then. Whatever you want," she says.

Art, I blurt, struggling to focus. There's a high-pitched ringing in my ears. *I met Sarah in art class. Is that what you wanted to know?*

"Sure," she says, but when I say Sarah's name, it breaks into a million soda bubbles that float to my brain.

Time slips again.

I shift my eyes to her wall, to the framed print there. White house, blue roof. Manicured lawn. Van Gogh's *Daubigny's Garden.*

It's because of that print that I stay.

"Really? I never liked it much."

The man with the straw hat squints at the painting and rubs his red beard thoughtfully. "It's not my best. Painted it on a goddamned tea cloth. And what's with the fucking cat?" He heads toward the house, gun in hand.

"Klee?" (Long *e*.) My eyes shift to Dr. Alvarez.

"Stay here with us!" The woman in the doorway calls.

A crow lands in a tall pine and the black cat skitters across the lawn.

The man turns. His finger twitches on the trigger, and the cat disappears.

"Tell me more about that," she says.

My eyes dart up.

Dr. Alvarez.

I rub my ear, alarmed.

I don't feel so great, I say.

"I know. I'm sorry. Hopefully I can help you with that. Tell me what you were saying about art class . . ."

What was I saying? I don't even know . . .

"About your girlfriend—"

She's not my girlfriend.

I've snapped at her. I squeeze my eyes shut. Tears leak out, and the soda bubbles pop inside my head.

"Klee, let me try this." She lifts a page or two on her clipboard and says, "So, you're a senior at Northhollow High, planning to major in art next fall? And you only transferred there this school year. Before that, you were at a private high school in the city. Is that right?"

I nod, and try to ignore the man.

"Your mother says it was your girlfr—a friend, Sarah, that went with you to the hospital." She flips a page. "And, it says here you have applied to go to the School of the Museum of Fine Arts in Boston." My eyes shift to hers. "I'd like to help you get well and get there."

I squinch my eyes shut tight, but more tears slip.

"We need to start somewhere," she says.

Sarah is singing and crawling toward me on her knees.

Her voice is breathy and sweet.

"Every cloud must have a silver lining . . ."

It's a hallucination, I think, but it seems real. Her eyes are warm and welcoming. I wedge my hand under my thigh so I don't reach out to her.

"Tell me your dreams, babe," she whispers.

I shake my head and a crow lands on the back of Dr. Alvarez's chair, turns a beady eye on me. It pivots, and I blink as it makes its way, talons tapping, impossibly up the wall.

I focus on Sarah's voice instead.

"Wait until the sun shines through
Smile, my honey dear
While I kiss away each tear . . ."

She moves slowly, her dark hair falling over her big blue eyes.

"Or else I'll be melancholy too."

I squirm as she gets closer, hoping I don't lose it. Sometimes, all I have to do is look at her. She slides her lips up my leg, her wide eyes watching, her tongue tracing the front of my jeans.

I close my eyes, and she stops and sits back.

"What the fuck, Klee? Are you crying?"

I shake my head, but she disappears anyway.

"Klee, you need to try to talk. I didn't want to push you yesterday during intake. Not while your mother was here."

Jesus. Yesterday? I was here with my mother yesterday.

The memory barrels in.

"Klee?"

She calls me Klee again, the wrong way. Like everyone else does when they meet me. It's Klee with a long-*a* sound. A Swiss name, after the painter.

Clay, as in "play," "say," and "day."

The mantra my mother taught me swims through my brain. More bubbles pop and fizz.

I ball my fists so I'll leave my ear alone.

Dr. Alvarez reaches into the drawer of the side table next to her and says, "Here, this might help." She rummages, before tossing a small purple stress ball to me. My hands move to catch it, but my reflexes are off. It bounces off my knuckles into my lap.

"It could be the sedatives," she says, watching me. "Or the painkillers. Those can really make you feel out of it. I'll talk to Dr. Ram. Your dose may be too high. There's a lot of trial and error at this point. It's common to take a few days to get adjusted."

I don't often take much more than Advil. I pick up the ball and squeeze it. It's a sales freebie advertising some pharmaceutical company or drug. Sand on the inside, stretched purple rubber on the outside, like a balloon. Stamped-on white letters read, **Rimmovin 5 (zopiclone 5 mg)** and below that, smaller, **"Sometimes a cigar is just a cigar."—Sigmund Freud**.

I must laugh a little because she says, "If you like it, keep it. I have plenty more."

I squeeze the ball harder and focus my brain.

Art class, I finally say again. *I met Sarah there.*

The crow crawls down the wall, hopping onto the table in Tarantoli's brightly-lit room, inches from Sarah's bent head.

She works across from me. Her hair spills onto her paper like a shiny black waterfall, and her hand moves the charcoal in tight gray lines.

Her drawing is of a girl on a bed looking out a window. *Girl in Repose,* she's named it.

Our drawing titles are written on a strip of masking tape on the table between us. Tarantoli makes us title our work so she can refer to them.

"The title was pretentious," the crow says. "She must have read one like it somewhere, called it that because she wanted to impress you."

I wave my hand to shoo the bird.

Sarah looks up at me and smiles.

Her drawing is decent, but safe.

"You can't be an artist and be safe," I say.

She wrinkles her nose at her paper, like she's considering. I can't take my eyes off of her.

She's the first thing I've been interested in at Northhollow.

"Because she's beautiful," the crow says, but that's not the only reason. There's something different about her. Open. Light. She stands out. You can tell she doesn't give a shit about anything.

I stare at her hair, then at her hand, then I reach out and trace the strands with my charcoal.

"Hey! What the fuck, Alden?" Her eyes search mine, then dart back to my marks on her paper. "What the hell is your deal?"

I yank my hand back, burnt, but it's too late, several kids have jerked their heads around. And, I'm already an alien for showing up here for senior year.

"Sorry, I didn't mean to . . ."

Tarantoli makes her way across the room. "Is there a problem here?"

There's a pause, then Sarah shakes her head. She leans in, retracing my lines, making them stand out darker on her paper.

"No, actually," she says, "it's better this way. We're good."

It's Sarah who says we are good.

"Can you tell me more?"

I shake my head. My mouth is dry, my words, thick and hard like concrete. The crow caws from somewhere I can't see.

The man's straw hat hangs motionless on the back of Dr. Alvarez's door.

She narrows her eyes and studies me, then presses the silver clamp at the top of her clipboard and slides out a sheet of paper. A form of some sort, flimsy, piss yellow. She turns it over, squints, scanning it. I can't make out what it says.

I bet it says how crazy I am. What I did. Maybe it says what happened with my dad.

Blood everywhere . . .

I block that out and try to focus. If I don't focus I'm not going to get better. I won't be able to see Sarah again.

"Idiot! Sarah's done with you," the crow calls. I can't see the dumb bird, but I know it's him.

But he's right. Sarah is done with me. Sarah is the reason I'm in here.

No. Not Sarah. My mother.

My mother is the real reason I'm here.

My mother, I ask suddenly. *That was yesterday?* I need to hold on to the facts so I can get out of here.

"Yes," Dr. Alvarez says. "We met briefly yesterday, Monday,

to do intake. Do you remember?" I nod, but I'm not sure. "Dr. Ram wanted to give you another day to rest and heal and get stronger. Get adjusted to your meds. Your mother has given her consent for me to work with you. This is *your* therapy. What you say here, stays here, like Las Vegas." She winks, and I try to smile at the butchered slogan. The skin on my face feels wonky. "Unless you tell me otherwise," she says.

Okay, yeah. I get it.

"You don't get it," the crow says. I see him now. He's wearing the straw hat and struts blindly, drunkenly, across Dr. Alvarez's rug. I watch until he disappears under her desk.

I do, I whisper in his direction. *I'm just trying to hold on to things.*

But I can't because it all slips.

Everything is liquid through gauze.

It's not Klee, I blurt, trying to focus on something solid. *My name,* I explain, *It's pronounced Clay, long a. After the famous Swiss painter, Paul Klee.*

"Oh, my goodness, I'm so sorry. I knew that. Your mother mentioned . . . You should have corrected me sooner." Dr. Alvarez looks away, embarrassed. "I'm so sorry, Klee." She pronounces it again, emphasizing the long *a*. "Now I'm going to have those *ee*'s stuck in my head."

It's okay, I say. *I'm used to it.*

I keep my gaze glued on her. I don't want to see the crow. I don't want to see anyone but her. She said she'd help. Help me to get out of here.

"No, of course it's not okay," Dr. Alvarez says. "I'll get it right from now on. Anyway, your mother is welcome back, to sit in, any time you want her to."

I don't want her to!

I close my eyes against all of it, against the memories that want to rush in—of my mother. Of Sarah. Of fucking Dunn's house in the rain. But it's too late. They slam in on me, knocking the wind from my chest.

Sarah, and Abbott, and all the blood.

Someone laughing at the door.

The images ambush me. I double over, head between my knees. Dr. Alvarez leans across the table.

"I didn't mean to upset you." She puts her hand on my shoulder. "We won't have her here unless you want her. Not until you're ready. Your choice. I promise. Nobody here is going to make you do anything. This is a safe haven. We want you to get better, okay?"

I nod. *I didn't want to . . . I didn't mean to . . .* I say, but keep my head down, waiting for the nausea to pass. Waiting for the crow to land again. Waiting for the field to fill with them, wings flapping, and the man with the gun in his hand.

But they don't return, and he doesn't return, and the moment passes and I can sit up again.

I open my eyes. Beneath me, a patterned burgundy rug.

"Do you want to take a break?" Dr. Alvarez asks.

I nod. *Yeah, okay.*

Everything is hypercolorful and liquid.

I'm a little queasy. I think I need a drink, is all.

"Sure," she says. "Let's get you some water. It's going to get better, Klee, I promise you that. From the sound of things, you've been through a lot. And it could be all the medication, too. I'll talk to Dr. Ram this afternoon and see if that's adding to the problem. Some of the stronger painkillers can wreak havoc."

"See?" the crow says. "You may not have meant it, but you clearly have a problem—*are* the problem. And now you're stuck in the Ape Can."

And it hits me: That's where I am. The Adolescent Psychiatric Center at Northhollow. The place the kids here all call the Ape Can.

". . . antidepressants, too," Dr. Alvarez is saying. "So, it's common for the doses to need adjusting." I nod again and try to keep the room from reeling. "Meanwhile, there's no rush. Try to relax. Take your time. And, breathe."

But I can't breathe because Sarah is crawling through my head.

I'd like to get a drink of water.

"Right, of course. Let's go get you one."

Okay, yes. My voice sounds too loud, and hoarse. It feels like days since it's been used. *I'd like to walk. Stretch my legs.*

"Perfectly okay. We don't want you to feel like a prisoner here. I know it can be scary, but we're here to help you, Klee." She walks to the office door, pulls it open, and stands in the frame. She points out and says, "Go through the waiting area the nurse walked you through, do you remember? Veer left when you reach the hall. Right there you'll find a fountain, and some cups if you need one. Do you want me to come with you?"

No. I'm okay.

I feel better now that I'm walking.

"Yes," she calls. "Like that. Cross through and make a left when you reach the hall." I feel her waiting, watching, but at least I'm in motion, away from her.

The hallway walls are Ace bandage beige. A hideous fish mural stretches half the length of the far wall, garish in primary colors. Cartoon fish swim about as if painted for five-year-olds by five-year-olds.

At the far edge of the waiting area, I stop in my tracks.

A girl sits in the corner, her back to me. Long, shiny black hair.

Sarah!

I must make a noise, because the girl turns and stares. Not Sarah. Not even close. The girl is young, Asian, pretty. She looks nothing like Sarah at all.

I find my breath, make my legs move again toward the fountain, but I feel clammy and my whole body shivers. The bright fluorescents overhead flicker and buzz, creating an insistent drumbeat in my ears. The air grows thick and swirling, as if I'm slogging through a blizzard to get there.

When I finally reach the fountain, I put my lips into the stream and drink.

I'm so cold and parched.

I feel like I'll never stop drinking.

I push my face farther down into the stream. The water shoots up, filling my mouth and my nose.

Sarah. My father . . .

The shower . . .

The drumbeat grows louder and louder.

The phone calls.

The fighting.

The blood.

My mother, packing our things—

I drink more, but can't steady myself. The blizzard takes over my brain.

"I don't want us to move, Mom. Jesus, not now. They say a year. He's barely dead three months."

I'm talking to her back. What else is new? She's in her favorite pink Chanel suit, leaning in toward her vanity mirror. Putting on lipstick, getting ready for an appointment with the broker. My mother is expert at this: managing her same mundane shit even after the world has fallen apart.

A cockroach after the apocalypse.

Her eyes go to mine in the mirror. I get that this is what *she* wants, but can't she wait one more year?

"Seriously, let me just graduate and get out of here. One measly school year and you're rid of me, too," I beg.

Her eyes flash soundless daggers, as only my mother can throw.

But I threw one first.

She recaps the lipstick and drops it into her handbag.

"There's practically a snowstorm out there, Klee. Do you think I want to be doing this? Sometimes . . ." She pauses, then says, "Look, I need to go sign the contracts."

She starts to get up, then sits back down heavily, waits for a moment, and searches for a tissue, which she presses to her lips to blot them.

As I watch her, this memory comes to me from not so long ago, of my father in a suit and tie, watching her as she readies for some formal event. He puts his hands on her shoulders and kisses the top of her head. His gesture is so tender, but she flinches. That's what I remember: how my mother flinches.

"Mom, please . . ."

She cuts me off and stands, determined.

"I've told you this already, Klee. You can stay and finish your senior year here if you need to. Graduate. I'll be okay. Aunt Margaret said you're welcome to stay with her. Then you'll come up and spend the summer with me after graduation. Before you head off to school." I can barely look at her. I've grown to hate her. She knows I'd never leave her alone. Not now. "Before you leave for Boston, for SMFA, in the fall." She gives this last statement a weak smile intended to impart that I have her vote of confidence as far as my art is concerned.

Her voice has softened and she thinks I'm a shoo-in there. I should appreciate that, but instead it makes me furious. Like art is good enough for me, even if she didn't think it was good enough for my father.

"The bottom line is, I don't have a choice here, Klee. They think it best if we sell by May, and close on the Ridge house by

June. As soon as school ends. More families are willing to move at that time. So at least you can finish the school year here." She sighs deeply, as if the choice is out of her hands, as if she's not the one who decided to trade in our whole life, or what's left of it, for a water view up in the boonies. "Either way, I cleared it with Aunt Maggie. She's happy to have you stay with her if you want. She's still a mess, too, so she'd love the company."

I glare at her until she turns back to the mirror. Because, first, there's the implication of the words "still" and "too," as if not being over the death of my father says something weak about my character. Just because she's some sort of fucking Ice Queen who is more than ready to move on. And, second, we both know Aunt Maggie's place isn't a viable option for me to spend an entire school year. She lives in a tiny studio apartment on the Upper West Side. Not exactly an ideal living situation for a seventeen-year-old. Besides, hate her or not, I'm not going to abandon my own mother a few months after her husband died. I'm not going to do that to my dad.

My mother grabs her purse and turns to go. "You could commute. That's an option, too. It's an hour. Hour and a half, tops. It wouldn't be the end of the world."

"Shouldn't the broker come here?" I ask, changing the subject. "Bring *you* the contracts? She's the one about to make a mint off you, right? Shouldn't she be the one pandering?"

"Klee! I don't want to fight over this anymore."

I follow her into the foyer to argue, but she yanks on her coat and bangs the door shut after her.

"Klee?"

Long e, *then whispering.*

"Klee!" *Same voice. Corrected, long* a.

I blink my eyes open.

I'm back in my room, in bed. My new room in the Ape Can, anyway.

"How are you feeling, hon?"

There's a cold cloth on my head. Dr. Alvarez's face looms over me.

"You fainted, that's all. No big deal. I just wanted to make sure you were okay. I'll leave you here with Carole, now. I have another patient . . ." A blond nurse smiles down at me. "We'll pick up fresh tomorrow. By then, Dr. Ram will have come by."

I nod. The fountain comes back to me, the girl with the black hair, the rush of snow swirling down.

How'd I get back in here?

An orderly. He stands near the door. Burly. Strong. "All good now?" he asks. "I can go?"

Carole nods, and he leaves. She stays, hovering over me. "Can you sit up, hon?" Her aqua scrubs with butterflies hurt my eyes. Worse than the cartoon fish.

"Okay, Klee, you're in good hands here," Dr. Alvarez says. "I'll see you tomorrow." She squeezes my foot and leaves. Nurse Carole pulls a rolling bedside table over, and I sit up against the prop of pillows she's situated behind me.

"Well, you look much better now! That's the way." Her voice matches the butterflies, overbright and cheerful, like I'm a child. She slides a food tray over to me. "How about some lunch? If you eat something, it might help."

The tray is the plastic cafeteria kind, a weird salmon color with white speckles. On it is a plate with one of those flat-topped domes covering it—both plastic, the lid, beige with a hole in the center. She lifts it to reveal a sandwich on white bread. Next to that, there's a small paper cup with orange juice, a piece of cling wrap stretched across its top.

"No glass or utensils for obvious reasons," the crow mocks just out of sight.

I'm not suicidal, I want to snap. *I'm not a danger to myself or others.* I've heard them say that, but it's the part nobody understands. I wasn't trying to kill myself. I just wasn't thinking straight. I shouldn't be here. I can go home now.

But I don't actually want to go home.

I focus on the tray. Next to the juice cup is a smaller paper cup, pleated, white, holding a bunch of pills. I grimace. Something yellow oozes out of the sandwich. Something I'm dreading might be egg salad. A wave of nausea rolls through me at the smell.

Nurse Carole wrinkles her nose. "Don't like egg salad? I can get you something else . . . You really should try to eat something. According to your chart, you haven't eaten much since you got here, and Dr. Alvarez says you're having some trouble with your meds. Trust me, you'll feel a whole lot better if you have some food in you. It's hard to handle all that," she nods at the little cup full of pills, "on an empty stomach. Those antipsychotics can wreak havoc your system."

Antipsychotics? What the fuck?

It's okay, I say anyway. *I'll eat it.*

She tilts her chin and offers the too-cheerful smile again. "Do you want me to scrounge you up something else for lunch?"

No. It's fine.

"Okay, good. Before I go—" She glances at her watch, takes my wrist in her hand, and feels for my pulse with her fingers. She presses her lips to indicate I should stay quiet, counts to herself, and drops my arm. "Pulse is good. You feeling better now? Dr. Ram should be in to see you soon."

Yes. Okay.

"Anything else you need before I go?"

No, thanks.

"Books? Magazines?"

Sarah struts across the rocky ledge, stops, posing topless, in just her underpants.

"You think I could be in a magazine, Klee?"

I nod and pull her to me . . .

"You do know there's a whole library down the hall? Has anyone shown you around this place properly? You're welcome to go in and borrow anything we have. You might even find some company in there."

"Give it up, Klee." The crow waggles a wing from the windowsill. The memory of Sarah is gone.

I think I'm good for right now.

"Okay, I get it," Nurse Carole says. "But in case you do—" she gestures at the far wall as if I can see through it—"it's just a few doors down on your right. There are puzzles and games in there, too." I nod. I have a vague recollection of someone pointing it out as they shuffled me down the hall. "Anyway, holler if you need anything. Otherwise, I'll be back later. And, eat."

I will.

"Oh, you need to take these before I go." She rattles the small cup at me, and I frown. I'm still feeling fuzzy and out of it. "Don't worry, hon. One is just an antibiotic for the wound. That one you'll take twice a day. And that other long capsule there? That's just plain old vitamin E. Omega 3. Like fish oil, you know? They've done more and more studies on the benefits of it."

I'm grateful for the information, but, really, at this point, what do I care? I dump them into my mouth and swallow.

When she's gone, I push the tray back and click on the television. I'm not a big TV watcher, but I don't have my other stuff for distraction. No laptops or cell phones allowed. Signs everywhere. They make that very clear.

The midday news is on, no sound. A crew is covering a fire

in downtown Manhattan. Even without the scroll at the bottom of the screen, anyone can tell it's the West Village. Flames lick up from the roof of three-story building; thick gray smoke fills the shot. The camera pans in on a reporter holding a cloth to his nose. He points his mic at a fireman, whose mouth moves soundlessly at me.

I pull the lunch tray over, take the top of the bread off and eat it, nearly gagging at the smell of the egg salad.

Antipsychotics. Jesus.

I get up and walk to the bathroom, trying to avoid my reflection in the wonky plastic mirror over the sink. But it can't be avoided. I look like hell. I don't look like me. My hair is a matted mess, flat on one side, poking up crazy on the other. My eyes are dull, ringed by a shadowed gray-purple. And the bandage on my ear seeps a weird yellow-brown ointment.

I'm an asshole. I just destroyed my fucking life, but whatever.

"Maybe, maybe not," the crow says, so at least he's throwing me a bone.

I take a piss and wash my hands, leaning against the sink to steady myself. I bend in and gulp water from the tap. It's lukewarm and metallic, and tastes like the smell of Lysol that fills my nose. When I right myself, I catch the reflection of the man in the hat with the red beard. He's sitting on the floor of the small doorless shower.

"Don't look, seriously. Just walk out." Another bone tossed by the crow.

I move back into the room and stare at the television. The fire is gone and a newscaster at a desk is laughing and waving her arms, like the news is some kind of comedy. I want the fire back. I want any old glimpse of Manhattan.

I peel off another triangle of bread and force it down with

the rest of the juice, then lie back, helplessly, letting my lids grow heavy and the cyclone take over my brain.

My mother is in the kitchen cooking dinner, my first clue it's only a dream.

The room smells of garlic and onions and sautéed things. I pull out a chair, sit, and watch her. She's humming some cheerful tune.

A manila envelope rests on the table in front of me. I unwind the red string and open it, letting the papers slide out. It's some sort of legal document:

Condominium Unit—Contract of Sale
Consult Your Lawyer before Signing.

I turn the page and read the first paragraph:

```
Contract (the "Contract") for the sale
of the Place you Live (without your
goddamned permission), made as of this
_____ [insert date] day of this
unbelievably terrible year, between the
Ice Queen (your Mother as "Seller") and
Someone You Don't Know and Don't Give a
Crap About (as "Purchaser").
```

I shove the document back in and push the envelope away. A small white rectangle has fallen out. A business card for one Judy Manson, licensed real estate broker. Puffy-faced Judy, with her bleached blond hair and blue eye shadow, smiles smugly from a box in the corner. Salivates for her 5 percent commission.

"One point three million," Judy says, winking. "Not bad at all." She winks at me from the goddamned card.

I look up. "Judy Manson just winked at me. She's salivating, Mom."

My mother whirls at me, hand to forehead, dramatic. "I've told you, Klee, I can't talk about this anymore. I won't. You'll just have to believe me. This is the best thing for us. A fresh start. To get away from all this!" She gestures wildly. "You can stay or you can come with me, but I need to get away from here. I hoped you'd understand."

Her words sting, reverberate.

She pours a glass of water, dumps two aspirin on the counter, and swallows them down, then walks back to the stove in her high-heeled shoes—*click, click, click*—and dumps the rest of the water on the pan. Steam sizzles and rises. She fans the smoke away.

"So much for dinner," I say.

She whirls again. "You don't understand, Klee. I just need to find some grass and trees, and water. Some peace. You don't know . . . I've been through hell, too. You have no idea the hell I've been through."

"*This* is hell," I say. I pull out the contract and toss it on the table, change my mind and rip it into shreds. I toss the pieces in the air and let them rain down, a flutter of expensive confetti.

"I expected more of you," she says. "And, anyway, that's only a copy. The original is already signed."

I don't say more, but she makes this hurt sound anyway, probably because she knows I'll feel sorry for her.

"Don't I deserve to be happy? There's a house—small, cozy—right on the river. It'll be healing for you. I never wanted to raise you in the city . . ."

"I don't want to heal!" I stand, knocking my chair over, kicking the bits of paper away.

"Jesus, Klee. There are things you're not privy to . . . despite what you think . . . you don't know everything." She takes the envelope, waves it twice, and disappears, like Dorothy clicking her ruby shoes.

I stare at the empty space where she was, then walk to the sink to get a drink of water. But when I turn on the tap, the water runs pink, then red, overflowing, filling the whole kitchen with blood.

Day ?—Afternoon

A knock on the door startles me awake.

My mouth is cotton. I'm drenched in sweat.

"Klee Alden?" A tall, thin man, brown-skinned with black hair, glasses, and a white lab coat, enters. He looks vaguely familiar, but I'm not sure.

"Do you remember me? I'm Dr. Ram. I examined you yesterday." He speaks with an accent, his vowels soft and drawn out, his consonants sharp. He pronounces my first name with something between the long *a* and long *e*. *Close enough.* I sit up and he shakes my hand. "How are we doing today?"

I shrug. "Okay, I guess."

He directs me to the edge of the bed, and pulls a blood pressure cuff from his pocket. "You look a little flushed."

"I had a bad dream."

He wraps the cuff around my upper arm, pumps and squeezes, closing his eyes to count. "Good, excellent," he says when he's done. "Dr. Alvarez said you were feeling a little light-headed."

I nod.

"Still?"

"Yeah, a little, but not as much. I mean, it's hard to tell . . . I just woke up."

"Well, good, then. Excellent. I'd like to keep you on this higher dose of the Aripiprazole for now, but I've had them decrease the pain medications. Those tend to be a more likely culprit. And you probably don't need them any longer." I nod again, wondering if I should tell him about the hallucinations. But, I don't want him to think I'm crazier than I must be, because who knows where they'll put me then.

My eyes dart for the crow and the red-bearded man, but thankfully, they're not around.

He undoes the cuff, jams it back in his pocket, and reaches into the opposite one, extracting a penlight.

"Look here," he says, moving the light from right to left, then back again. My eyes follow. "Good," he says. "Any blurred vision?"

Turn off that fucking light, asshole!

I shake my head, dislodge the memory. "No," I say, "I don't think so."

"Excellent, I think we're good for now."

Whatever you say, Doc.

He slips the penlight away, puts his hands on my throat, and gently presses at my glands. His fingers are soft and cold. The cold feels good on my skin.

"Sore throat?"

"No."

"Good."

Right, good.

He looks at me and waits. I look away.

"Are you sleeping at all?"

"Yeah, a lot. But I wake up constantly . . . my dreams are vivid, and weird."

"To be expected. You've been working with Dr. Alvarez." A statement, not a question, so I nod. "Good. Excellent."

I almost laugh. Apparently everything about my situation so far ranges from good to excellent.

He writes something in my chart. Paranoid, I stare hard at his pen.

"Mr. Alden, make sure you eat." He looks down his glasses at me and frowns. "It will help if you keep your stomach full. But for now, I think we should stay the course. Looks like everything is adjusting nicely."

"Okay."

"Let Dr. Alvarez know if you have any additional concerns."

"Right," I say. "I will."

He puts his hands back in his coat pockets and *tsks* at the window beyond me. I twist around to see. Construction equipment has lumbered into view. "A shame," he says, indicating a large excavator that may as well have parked in front of my window. "It's been this way for months. An earache and an eyesore." He shakes his head at the yellow, prehistoric silhouette. "All right, son, I think we're good for now. We'll see how you're feeling tomorrow." The word "son" makes me flinch. "Holler if you need something." He heads toward the door.

"Okay, thank you. I will."

The door closes slowly behind him all but the last few inches.

I lie back down and stare at the excavator, then close my eyes, grateful for its noisy rattle and hum.

Dr. Ram is right: Except for the part where my father is gone and I'm lying here alone in the Adolescent Psychiatric Center at Northhollow missing Sarah so bad I can't breathe, everything is adjusting just fine.

Day ?—Evening

"Come to me my melancholy baby . . ."

The room is dark, and Sarah is crawling again.

"Cuddle up and don't be blue
All your fears are foolish fancies, dear . . ."
I sit up.
Not Sarah. I'm in bed. In the Ape Can.
But there was a noise.
Someone is in my room.
But when I switch on the reading light, the room is empty, the rolling table pushed over, alongside my bed. A note and a two-pack of Yodels sit there.
I pick up the paper and read:

Welcome to APCN.
You're early to bed so I've left something sweet to welcome you.
Hope to chat with you soon.

It's signed:

Sister Agnes Teresa

I pick up the Yodels and turn them in my hand, not trusting if they're real or some looped-up-on-drugs hallucination. Whatever the case, I'm starving, so I rip open the wrapper and scarf them down.

Day 3—Morning

Sunlight streams in the window.
Someone has let the shades up. I'm not usually such a heavy sleeper.
I move my tongue around and glance at the table. The note is there, and I still taste the chocolate in my teeth.
Not a hallucination, then.
Maybe I'm stabilizing. I do feel a little more like me.

Is that a good or a bad thing?

I roll my head to the side and stare out the window. The tree branches sway in a breeze, their shadowed silhouettes dappled cave paintings that play across the canvas of the shades. I sit up and search for the yellow dinosaur, but he's beyond the scope of my view.

Something else I notice now, too: There are no strings or cables on the shades. They lift and lower by touch. *The better not to hang ourselves with.*

A salmon-colored breakfast tray sits on the bedside table next to the note and the empty Yodels wrapper. A too-sweet syrupy smell emanates from under its lid.

What day is it? I count forward from Saturday trying to keep track. *Wednesday, I think. Already Wednesday.*

I swing my legs over the side of my bed, walk to the window, and look out. In the far corner of the courtyard, the yellow excavator hulks, neck extended high, but digger slack-jawed, saw teeth down. A brachiosaurus, time-traveled through history to get here. Just me and a dinosaur, in this place where we don't belong.

But, I do belong, don't I? I did what I did, so I must.

I move my hand to the bandaged itch that's my ear.

Who am I kidding? Of course I belong here.

Beneath the excavator, a trench is being dug. Across from that rests a giant spool of thick black cable.

I'm overwhelmed by the urge to walk outside, climb up into the excavator's cab, and push all its gears and levers, making its jaws plunge down and bite into earth, bringing up chunks of concrete, dirt, and sand.

It occurs to me that I don't know if I'm allowed to leave this place at all, even for a walk. I have no idea what the rules are. I've just been plodding around like some crazier-than-fuck zombie, numb from the shoulders up.

This is my life now. This is what I have to look forward to.

Except, deep inside, I don't believe it. I know I'm not crazy. *At least I don't think I am.*

I stare past the brachiosaurus to the grassy courtyard, to the trees starting to show off their purple-red buds. Technically it's spring, and it's bright and sunny outside. I should get dressed and walk out of here, prove to myself I can. Do something normal for a change.

The thought slams me hard: *I'm not normal. When is the last time I felt like I was?* Was it with Sarah, or not since my father died?

But I did, right? There was a time when I felt happy and normal. I want to go back there, back a year ago—more—back to my city, my home. Back to when I had friends, and had fun.

Back with Cleto and Dan.

"Where'd you find this place?" Dan asks. "It's a chick magnet!"

Dan is hyper, per usual, talking too much, and messing up metaphors. Hopping up and down like an idiot. Fake IDs or not, he's going to get us kicked out before we get in. We've been on this line for an hour, and we're finally getting close to the door.

"Take it down a notch," Cleto says, putting a hand on Dan's shoulder. "I told y'all my cousin works here. But you need to let me do the talking when we get up there. He ain't gonna let us in if you act like a fool." Dan shuts up. He would never listen to me that fast, but he listens to Cleto. Cleto has this power over people. "Y'all need to chill. I know I'm asking a lot of you assclowns. But humor me. Try to seem like you've done this before. Not like you never set foot in no bar." To prove his chillness, Cleto pulls a water bottle from his jacket pocket and swigs some down. It's vodka, not water, we know. But he drinks it down easy, which is part of his charm.

"Don't look at me," I say, holding my hand out for a swig. "I'm just standing here."

Cleto nods. "Right, be like Alden, here. Nice and cool." He hands me the bottle. I take a sip, alcohol burning my throat as I pass it on to Dan.

"Aye, aye, Captain," Dan says. "I'm cool. Swear. Thanks for getting us into this place."

"We ain't in no place yet," Cleto says. "That's the point I'm trying to impress upon y'all."

The place, for the record, is some new kitsch bar down on Sullivan Street called Hi-Ho Silvers! that is frequented by everyone from ironically Teenage Mutant Ninja Turtle T-shirt-clad biker dudes, to stuffed-shirt Wall Street types who want to prove they're something other than that, to the hottest college girls from nearby Cooper Union and NYU. Cleto's cousin said it got popular because Taylor Swift and some of her friends came in one night. We don't usually go for the trendy places, but then again, we don't usually go for the bar scene at all since the fake IDs are a pretty new acquisition. We're not even sure they'll fly. So knowing someone who can put a good word in for us is key. And, according to Cleto, despite the physical heft of the very intimidating bouncers at the door, they're pretty lax about checking IDs.

"So long as you have one," Cleto had told us, "my cousin says he'll make sure we get in. It ain't like they gonna be quizzing y'all, just don't act like no jackasses."

Dan still seems nervous. I am, too. I don't exactly feel like getting kicked to the curb in front of a bunch of people, including girls who may or may not be Taylor Swift's friends. But junior year has been crushing us with its months of SATs, AP exams, and college visits, and we just need to blow off some steam.

I glance at Cleto and try to emulate the way he looks and stands. Cleto was born to do shit like this. Nothing rattles him. He knows how to get anyone to buy what he's selling. I'm guessing it's the southern accent. He's originally from Alabama. His real name is Jared, but we started calling him Cleto after Cletus, the stereotypical hillbilly character from *The Simpsons*. When we first met, he was always going on about how it was his favorite show. He was always quoting it and shit, so we figured he wouldn't get mad.

He didn't. He thought it was so funny, he calls himself Cleto now, too. Like I said, laid back. Take the whole drinking thing. He'll be the first one to tell you he's been drinking since the tender age of ten.

"And, not your fancy liquor store bullshit either," he likes to remind us. "Homemade rotgut hooch. The kind that'll literally singe your nose hairs. You pussies would be dead after one sip." He doesn't drink that much, but still. Sometimes I do kind of worry about him.

Dan passes the water bottle back to Cleto as we move a few spots closer. I fumble for my wallet, trying to figure out if I should leave my fake ID in its clear plastic slot and flash the whole thing, or pull it out in advance.

When we finally reach the head of the line, Cleto flashes his ID and mentions his cousin's name. Dan and I follow suit, and the bouncer just lowers his shades (Ray-Bans even though it's nighttime) and waves us in.

"That's it? Motherfucker!" Dan exclaims before we've even cleared the door, causing Cleto to give him a death glare.

The place is crawling with people. Dan is hyper again, sure that he sees Taylor Swift. Cleto elbows his way to the bar and orders us drinks I've never heard of, and before you know it, we're standing next to some cute girls, flirting and getting buzzed.

Life is good, everything is good, until I realize I'm more than a little drunk, like close-to-puking drunk, and the room is starting to spin.

"Cleto," I say, leaning in and nearly falling on him, "I thinkh I needa geh air . . ." I motion toward the door, but Cleto just laughs and turns his back on me, says something to Dan, who is holding his own with a spectacularly pretty redhaired girl. I tap his shoulder again. "Cle-oh . . . for real . . ."

I must look desperate because he says, "Gimme a minute. My sister here can't hold her liquor. We need to get her some fresh air." He gets up and steers me toward the front door, which, one second I'm super happy and relieved to be headed toward, but the next, I've decided I'm sober enough and we should go back to the girls.

I say this to Cleto, but he says, "It's okay, Romeo, I think we should get you outside."

I try to twist away from him—he's a skinny motherfucker, so I can usually break free. But drunk, not so much, and when he refuses to let go, I haul off on him, missing completely, and slamming my fist into the chest of a life-size stuffed bear that stands off to the side of the front door.

I take the bear out. I mean, the motherfucking animal goes flying, me with it, and we both land several feet away, facedown, on the beer-sticky floor. Cleto stands over me, laughing.

"Time to go home, man." A thick hand drags me up without effort, and I'm staring into the face of the Ray-Banned bouncer.

I hold up my hands in surrender, but Cleto steps in for me. "He's okay now," Cleto says. He nods toward the bar. "Farkus is my cousin. But, we're leaving now, I swear. We'll make sure to get Ole Revenant, here, home in one piece."

"The Revenant!" Dan has righted the bear, and he's growling and moving it toward me, and a crowd has gathered, and pretty much everyone is dying laughing.

"Go, Leo!" someone yells, and someone else shoves Dan and the bear into me and I stumble backward, the bear landing on top of me as the crowd breaks into an uproar.

Now Ray-Banned Bouncer is back, and this time he's got both Dan and me by an arm.

Dan looks up in all sincerity and says, "Hey, chill out. You can't just boot the Revenant, man!"

And then I'm laughing, and Cleto is laughing, and Dan is laughing, and we're all kicked out, and we're rolling with laughter toward home.

The whole thing was hilarious. The goddamned funniest thing that ever happened. So why am I crying thinking about it now?

I miss those guys, Cleto and Dan. And that's on me, not them. I'm the one who dropped the ball. After I moved. Even before that. After my father died. They tried, but I shut down. I blew them off. They didn't know how to help me anymore.

They tried, though. They texted. They called.

"Can't, dude. Sorry. Next time," I'd respond. I made no effort. I wanted to make plans with Sarah instead.

I screwed up.

Because I couldn't see it. I couldn't be us. I just couldn't feel it anymore.

Across the room, I walk to the bureau and slide open its few flimsy drawers, one after another, though I don't know what I'm looking for. Nothing, really. I'm just looking. Like I'm at a hotel and I'll find a nice brochure or something. Glossy, with photographs of pristine rooms and smiling visitors. Some catchy slogan: *Things to Do and See During Your Stay at the Ape Can.* Instead, I find a small laundry sack (no drawstring or ties) and three books: a black paperback Bible with gold lettering, a pale blue book called *Twelve Steps and Twelve Traditions,* and a navy blue paperback that looks like it's from the 1970s called *One Day at a Time in Al-Anon.* I pick up the twelve-steps one and open to the first page: *"We admitted we were powerless over alcohol—that our lives had become unmanageable."*

I know it shouldn't, but it makes me laugh, thinking of that night with Cleto and Dan again. I toss it back in the drawer, missing my cell phone, feeling glad, at least, that I'm not *that* kind of a fuck-up.

Then again, maybe that would be better than this.

I sit back heavily on the bed, wondering when I might feel like I can breathe again.

All I do lately is suck wind, and fight back tears.

Some Revenant I am.

Cleto would have my head.

A nurse stands at the door to my room. Nurse Carole with the blond hair and the too-bright smile. She holds a cup of water in one hand and the little paper cup with my pills in the other.

"Good morning, Mr. Alden. We need to get going. You meet with Dr. Alvarez now. You don't want to keep her waiting."

I take the pills and follow her. When we reach the corridor with the hideous fish mural, Nurse Carole places a hand on the small of my back, veering me through the waiting area to a section of chairs across from Dr. Alvarez's closed door.

"She'll be out in a minute. There's help over there if you need any." She nods at the nurses' station across the hall, where one woman sits with her head bowed and an orderly is mopping the floor. "You good here for the time being?" I nod. I'm happy not to have her wait with me. "Okay. Holler if you need anything. Otherwise, I'll see you after."

I sit and try not to think about anything. I'm feeling off balance again.

I thumb through magazines until I find an old *Highlights,* then flip through until I find the dumb old Hidden Pictures game. It's still there, just like when I was a kid. I scan the scene, a family of pigs outside a barn, and search for the objects without bothering to look at the crappy illustrations in the key. The objects are always the same, anyway: a pencil, a toothbrush, a hockey stick, ridiculous likenesses, at best. I find a teacup and saucer, a spoon, and a thing that doesn't really look like anything but I'm pretty sure is supposed to be a tree limb, before I hear a click and the door behind me opening.

"Oh, good, you're here, Klee! You're my first on Wednesdays, so from now on just knock and come on in."

She pronounces my name the right way, which is promising, but I'm stuck on the fact that she says "Wednesdays," plural, as if there are many more weeks that I'll be here. I close the magazine and walk toward her, my legs feeling unsteady.

In her office, I sit quickly and focus on the print of *Daubigny's Garden*. It was one of Van Gogh's last paintings, painted at Auvers, the home and garden of a painter he admired.

There are actually a few versions floating around. The original was done on a tea cloth because Van Gogh had run out of canvas. This print isn't from the original because in that one a black cat scampers across the foreground.

"So, I take it you like it?" Dr. Alvarez follows my gaze to the print, but she doesn't wait for an answer. "How are you feeling this morning?"

The crow swoops in, lands in the grass, and the man with the straw hat appears among the flowers . . .

I shake my head to make them scatter, disappear. Dr. Alvarez waits patiently, but my mouth feels dry and my words stick heavy and unformed in my throat. I don't know what I'm supposed to say. About anything.

"That good, huh? Well, I did speak with Dr. Ram, and he said your vitals are good. He says to be patient, another day or two, and your body will start to adjust to the medication. It can take the body longer with this particular one, but they've been seeing good, long-term results. If you're still feeling groggy tomorrow, we can talk again."

Groggy. That is the word I've been looking for.

"Okay," I say.

"All right. Good. We're making some progress, here." She smiles warmly, slips her shoes off under the table, and crosses her bare feet at the ankles. Her ankles are thick; her toenails are polished bright red.

My eyes go to her face. It isn't young or model-like or anything, but it's pleasant and kind. She looks Spanish or something, but maybe I just think that because of her name. My eyes dart to her feet. She straightens up and slips them back into her shoes.

"So, tell me, how was the rest of yesterday? Are you getting settled here?"

Am I supposed to get settled?

I stare at the spot where Van Gogh's cat should be and try to remember how yesterday was. I watched TV. Dr. Ram came in. Someone delivered trays of barely edible food. A nurse repeatedly took my blood pressure and listened to my heart, then told me to check out the dining hall and game room. Like the Ape Can is a freaking resort.

"Mostly a blur, I guess," I say. "I slept a lot. My dreams were really weird."

And, in the middle of the night, Sister Agnes Something left me a note and some Yodels.

I leave that last part out. I'm not even sure it was real.

I leave this out, too: *I can't stop thinking about Sarah.*

"Quiet," I say instead. "It's so quiet here. Not just in here, but in all of Northhollow. I miss the city. I miss the noise. The noise blocks out all the other crap in your head."

"That it does," she says. "I get that completely. So, tell me more about the city."

I swallow, and scratch at the bandage, and try to cement the order of things. The city and Dad, counting backward. North-hollow. My life before and after he died. Me, here, now. And more recently, I sort days. Yesterday was Tuesday. Monday was the day Dr. Alvarez says my mother was here. So, Sunday I was still in the hospital. Or maybe that was the night they brought me here.

And, before that?

Saturday. Dunn's house.

The stupid party.

My stomach churns. I don't want to think about that. I can't if I want to get out of here.

"What about this morning?"

"Sorry?"

"This morning," Dr. Alvarez says. "Have you been out of your room? Met the others? We have a small inpatient group . . . and a pretty nice dining hall here. Breakfast is best. Decent waffles." She winks. "Passable, anyway. I wondered if you ventured down?"

"Not yet," I say. "I ate in my room. They told me it was okay."

She nods. "Of course. Take your time. It will all be there when you're ready. But I'd like you to assimilate and get started in group therapy. At least by the end of the week. And, of course, family therapy. But not yet. In the next few days."

Family. I feel dizzy again. "I'm not feeling too social," I say.

I mess with the bandage some more, and Dr. Alvarez pulls a bright orange stress ball from the drawer. She tosses it to me and I manage to catch it this time. ***Rimmovin 5 (zopiclone 5 mg). "We cannot solve life's problems except by solving them."—M. Scott Peck.***

I turn it and squeeze it in my hand. "The people at Rimmovin sure have a sense of humor."

Dr. Alvarez smiles. "I suppose they do. Keep it. You can start a collection. One of every color." She shifts her position and grows serious again. "So, besides the noise, tell me what else you miss about Manhattan."

The word "Manhattan" clobbers me, suffocating me as if yards of sand have been dumped from a flatbed truck on top of me.

"My father," I say, caving to the avalanche. "I fucking miss my father."

The words, choked out through the grains, crush me further, finish me off, letting the whole of it bury me. I'm not ready to talk about my father. Not after everything else that has happened.

Besides, that's what I miss about *everything*, not just Manhattan.

My father.

My father and Sarah.

And Sarah was the only good thing *after*.

The crow eyes me from Tarantoli's desk, daring me to come in. On the whiteboard behind him, the date reads October 3rd.

The day I drew on Sarah's paper.

The day Tarantoli asked me to stay after.

"She wanted to chat with you, remember?" the crow says. "Make sure you weren't some sort of lunatic. But you are, aren't you? You, of all people, know you can't go messing with other people's artwork."

I block the crow out. I want to see Sarah. I want to go back to that day, that room, before all this other shit happened.

"Mr. Alden?" Tarantoli is waiting for me. But Sarah is up, leaving.

"I have a quiz fourth period," I call to Tarantoli over my shoulder, "I have to study . . ."

"Okay, tomorrow, then," she says, but I'm already gone, chasing after Sarah.

"The teachers go easy on you," the crow calls after me. "Because they feel sorry for you. Because they all know why you're here."

I ignore it. I need to catch Sarah. I need to see the way she looks when she turns and sees me, the way she smiles, the way she takes me in completely. Like she's open to anything. Like she doesn't give a shit what she's heard, or if anyone else will care.

I grab her shoulder, and she turns.

"Hey, what's up, Alden?"

Yes! That's it! Something in her expression. It makes my heart fill.

"She was happy to see you," the crow says. "It surprised you that she didn't think you were some loner weirdo like everyone else did. Like you *are*."

I shoo it away. I only want to think about Sarah.

"I wanted to apologize," I say. "I didn't mean to touch your work. Your drawing, it was really good. I swear. I just wanted to help you a little, to, uh, loosen it up, make it less stiff, and more organic like—"

"Organic?" She rolls her eyes, but she's smiling.

"I don't know. Something like that."

"Like I said, no problem. I get it. Anyway, I liked what you did. What you said. It *was* too safe. It's not so safe anymore." She looks at me fully, studying me. Against her pale skin, her eyes are the color of one of Van Gogh's evening skies. "So, no biggie, okay? Consider you did me a favor. Anyway, I've gotta go. I'll see you around."

"She blew you off," the bird says, returning. I shake my head. *Wrong.* Because the next morning, when I get to Taran-toli's room early, Sarah is there, waiting, the only other person in the room. And, when I sit, the sides of her mouth curl up into a definite smile.

"So, she liked you. That seems clear." I look up, relieved at how the crow has come around, but it's Dr. Alvarez speaking, which confuses me more. I wasn't intending to say all of this stuff aloud. "From what you've told me so far, your girlf—your friend, Sarah, she liked you. And she was worried. She cared you were hurt. It says here . . ." She rifles through the pages in her lap, "She tried to go in the ambulance with you. She wanted to go to the hospital." I look away. I hadn't remembered that. I was pretty out of it by then. "Of course, I don't yet know what happened before . . ." I swallow hard, shake my head. "Whatever it is, Klee—or, was—it must have been pretty painful to upset you so much, to land you here. And it's not a bad thing to cry if you need to. I bet you've been working overtime to hold it in. Sometimes, letting it out once and for all can help more than you'd ever imagine."

"Crying seems pointless," I say. "Like spilt milk, right?"

"According to whom? Is this an issue with your family?"

I shrug. "You mean with my mother? She's pretty much the only family I've got left."

"Yes. Your mother, then."

I squeeze the orange stress ball, then pick at a cuticle on my thumb.

"Let's just say she isn't much of a crier." I can hear the crackle of anger in my voice, but I can't control it. "Anyway, she's right. Crying proves nothing."

"What are you referring to, here? Something specific? Klee, did she not cry when your father died?"

I inhale sharply and stare up at *Daubigny's Garden*. The room is a vortex, the missing cat a big black hole in my heart.

It's after school, late, and I have to take a piss bad. The subway was delayed nearly half an hour.

I drop my jacket and portfolio inside the front door as I call out, but my mother doesn't answer. Right. She's not home. She's *never* home. Probably has some fund-raiser or something.

"Order in if I'm not back by dinner," she always says. "I'll leave a credit card on the kitchen counter."

I rush to the bathroom, unzip, and go—sweet relief—then walk to the sink to wash. But a shadowy darkness stops me, hulks through the frosted shower doors.

Dirt spatters. Sprayed across them.

No, not dirt. Not brown.

Red.

Crimson across both shower doors.

Something is wrong.

An ice-cold feeling washes over me.

I walk over and slide them carefully open.

He's in there, my father, crumpled, on the shower floor. Blood and bits of skin everywhere.

But no, he's at work! It's not him!

I scream—I must, because she's here now, too. My mother has come in. I don't even know where she came from.

"Jesus! Klee!" She screams, then lets out a strange, hollow sound, before pushing me away from the shower door. "Get out of here! Don't look! Go away!" She falls against it, trying to shield the whole scene with her body.

"I. Said. Get. OUT."

We stand, motionless. Me, I don't know what I am doing. I feel frozen. My body trembles in fear. She seems so small and frail, collapsed in her pink suit and her fancy, high-heeled shoes. Her coat hangs open, her leather handbag is still slung over her shoulder.

She's breathless. I can smell the city, the cold winter air on her coat.

A sound escapes again. Not words. Something foreign and animalistic.

"Jesus Christ!" she finally says, her voice charged with anger. "Not this. Not *this*! I can't . . . I won't . . ."

She shakes her head, hands over her face, as if this will help her unsee it. Unsee his skin and blood and shattered bone.

"I. Just. Cannot." My mother's fury crackles. She rights herself and moves forward, leaving the gun, the mess of blood, the pieces of skin.

She walks out. I stand, frozen.

"Klee! Out! Now!" She grabs my arm, pulling the door shut hard behind us.

In the hallway, she inhales sharply, and says, "I'll call nine-one-one." I nod, every inch of me still quaking. "And Isabella," she adds, moving toward another room. "Someone . . . Some kind of service to clean this all up."

"Klee?"

I can't answer because I'm all choked up again.

"Did you need her to express that she cared in a different, more definitive way?"

I close my eyes because the room is reeling.

Maybe I did. Who knows what I needed back then? Whatever I needed, she didn't offer it. Not to me, or to him.

"Okay, too soon," Dr. Alvarez says, more to herself than me. "Maybe we can explore that later. For now, let's stay on more concrete things. You were talking about the city, how you miss the noise. Let's go back to that."

I breathe more slowly, open my eyes again. "I didn't want to move . . . I only had to finish my senior year. I had my life, my friends . . . but she insisted."

"And you miss them."

"Not just them. My school. The city. Everything."

"I can imagine."

"But yeah, my friends. My friend Cleto, especially. The people and the traffic, and the garbage. The asswipe bicyclists who don't give a shit if you're in a Hummer or a delivery truck, or on foot." She laughs a little at that, like she appreciates the sentiment. "And, the pigeons," I add. "I know it's not possible, but I miss the fucking pigeons."

"Well, I have good news for you, then. We have plenty of pigeons here in Northhollow."

I let my eyes meet hers. "Only lame-ass suburban ones."

"You have a good sense of humor," she says. "I bet that has served you well."

Maybe. But, it sure as hell hasn't saved me. "It didn't stop me from acting crazy," I say. Saying it makes my chest constrict so tightly it feels like I can't get air in.

I don't want to be crazy. I don't want to be in here.

I suck wind and put my head between my knees.

"What if I am crazy?" I say, trying to sit up again. "What if I can never be normal again?"

"I don't think you are. And, more than that, I think you'll be feeling better again, soon."

I give her a dubious look as if to say, *Do you not see me sitting here in the Ape Can?*

"What I mean is, it seems clear you had a break—a serious one, not to be messed with—so we need to get to the root of it, to get you on a path of being well. But, just the fact that you're asking that question and worrying about it is a good sign, a promising one. That, with help, you'll feel better . . . feel well. So, how about we go with that for now?"

I nod, wanting to believe her, to trust her. I stare down at the stress ball and squeeze.

"We can only solve our problems by solving them," I read aloud. "But what if I don't know how to solve them?"

"That's why I'm here, Klee. That's my job. I'll help you. If you'll give me the chance—"

I want to—I do—but the room is whirling again.

"I need a drink," I choke out. "I'm going to get some water."

"Here, I'll come with you." She stands and follows me through the waiting area.

Nice work, loser. Can't even get a drink of water alone.

I look for the crow, but I don't need him to tell me what I already know in my head.

At the end of the waiting area, Dr. Alvarez stops and says, "How about you go on ahead. I'll wait here."

I walk, dizzy but grateful for her little bit of faith in me, past that stupid, garish *Finding Nemo* scene, and toward the fountain. I want to take my own paints to the blasted thing and redo it, make it good. *That* would make me feel better, taking my paints to it.

At least I'm upright. At least I'm getting a drink on my own.

After the fish, but before the fountain, there's the Asian girl again with the long black hair, sitting and waiting, her back to me, trying to trick me that she's Sarah.

I know it's a trick, but my heart ramps up anyway, and the blizzard beat rushes my ears. I grow clammy and the girl turns and stares.

Not Sarah, Klee. Not Sarah, I say, but she slides to the floor, comes crawling toward me.

"All your fears are foolish fancies, baby . . ."

Closer and closer . . .

"You know that I'm in love with you"

She isn't. She's lying.

Don't believe her.

We're in Tarantoli's room and Sarah is working on her drawing, *Girl in Repose.*

She's darkened in the lines I made yesterday, letting them flow off the paper like water. The girl's shirt now blends and fades into the background, and flowers fall out of her hair.

I slide out a blank sheet from the paper cubbies in the back of the room and start fresh on something new. I hate the other piece I've been working on. I haven't been able to concentrate since I got here, and it shows. But I need to focus. I need at least four worthy portfolio pieces to submit to SMFA by early spring.

We work across from one another, while the rest of the class comes in and settles. After several minutes Sarah finally looks up. Our eyes meet, and she pushes her paper over, spinning it so it faces me.

"Better, right?"

I nod. "Yeah. It's looser, you see?"

"Yes. Freer. Not so safe anymore." She smiles, satisfied.

Encouraged, I say, "It feels a little like an early Van Gogh." She rolls her eyes. It's not as good, of course, but it does remind me a little of one of his drawings. "Most people only know him as a painter, but he was an illustrator first. A lot of his early work was pen and ink. That's all I meant." Her eyes meet mine again. This time there's something softer in them. "Go ahead, Google Van Gogh's *Seated Girl,* or *Sorrow,* or *Pine Trees.* They're some of my favorites of his."

I should shut up. I've entered full-on art-geek mode, and Cleto, in his sarcastic drawl, is calling me out in my head: "Seriously, dude, you're all kinds of lame, you know that, right?"

Cleto was always giving me shit about my art talk, especially when we were out trying to meet girls. "Keep all that big city, elitist shit to yourself," he'd say, jokingly. "Talk about sports or something manly like that."

"Van Gogh was manly," I'd shoot back. "Toulouse-Lautrec,

too. Matisse. Picasso. Monet. If you knew anything at all about culture, you'd know that all the great masters were manly, manly men."

"Your funeral." Cleto would laugh. "But, trust me, dude, save it for the second date."

Yet here I am, hearing myself say, "I could take you to an exhibit, or something. There's a Van Gogh exhibit at MoMA this weekend." The minute I say it, I'm sorry. Cleto is right. I should ask her to a movie instead. "Or, we don't have to do that. We can do something else . . . anything else . . ." Because, now that I've said it, it occurs to me that going to the Van Gogh exhibit will be totally brutal without my dad.

Her eyes dart to mine. "No, that sounds great. I'd really like that, Alden." Then, without another word, she reaches across and draws a large charcoal smiley face right in the center of my paper. On top of the halfway decent drawing I had started. "See?" she says, laughing. "So much better unsafe."

Somehow I manage to shake Sarah from my brain and get a drink of water from the fountain. It's not much, but maybe it's not nothing either. I don't pass out. I don't make a fool of myself. And I make it through the rest of my session with Dr. Alvarez.

Progress, right?

You're a goddamned superstar, Alden.

Day 3—Afternoon

A lunch tray sits by the side of my bed. The pleated paper cup filled with pills. I slept through their delivery. I sleep through a whole lot these days.

I force myself to sit up to take them.

Something feels different. Shifted.

No, *present.*

Something feels present.

Someone.

My eyes move to the door.

A navy blue duffel bag.

Mine.

And another thing: my leather art portfolio.

The Ice Queen was here.

Day 3—Evening

Mistake: To make up for sleeping through the rest of the afternoon, I tell the shift nurse I'm going to brave the dining hall for dinner. Like Dr. Alvarez says, I need to assimilate, get out of this room, even if I still feel like garbage. "No one here is going to judge you, Klee," she had told me. "Remember, everyone here is busy fighting their own battles."

Is that what I'm doing? Fighting a battle?

She also wants me to join group therapy. "By the end of the week if you can." She says I'm in for two weeks, minimum, but that individual and group therapy both will continue after.

"It's a very small group, right now," she had clarified. "One of the things I like best about our facility. Presently, there are only four other kids inpatient. We're one of the first all-private-room acute treatment centers in the country."

Only five of us. Apparently there's not a whole lot of mental instability in Northhollow.

I had said that to her and she had explained that kids come here from all over, not just Northollow. The city. The Northeast. "Certain times of year we get busier. I guess no one really oriented you," she had said, pulling out a brochure for the facility, then sounding like an infomercial for the Ape Can. "Our inpatient beds are limited, and our staff as well, small, well trained, and intimate. There are only twelve extended-stay rooms. But, we're outpatient, too. In fact, we're mostly outpatient. Our community takes advantage of that, too. But, this time of year—spring into summer—well, it's typically quieter here."

This time of year. Spring. When life has turned green and promising. When life is supposed to look up. Unless you're me. Unless you're pathetic Klee Alden.

Dad killed himself in January, in the stark, post-holiday days of winter. Maybe he'd still be here if he'd managed to hold on another month or two.

"Did you know, Dr. Alvarez," I'd said, "that more deaths take place in January than any other month of the year? The school psychologist told me that. So, if I was going to end up here, shouldn't I have imploded back then?"

"Not necessarily," she'd said. "Maybe you're not the imploding type. Maybe you're pretty strong and resilient, and can withstand a whole lot in a typical year, and this was—and is—an aberration. Sometimes we have a long-standing, serious disorder or form of mental illness—say, anxiety or depression—but sometimes we don't. Sometimes the very real pressures of life—tragedy, illness—can become cumulative, adding up to more than even the most solid and stable of us can handle. Sometimes, we bear three, four tremendously difficult things, before the fifth one shows up and takes us out at the knees."

A series of images had flashed through my brain then, and I fight to keep them from coming back now: *My father in the shower . . . the first day at Northhollow . . . the guest room with the fucking box of letters . . .*

Dunn's house in the rain . . .

Sarah.

"In the meantime," Dr. Alvarez had said, "we're, here,

doing our best. Maybe we even appear to be dealing. Going about our business. But the problem is, we're really just tamping things down. We're in a state of serious denial.

"Don't get me wrong, employing a little healthy denial now and again can be good thing—a very good thing. But ignoring things as they pile up, well, that's different. That's when we might reach a breaking point, a point where we can't stay in denial anymore."

After my father died, I was forced to go see the school psychologist. I'd told him I didn't need any help, I was okay, that I could barely remember the details. It was the truth at the time. I had managed to block it out, as if it were a distant story I'd heard about someone else's father, rather than something that happened to me. The psychologist told me the brain does that sometimes, shuts down, cuts off the flow, like a gift, to keep the tragedy from replaying in your head.

"But if you don't talk about it," he had warned me, "at some point those memories are going to come flooding in."

And he was right. Those shut-out details, they do come back. Sometimes as dreams, free-floating and viscous, but other times while you're wide awake, without warning, in sharp and horrifying detail.

But not at first.

At first, it was the opposite. In those early days of January, I was so numb from shock, the event seemed to disappear altogether, leaving me only to focus on the minutiae. In the days that followed, the minor nothingness of my life played out in what felt like excruciating technicolor. Not what I did or where I went, but more what I saw outside my own body: the world, still existing; the cruel bits of living that continued to go on around me. So that, as I walked the streets to school in the mornings, I'd notice every little thing. Every sight. Every sound. Every smell. Which seemed like the opposite of what it should be. Because it proved that the rest of the world was still here—alive and in motion—while my father was permanently gone.

Which only made it all more unbearable.

What I remember most in those first days was passing the endless ragged Christmas trees, dragged half dead from their cozy brownstones, and left curbside for pickup like so many abandoned bodies. Their dried, brittle pine needles peppering the sidewalks, bare branches still boasting stubborn strands of glittering tinsel, or a felt snowman, or a forgotten red silk ball. As if refusing to believe the holiday season was over. One still bore all its fancy antique ornaments, plus a broken angel on top, as if its owners had said, "Fuck it," and dumped it along with everything that ever mattered to them.

Kindred spirits, then.

"Mr. Alden, are you ready? Shall we go down now?" The shift nurse stands eyeing me from the doorway.

Right. I said I'd go down to the dining hall.

Of course, now I've lost my will to go down. I don't want to see or talk to anyone. I'd rather curl up, pull the blankets over my head again.

"Shall we?"

I stare at my feet in my gray and orange Vans, my frayed Levi's, my gray-striped T-shirt, none of which feel like they actually belong to me.

"Okay, yeah, sure," I say, following her out and down the hall.

The dining hall is a glorified cafeteria with honey-colored wood tables and chairs with mauve cushions. White plastic salt and pepper shakers and a small plastic bud vase with fake red and white carnations grace each table. Only two of the tables are occupied, one by staff at the far side of the room, and the other, the one nearer to me, by the girl with the long black hair (*not Sarah . . . not Sarah . . .*) and another kid, scrawny and younger, with a flop of brownish-orange hair sweeping across his forehead and eyes.

The girl faces the entrance. Her eyes shift to mine, then quickly away. But I see the corner of her mouth turn up in a smile, as if she's somehow relieved to see me. Someone closer to her age, maybe. She looks younger than I am, but not by much, while the boy looks nine, maybe ten, tops.

"Oh, good! Martin and Sabrina are here. I'll leave you with them." The nurse pulls out a chair like a hostess.

"It's okay, you can sit," the scrawny kid says.

"Hey, I'm Klee," I say, obeying.

"You rhyme," the girl answers softly. She's normal looking from what I can tell, nothing discernibly wrong with her. My hand self-consciously goes to the bandage on the side of my head. Not that it matters, I guess. Visible or not, we all must have a reason to be here. "I've seen you around," she says, and my brain calculates: *the dumb fish mural, the fountain; me, passing out like a loser.* A great first impression. "Down in the South wing," is all she adds.

"Yeah, same."

"The burgers are decent if you want to get some food," the boy says.

I don't really, but do anyway, returning with a thin-looking gray slab between two buns, a large leaf of wilted lettuce, and a mealy tomato poking out the side. I sit again.

The boy scarfs down his burger with gusto. His eye closer to me has a twitch or a tic. I try not to stare when he turns.

"So, she's Sabrina," he says, mouth full. "And I'm Martin."

"Geez," Sabrina says, "Wait till you're done before you talk."

"Where you guys from?" It's a dumb question, I know, but, "What are you in for?" seems like a weird question. And, anyway, I don't want to share my own reasons yet, either. Especially not with some kid who probably hasn't even sprouted pubic hair.

I stare down at my plate feeling queasy and unhungry, but since I don't want to be in charge of talking anymore, I lean in and take a big bite, waiting for someone else to carry the conversation.

"I'm from here," Martin says, obliging. "And Sabrina is from Westchester." Sabrina nods, picks up a carrot, takes a nibble and puts it back down. Her nails are chewed down to the quick, the skin raw and bloody on the edges. "And the other guy that shows up sometimes, the one with the tattoos, that kid Euclid? I think he's from Manhattan."

"Brooklyn. And, that's not his name," Sabrina whispers.

"Yes, it is," Martin says.

"No, it isn't." She drops her carrot, pulls her sleeves down over her hands, and buries them in her lap, under the table.

"Whatever," Martin says. "And there's some other kid, a girl, but you don't need to bother with her, I hear she's leaving tomorrow."

"Martin knows everything," Sabrina says.

"I see that. How old are you two?" I ask, forcing another bite of burger in.

"She's fifteen," Martin says, "And I'm twelve. Almost thirteen, though. Thirteen in two weeks, so technically thirteen. And, anyway, my intellectual age is way older than most kids' my age."

"Really?" I say, not meaning it to come out as sarcastic as it does. I'm not questioning his intellect. The kid barely looks a day over ten.

"I get that a lot. I'm told I'm very youthful looking." He bats his eyelashes, takes another bite of burger, and continues to talk with his mouth full. "I go to Northhollow Middle. Eighth grade. I skipped a year after first grade. IQ-wise, it should have been two. Keeping me back was probably a mistake. I'm on the debate team, which is technically only for eighth graders, but I hold my own. I act with an improv group, too, but that's extracurricular. We're called the On-the-Spotters. Get it? It's very clever."

"It's not that clever," Sabrina says under her breath, making me like her more by the minute.

I watch as she arranges the carrots on her plate into a starburst. It makes me wish I'd taken some. The carrots seem better than the burger. For art purposes, anyway. At any rate, I'm getting the sense that this Martin kid is the reason she seemed relieved when I—any other person—walked in. Poor girl. Wonder how many meals she's been stuck alone with him.

"And she plays violin," Martin is saying. "She's supertalented but way more humble than I am. But trust me, I've heard her. There's a room here for music therapy, right next to the room where we do GT."

"GT?" I ask, looking at Sabrina.

"Group therapy," Martin answers, without giving her a chance. "She played at Carnegie Hall once, did you know that? And, not with her school, but by invitation. Well, of course you don't know, you haven't been to group yet. Dr. Howe says you're going to be joining us soon. Euclid doesn't like to come either, so some days it's just the two of us, so we basically know each other's whole life stories."

"No we don't," Sabrina says, "and his name isn't Euclid." Martin's eyes dart to hers, this time with alarm, which makes me feel bad for the kid.

I push my plate away, vaguely wondering how many times he's gotten beaten up. I'm betting more than once. Which is cruel of me, I know. I get that it's just his insecurity speaking. But seriously, he's the kind of kid that annoys everyone except his grandparents, who probably think he's the smartest, cutest kid in the whole world.

My eyes move back to Sabrina. She shifts uncomfortably, which makes me feel worse for her, like I should at least try to acknowledge the stuff that he's said about her.

"That is pretty cool," I say, "to have played at Carnegie Hall." I turn back to Martin. "And you sound pretty accomplished, too."

"I am," Martin says, "but with great genius comes great madness, you know?"

"Isn't that power and responsibility?" I ask, and Sabrina's eyes meet mine and she laughs.

"Whatever," Martin says. "I'm not dumb. I know that's Spider-Man you're quoting from. So, what about you?"

"What about me?"

"Your deal?" he asks. "What is it?"

"I'm a senior. From the city." I leave out the part about Northhollow. I've lived here for less than a year, and I don't want him asking if I know so-and-so's older brother or sister. Bottom line is, I'm not about to tell this kid my life story.

"What else . . . ?"

"Not much." I look back at Sabrina and decide to offer a little more. "I paint. I'm hoping to go to the School of the Museum of Fine Arts in Boston this fall."

"Aha!" Martin says. "See? An artiste! I rest my case. Genius. Madness. Art."

I awaken to a stubby dwarf nun in a black habit with white collar and headpiece, standing at the door of my room. It's dark, save for the low blue light of the television, so her figure is backlit, like some strange apparition, from the brightness from the hall.

"Good evening, Mr. Alden." I blink and wait for my eyes

to adjust. "I brought a little treat for you. I didn't expect you to be sleeping so early. Seems to be a habit of yours."

I push up on an elbow and try to make sense of things.

She moves toward me, purposefully, and I blink again. The combination of short and heavy makes her waddle, and with the get-up she's wearing, she looks uncannily like a sturdy penguin. At the side of the bed, she stops and sets down a two-pack of Twinkies. My mind slips back to the Yodels and the note. This must be Sister Agnes Whatever.

"I've been anxious to meet you. You're quite the heavy sleeper."

"Not usually," I say. "I think it may be the medication." She reaches over me with effort to turn on the overhead light. I squint against the onslaught.

Dunn's house . . . the lights in my eyes . . .

"Too bright?" She switches it off again. "The TV is fine. Anyway, I'm Sister Agnes Teresa," she says. "Very nice to finally meet you."

Sister Agnes Teresa. Right. That's what it was. I crane my neck to look past her to the old-fashioned digital clock by the side of the bed, but it's turned on an angle, so I can't make it out.

"Barely nine P.M.," she says.

I fell asleep after dinner.

The dining hall with Martin and Sabrina.

"It's easy to lose track of time here," she says, moving to the end of the bed. She folds her too-short arms across her chest and studies me. I'm suddenly starving. I eye the Twinkies.

"Well, good, here we are." She nods at the table. "Go ahead. Eat them. That's why I brought them to you. Not that they won't stay fresh for a lifetime." She chuckles. I unwrap them and scarf one down, enjoying the sugary goodness. "Would you like some water?" She waddles to the pitcher on the table near the head of my bed.

"Yes. Thanks. But I can get it."

"Nonsense." She works hard to lift the plastic pitcher, stretches to retrieve my plastic cup from the rolling table.

I don't mean to stare, but it's hard not to. Honestly, there must be a dozen things wrong with her. Not just her stature, but her proportions. Her hands are thick—too thick for her size—and her fingers are bratwurst sausages. Her torso is too long for her legs. And her voice, too, has an odd froggish quality to it, as if she's swallowed both sandpaper and helium. On the other hand, her face is normal. Nice, even. Pleasant and round, and beneath the white hat, her eyes sparkle friendly and warm.

While I eat the second Twinkie, Sister Agnes Teresa moves awkwardly around my bed, smoothing my blankets. Finally, she waddles back to the window, where the shades are pulled down. She lifts them halfway and peers out over the courtyard, now lit by sodium lamps that bathe it in a yellow, melancholy glow. The brachiosaurus looms stark and lonely in the stillness.

After another minute, she lowers them again. "All right, it's been a long night and I don't want to impose on you more. You be well, Mr. Alden," she says, making her way to the door and pulling it closed all but those last few inches behind her.

Day 4—Morning

"Daubigny's Garden."

I say this aloud to Dr. Alvarez—Daubigny's Garden—for no other reason than it's there. Or maybe I say it because it's art, and sometimes that's all there is.

Dr. Alvarez turns to where its blue-roofed house rises into yellow and blue clouds. "So that's what it's called?"

"Yes. But that's not the real version. Or, at least not the *original* version."

"No?"

"No. In the original there's a black cat, there, in the foreground." I point near the bottom of the print. "Just below the lavender area."

"How interesting!" She twists back to take it in again, before turning back to me. "You know your stuff, don't you?" I shrug. "I've always liked it," she says, "but to be honest, I didn't put it there. I'd like to take credit, but it was already here when I inherited this office, so, perhaps a bit of kismet at work. Speaking of which, I'm told your mother visited. How was that?"

I shift, uncomfortably. "Not really visited," I say. "Just dropped some things off. I was asleep. I didn't even know she was here." I don't elaborate. And I haven't opened the portfolio since she left it, just shoved it in the corner near the closet. I did open the duffel bag, where she packed me some extra clothes and other necessities.

"Art can be great therapy . . ." Dr. Alvarez says, so I'm guessing she knows about the portfolio. "We can arrange for you to get some work done in here if you'd like, and I'd love to see some of your pieces if you're willing." I must flinch because she quickly adds, "Only if you want to at some point. I know art can be quite personal. So, how are you feeling? Are you adjusting to the meds any better?"

"A little, I guess." *If only you wouldn't keep bringing up my mother.*

"Tell me."

"I went down to the dining hall. And I slept better last night, so there's that." Sister Agnes Teresa waddles across my brain, staring out my window into the night. I don't mention her. I'm still partly afraid I hallucinated her.

"Glad to hear it. Your body needs rest. Not just emotionally, but physically. You're healing physical wounds, which takes energy, did you know that?"

I don't know what I know.

I turn and look out her window. It's April. I'm done with school in the middle of June. Less than three months. But the thought of going back to Northhollow, of facing Abbott and the others, makes my stomach roil.

Of facing Sarah.

But if I miss too much time, I may have an issue graduating, and I don't want that either. I'm already on extension to complete my portfolio for Boston. "Extenuating circumstances," they noted. But they're not going to give me much more time. The best thing I can do now is get out of here. Get accepted. Go there. Get away from the Ice Queen and Northhollow.

Jesus, how I've screwed things up.

No. They were screwed up already. They were screwed up long before Saturday.

Dr. Alvarez glances up from her clipboard, where she's been flipping pages. "Tell me what you're thinking, Klee." But, that's the problem. I don't want to talk about any of it. My father. What happened with my mother. Or with Sarah. "How about we go back to where we left off yesterday?" Dr. Alvarez smiles gently. "You were telling me about that first day in the city with Sarah."

The portfolio slips through my head again. Not because of what's in it, but what's on it. I saw it yesterday. The little piece of masking tape on the handle.

K EE HA WOO .

Her words. Still scrawled there like a faded promise.

Sarah and I take the train into the city.

Mom lets me use Dad's car locally, but she won't let me drive it into Manhattan. "Klee, the taxis . . . they're dangerous, and you just got your license when we got up here. Besides, do you know what that car is worth? What repairs cost? And I can't have anything happen to you . . ."

Me, or the car? Always so hard to tell what her real concerns are. It doesn't matter anyway. I'm happy to take the train if I'm with Sarah.

Sarah is waiting near the stationhouse when I get there. I let out a sigh of relief. I was afraid she'd blow me off. But, there she is, looking incredible. Ripped jeans, a white T-shirt, some sort of crocheted green sweater that has holes so you see her skin. Her long black hair, pulled back into a ponytail. She waves as I pull in, dangling a pair of rainbow-colored Vans in her hands.

October and she's outside with bare feet. A smile forms at the edge of my lips.

I park and get out as the train pulls into the station.

"Hey," I say heading over, the smile on my face so big now I must look like the Joker from *Batman*. I nod at the train. "I don't think they'll let you on without shoes."

"Fuck 'em," she says, batting her eyelashes, and we head up to the platform together.

The train is empty, so we have our choice of seats. I slide into a window seat halfway down the aisle, and Sarah slips in next to me and slouches, knees bent up and pressed against the seat in front of us. She smells spicy, like cinnamon, and suddenly all I can think about is kissing her.

"You got something against shoes?" I ask, trying to distract myself with something, anything, else. "The floors aren't particularly clean in here, I'm guessing."

"I like to live dangerously," she says.

Her toenails are painted a deep Prussian blue. This, too, makes me want to kiss her.

I focus on her jeans instead. There are holes in the knees, and she's drawn flowers on the skin of each in blue ink. I reach out and trace one, and she smiles down at the floor.

Is this a date? I'm not quite sure what it is.

It's weird how awkward I feel around Sarah. It's not like I've never dated before. More than date, actually. I haven't been a virgin since summer before junior year. But since my father died, I haven't felt like doing much of anything with anyone.

But, now, here, with Sarah, I feel different. Or maybe I'm kidding myself. I don't really know her. At all. And from what I've seen, she's not my usual type. The way she hangs out with the popular kids and the football players. The Keith Abbotts and Scott Dunns of the world. Not exactly the sharpest tools in the shed. At first, I thought the blond one, Abbott, was her boyfriend. He's always hanging around her, like some sort of lumbering, lost dog.

I turn and stare out the window as the train pulls out of the station, wondering if I've made a mistake even bothering.

"Where'd you go, Alden? You disappeared on me." Sarah sits up straight and bumps her knee against mine. "Have you gone all broody on me again?"

"No. Not at all. Sorry. I'm really glad you're here."

"Could have fooled me." She slips her Vans on as the conductor makes his way down the aisle, and says, "Here, I'll be good and follow the rules." She's quiet while he checks her ticket. "So, is this a date?" she asks when he's gone, and flutters her eyelashes.

"I don't know. You tell me . . . I wasn't sure if maybe you were with someone already."

"I'm not. So is that why all the brooding? Because seriously, what is with that, anyway?"

"With what?"

She gives me a look. "You know, the whole dark and mysterious dude from the city thing. The whole—I don't know—emo artist thing. Is that for real, or put on?"

"Emo? I am so *not* emo," I say, offended.

"I wasn't being mean. I guess I figured maybe it was protective, or something. Because that I would get." Heat rushes my ears, spreading down my cheeks to my neck. "I'm just saying, super cute guy sweeps in senior year, all artsy and shit. Talks to no one. So, I'm just wondering?"

Now I look at her. Maybe it's the word "cute," or maybe it's the half smile on her face, like she wants me to know she's partly egging me on. But I want to set her straight, too, make it clear that I'm not emo. I'm not anything. I'm just your typical kid who's been through hell, who didn't want to be here, didn't ask to be here. I'm just trying to get through the days.

Instead, I say, "Do people do that around here? Put things on for effect? Abbott, and those guys? Act one way when they're really another?"

"Aw, don't make this about them. Abbott is a decent guy, really. Maybe not a brain surgeon, okay. But, we've been friends for a long time, since we were little. He sticks up for me . . . he doesn't ask anything of me. Unlike . . ." She closes her eyes, exhales, then says, "Well, unlike everyone else. Trust me. I'm just saying, they're not like you think they are."

Our eyes meet, and I want to be sarcastic, but there's something in the way she looks at me that tells me she needs me to let it go. She wants to be here with me, and I'm acting like a jerk. Getting defensive. Of course she has a right to know what my deal is.

"Seriously," I say, "I'm just trying to be me. You have no idea. It's been a fucking rough year."

"So, tell me, then."

I swallow hard, choosing what information to give. It's not really something you want to share with a girl you barely know and are trying to impress. That your father killed himself, that you don't even matter enough for your own dad to want to stick around.

The train lurches to a stop, and the doors chime and open, letting a handful of new passengers on. When the doors close again, I say, "My father died. Unexpectedly. Last January. It's still hard to talk about right now."

"Oh, that sucks! I'm so, so sorry," she says. She bumps her shoulder against mine, feeling badly. This is why I don't tell people the full truth. It makes me seem pathetic. I don't want her pity. I just want her to like me. "So, that's why you're up here, then?" she asks.

"To tell the truth, I'm not sure why we're here. My mother wanted a water view." She looks at me and raises an eyebrow. "You know, a 'fresh start' and all that. Not me. But she didn't care. So, I'm here, just biding my time."

"Well, fair enough. I take it back. You may go ahead and keep on brooding, then." She reaches out and runs her thumb along the top of my hand, then pulls her hand back again.

I wish she'd leave it there.

I wish she'd keep it there forever.

I pause and look up. Dr. Alvarez stops jotting notes down on the clipboard.

"I'm listening," she says.

"I know. I'm just thirsty. Could I get a drink of water?" I stand, anxious to walk, to move. To leave the room and stop thinking about it all. Because it makes me want to believe that she meant what she said. What she wrote. It makes me want to believe that everything wasn't a lie.

"Oh, right, give me a sec. I almost forgot!" Dr. Alvarez is up and bending down next to her desk, where she drags out a case of Poland Spring water.

She brings two bottles over and hands one to me.

"Let's keep going. I know it's hard. But we're making some progress here."

By the time we reach Grand Central Station, I'm feeling more like my old self again. The "before" Klee. The one from before my father died.

"I forgot how awesome it is here," Sarah says, spinning as we climb up out of the terminal.

"You forgot? You barely live an hour away."

"Yeah, I know. But I can't remember the last time I was here. We used to come a lot when I was little, to see shows for our birthdays. The last one was *Lion King*. Not since the split, though." She sings the opening line from *The Lion King*'s theme song, the "Nants ingonyama" thing, then skips ahead of me. I run to catch up. "I used to love that movie so much," she says when I reach her. "I still watch it with my little brother."

"You have a brother? Does he go to Northhollow?" I don't know why I sound surprised. Obviously I don't know much about her. But I want to. I want to know everything.

She laughs. "Yes. I mean, no. I mean, yes, I have a little brother, but, no, he's not at Northhollow. He's only eight. And he doesn't live here. He's my half brother. Tyler. He's super adorable. And, yes, if you're doing the math, that is older than my parents' divorce, which was when I was twelve, so you figure it out. Anyway, they're not here. He went to work for his new wife's brother in Pennsylvania, so it's not like I get to see him much. They moved there right after the divorce."

"Nice," I say sarcastically.

"Right?" She wraps her arms to her chest. "My mom went apeshit when she found out, and not just because he had some other kid, but because the new wife is practically my age. So, you can imagine how happy that made her."

"Ugh, seriously? Do you hate her?"

"Well, close. She's twenty-four. And, actually, no, I don't. In fact, I kind of like her. Better than my mother anyway, because my mother is a miserable, insane witch. Depressed insane. Needs-to-be-medicated-but-isn't insane. So, it's hard to blame him. She wasn't fun. Ever. You should've heard the crying jags she used to go off on . . . which pale in comparison to the ones she can go off on now." Sarah smiles sadly and shrugs. "I wouldn't have wanted to stay with her either."

"So, why didn't you go with him?"

She jams her hands in her pockets. "Because she may be a miserable witch, but she's my mother? And, anyway, my older sister wasn't going to . . . Well, never mind. Forget that. She's already gone and never coming home."

"Wait. Older sister?"

"Got pregnant. Dropped out of Northhollow. Went to hair school," she says, ticking items off on her fingers. "Left for California with her boyfriend. In a nutshell. 'Nut' being the operative word. In case you think your life is a mess."

"So you're an aunt, then?"

"Nope," she says. "Miscarried. Which I guess was maybe a blessing. But my mother went batshit anyway. So now my sister is in California, my brother is in Pennsylvania, and I'm the one stuck here with the loon. Anyway, now you know everything there is to know about me. More than you'd ever actually want to know."

"Not true," I say. "I'm sorry about all of it, but I like knowing."

"Well, great, whatever. So, basically, if I had gone with him, it would have killed her. I may hate her, but there's no way I'm going to be responsible for killing my own mother." I get that, but don't say it, because, that's pretty much what I'm doing here in Northhollow. "And, by the way, Alden, now we're done. Seriously. Enough of this drama and self-pity. Starting now, we make a pact. No more talking about bad things for the rest of the day. No parent shit, or home shit, or school shit. And no Northhollow, either. Northhollow sucks, so we're totally agreed on that one. And, it's Saturday and we're free, right? So, let's have a happy day in the city."

"Good with me," I say. I want to forget everything, everything except spending a day in the city with Sarah Wood. She lets me take her hand, and we walk through the corridor until we reach the marble walls and high, ornate ceiling of the Main Concourse. In the center, I stop and say, "Look up," and I point out the constellations in the blue-green ceiling.

"Wow," she says. "I never realized those were there."

"And, see that?" I indicate the westernmost corner of the ceiling. "The crab, Cancer, over there?" She nods. "Now, look at its left claw, then follow that straight ahead to where the green part meets the cream." She squints, confused, like she can't see what I'm pointing to, and I say, "Do you see that small dark square?"

"Now I do. Yeah," she says excitedly.

"That's there on purpose. It's part of a restoration they did years ago to clean the ceiling, the mural, the whole nine yards. They left that little square to show the accumulation of dirt. And to make sure the restoration didn't hurt the artwork."

"Really?"

"I swear. That square is a mix of dirt, fumes, and cigarette smoke."

"Gross," she says. "But fascinating."

"And, this," I say, steering her to the gold, four-faced clock over the pagoda, "is worth millions. And, beneath it is supposedly a secret spiral staircase that goes to the lower level and a top-secret room."

"Seriously?"

"Seriously."

"How do you know all this?" she asks.

"My father." I swallow back a lump and plow forward now that I've started. "He loved this kind of stuff. He was always telling me myths and stories about the city, and the world and—" But, I stop. I can't. We've made a pact, and I don't want to get all choked up thinking about him. It's the first time I've been back to the city since we moved, and I already feel him everywhere around me.

"Klee?"

"Yeah?"

"You're awesome. Stop brooding." She swings my hand, then skips to the exit, pulling me along with her into the bright outdoors.

At MoMA, I find myself mimicking my father's stories as I tell her about the exhibits. Like in the Matisse room, when we reach his *Swimming Pool* cutout: "Can you imagine," I say, "two thousand hours to replace the burlap, fiber by fiber . . ."

I should heed Cleto's advice, but Sarah seems interested and, maybe, impressed. And, anyway, it's not like I know how to help myself.

After the Van Goghs, which don't include *Sorrow* like I was hoping but do include his olive tree series from Arles, the period during which he became obsessed with Japanese printmaking, I decide we've seen enough and head us up

7th Avenue toward the park. Things grow quiet between us, though I'm not sure why. Maybe we're still in hushed mode from the museum, or maybe it's the ghosts of my father that seem to pop up on every corner.

"Did I ever tell you about the ship carpenter, Lozier?" Dad asks.

"Yes, the guy who convinced everyone they should try to saw Manhattan in half . . ."

My chest tightens as I shake off the memory. It's unseasonably warm for October, and I pull off my sweatshirt and carry it in my hands. Sarah keeps pace next to me, though every once in a while she has to do a little skip to keep up. I turn and watch her, and smile. I need to stay light. I need to be fun. She won't want anything to do with some fragile wuss who keeps losing it over his dead father.

At 59th Street we cross Columbus Circle and head north up Central Park West.

Sarah leans into me. "You sure know a lot about Van Gogh." She nudges me when I don't answer.

"My father loved him."

"What happened to him?"

"Van Gogh?"

"No, your father."

I shake my head, heart pounding. I really can't talk about this now. "We made a pact, remember?" Blood rushes to my ears. "Nothing but good stuff. Like *you* said."

"Okay, fine, so tell me about you. Is that what you want, to be able to paint like Van Gogh?" The question makes me dizzy. I try not to think big, or in the future tense about my own art. My father proved it wasn't a real career.

"Who doesn't?" I say finally. "But, it's pretty naïve, because, seriously, what are the chances? That's why I picked Fine Arts, Boston. They have a dual major, business and art, so I can do anything after. I could go to law school like my father . . ." I swallow hard, trying not to hate myself for sounding like him. Well, not him, but my mother. "It's hard to make a living as an artist, is all."

"I bet you could." She squeezes my arm. "I tease you, but you're really, really good."

Warmth creeps up my neck, my cheeks. "Those pieces in Tarantoli's? Those aren't my best. I haven't felt much like painting since . . ." I stop again. "It's been hard to find my rhythm here at Northhollow."

"Well, if that's not your best, then you must be awesome," she says. "Everyone talks about it. About how talented you are. I'm not the only one who's noticed, Klee."

I give her a look because I'm pretty sure exactly zero and a half percent of the population of Northhollow know, or care, what I do or who I am. "Everyone?"

"Okay, fine. Maybe not *everyone*. But everyone in Tarantoli's class, for sure."

"Whatever," I say. "I'm okay. But, my dad, he was amazing. Way better than I'll ever be. And I know from him that most of us will never make a living—"

"Maybe," she says, cutting me off. "So he was a lawyer?"

"Yeah. Corporate. Securities. Tax work. Pretty boring stuff. He made good money, but he hated it. Hey, it was *your* pact. Do we really need to keep talking about this?"

"No. You're right. If it makes you feel better, my mother is a nurse and she hates it, too. She used to like it when she first started, but it's hard, with crazy hours, and there are all these hospital politics she's always bitching about. And they don't pay her nearly enough. She's always complaining, and always tired, and, I swear, it seems like babies are always dying on her."

"Babies?"

"Yeah, she works with preemies in neonatal. It can be brutal sometimes."

"Wow, that's hard. See? This is why I shouldn't give a shit if I'm poor. Money never makes anyone happy. That's one thing I know. I can't work a shit job I hate, just so I can buy someone else fancy things." My voice hitches with anger. "So, I guess that's one difference between my dad and me."

"So, he was rich, then? I mean, you are . . . ? I mean, it's clear you're not poor."

"Come on." I start walking again and she follows.

"I mean, I knew that from where you live, obviously. The Ridge neighborhood is pretty exclusive. Not like my neighborhood. Wait till you see."

It isn't lost on me that she knows where I live, but it makes me wonder why she does. "I won't care," I say, pressing forward, warding off the growing knot in my stomach. "But you keep bringing all this up, when it was your pact not to in the first place. I'm going to have to remember that about you: You're a crap dealmaker. Or at least a crap deal *keeper*."

She laughs and I glance up, relieved. We've reached the 72nd Street entrance to Central Park.

"Forget all that," I say. "We're here. Let me show you my favorite place in the whole city." I grab her hand and pull her into a run.

Dr. Alvarez has put her pen down. Her eyes are closed, and for a second I wonder if she's sleeping. I can't believe I'm telling her all this stupid stuff anyway. The small things. The private things. What do they even matter now?

She shifts her feet under the table, opens her eyes, and studies me. "I love Central Park," she says. "And, don't be fooled by my eyes," she says, closing them again. "Sometimes I just listen best this way."

In the park, Sarah takes my hand again, which makes me dizzy in a good way. It's as if I can feel the electricity pass from her fingers into mine, traveling like a current up my arms and through my chest, thawing the cold numbness I hadn't even realized had settled there.

"This is Bethesda Terrace," I say, when we finally reach the fountain, its towering *Angel of the Waters* cascading her circular waterfall from her feet to the basin below.

"She's beautiful," Sarah says.

As the mist dampens our faces, I explain how the angel is actually a goddess or something more secular, not religious. "She's supposed to be the purifier of the city's water supply," I say, less worried than I should be about the total geek I keep sounding like. "Which is ironic, I guess, since a guy has to come clean the coins and garbage out from under her pretty much every day."

She laughs. "Is that true?"

"Yeah. It's actually his job."

"It's crazy how much stuff you know." I give her a look, and she adds, "Good crazy, not bad. Seriously. I like that about you. It's different. You're different. Weird, but hot." She gives me this smile, which kills me, then walks off, trawling her fingers along the edge of the fountain's coping. I follow, watching the spray catch in her hair like tiny, mystical crystals.

At the far side of the fountain she stops again and leans so far over to cup her hand under the cascade of water, I'm sure she's going to fall in.

"Hey, Klee," she says, turning to me finally, "out of all those wishes, how many do you think come true? I mean, there must be thousands of coins in here, so thousands of wishes every day, right?" She looks down again. "I hope at least some of them come true."

"Me, too," I say, nodding, as she starts off again. I follow silently, wondering what it is about her that breaks my heart and fills it at the same time, that scares me but comforts me, that makes me want to tell her things I can't begin to find words for.

When she stops again, she tilts her face to the sun and closes her eyes and inhales deeply. I stop next to her and do the same. I know what she's doing because I've done it myself before. She's letting the mist collect on her face, on her shoulders, her body, hoping in some magical way it might anoint her.

"I know it's not a story exactly, but you're a good storyteller," Dr. Alvarez says when I pause again to collect myself. "You have a way with words, as well as art, I suppose. Has anyone ever told you that?"

I shake my head and look away, embarrassed at how love-sick I sound. I don't know why I'm telling her all this. And yet now that I've started, I don't want to stop. It's like I need to. I need to go back there myself to know I didn't imagine it. That I wasn't crazy.

That she liked me as much as I thought she did.

"Can I kiss you?"

Sarah jerks her gaze back to me, her face damp and sparkling, then tilts her head back and bursts out laughing. When she straightens again, she says, "Jesus, Alden, you're adorable. You're *asking* me if you can kiss me? You're just supposed to do it." Then she takes my hand and leads me definitively across the terrazzo to the grass, and pulls me down onto her, and we make out intensely, just like that. No further conversation, no fanfare. Just her and me, our tongues mixing, our bodies pressed tightly together in the middle of Central Park. Me, desperate beyond desperate with wanting her.

I'm not usually one for public displays of affection, but she started it. And, I'm so freaking happy and awake now that she has, that I'm pretty sure I won't ever be the one to calm us down. This, now, here, is everything. She is everything. Like a vacuum and an eddy and a tornado all mixed up together, pulling me down, but lifting me up, swirling us like a tumult through eternity.

"I can't explain it," I say sheepishly to Dr. Alvarez. "I know I sound naïve, but it was like . . ." I search for the words. "I had been so checked out before, but I didn't know it. And, then, there I was, for the first time in a long time, feeling totally happy and alive again. That's it, I think: alive. And I remember thinking, 'I don't want to move from here. I just need to stay here. I never want to go back there, to Northhollow.'"

"But you did have to," Dr. Alvarez says, nodding in understanding. "You had to go back. Bring her home. Go to school. Go about your routine. And some things work better in a vacuum."

"What do you mean?"

She glances at her watch. "We need to stop for today. I'm glad you've opened up. You shared a lot, and I know it's hard to talk about this, so I appreciate your willingess to try. In the meantime, it doesn't sound crazy, Klee. None of it sounds crazy. It sounds like you and Sarah had found an important connection, one she wanted. It sounds like she probably cared for you deeply."

I shrug, but my heart aches.

K EE HA WOO. I haven't told her that part yet.

Her words, that she spoke. That she wrote.

How badly I wanted to believe that they were true.

Day 4—Evening

"So, you didn't come to group today?" Martin asks as if he doesn't know the answer already. He takes a bite of his sandwich, chews for a while, and waits. Then he says, "You really should come." Sabrina kicks him under the table with a thud. "Ow! What? He should. It's useful."

I sit, tray heaped with food there's little chance I'm going to feel like eating.

"I didn't feel much like talking. Dr. Alvarez said it's fine if I'm not ready." Martin's gaze moves to mine, and suddenly I feel lame telling a twelve-year-old I'm not ready. If he can go, I should be able to, right? I wonder if Martin sees Dr. Alvarez, or a different therapist. I've never seen him going in there, and I'm pretty sure Sabrina doesn't since she's always at the other end of the hall. If there's more than one therapist here, I feel lucky to have gotten Dr. Alvarez. I can talk to her, at least. As much as I don't really want to talk to anyone.

Sabrina nods and pushes her tray away. "Take your time. Don't let the Mayor of Madness here pressure you." I laugh. Sabrina is quiet, but she packs a punch. "But you *should* eat," she says, nodding at my untouched meal. "I've never seen you eat when you're in here."

"I haven't been hungry."

"I'm always hungry," Martin says. "I can eat through anything, pretty much. Earthquakes, tornadoes, suicide attempts. My mother's boyfriend going to town on me with some endless string of verbal assaults."

"Martin!" Sabrina glares at him. "Why do you have to be

like that?" She shakes her head and turns to me. "I swear it's for shock value, or something. Even Dr. Howe said—"

"It's a defense mechanism," Martin cuts in. "Psychology 101. I say crap because it helps me to process it. So, I really can't worry about whether it's bothering you." He turns to me. "So, enough about my troubles, what happened to you?" He indicates my bandaged ear. "You never did tell us. If you want to, of course. No pressure." He makes bug eyes at Sabrina.

Sabrina rolls her eyes. "Way to be subtle, Martin."

Ignoring his question, I bite into my sandwich, then, even though I'm not sure I want to know, ask, "Wait . . . Suicide attempts?"

"Well, more like ideations, I guess. I've mapped them out, but never really attempted to carry them out. But I'm pretty sure I want to."

"I'm sorry. That's awful. Don't think that . . . You have no idea . . ." I look away. I don't want to share anymore.

Martin shrugs. "It's okay. At least my mom figures it out before and brings me here."

"So, you've been here before?"

"Twice. Plus now. So, three, if you're counting. And, you?" I shake my head. "No, not that. I meant your bandage, there. Fess up."

"Oh." My hand moves reflexively to my ear. "I had a fight with a bad day. Well, actually, a bad night. And the night won."

Sabrina smiles. "I've lost my share of those."

"Actually, it was a few bad months. Well, really the whole, entire, freaking, goddamned year." I push my plate away. I can't eat through the lump that's taken up residence in my throat.

"I hear you," Sabrina says, trying to commiserate. But it's too late. Thoughts of Sarah, of my father, slam me. Of my mother's letters. Sabrina nudges my plate back toward me.

"Trust me. Sometimes you just need to talk about it. Maybe not right now. But soon."

Martin nods, taking some fries from my plate. "We've all done stupid things we regret around here."

"No one said it was stupid, Martin. And sometimes you just need to *not* talk about it, too." Sabrina smiles at me again. "Especially with food in your mouth. Geez."

And, I can't help it. I laugh. "It's okay. I guess it was pretty stupid," I say.

"See?" Martin says. "We're all brilliant and stupid. Geniuses and losers." And he sits back, satisfied, content with whatever debate he thinks he might have just won.

"Mr. Alden, not asleep?" Sister Agnes Teresa waddles forth, sounding surprised as she drops a Hostess Fruit Pie on my table. Its cheerful cherry label stares up at me.

"Do you own stock?" I ask.

Sister Agnes Teresa frowns and says, "Ah, in Hostess, you mean. But Yodels are Drake's Cakes, my friend." She nods toward the window, where the shades are up, letting in the melancholy glow of the courtyard. "Awake *and* you let the outside in. Good signs this evening. Plus, always smart to have the reminder."

I'm not sure what she's referring to, but don't ask, just watch as she moves to the window and stares out, her tunic rising and falling with her breath. She crosses herself before finally turning back to me.

"Don't you like cherry pie, Mr. Alden?"

"I do, thanks. I'm just not hungry yet." I pick it up anyway and examine the label, then hold it out to her. "It says fruit but shows cherry. Is it fruit or cherry, do you think?"

"Ha, we could ask Annie, right? See if she likes it."

"Annie?" I rack my brain, worried the crow is lurking, about to make some grand entrance, proving I'm no better than I was a few days ago. That even Sister Agnes Teresa is a hallucination.

"Annie," she repeats. "Don't you know her? She's odd and funny, but not peculiar."

"O-kay?" I search beyond her to the top of the window sash, but no crow.

"Such a shame you haven't heard of her," she says, determined. "Annie, Annie? No? Well now you have. She likes cookies but not tarts; she likes apples but not peaches; and for sure she likes cherry pies but would never eat a fruit one."

"Ah. Okay. A riddle, then?" I ask, more confused than ever.

"For me to know and you to figure out," Sister Agnes Teresa says, moving from the window toward the door. "Well, I can see you've had enough of me for one night. And, it's almost lights-out anyway." She pulls the door open and turns back again. "She reads books but not magazines. Loves puppies but not dogs. Chews peppermint but not ever spearmint gum."

"Annie," I confirm.

"Indeed. I have faith in you. You'll figure it out," she says.

I slide the cherry pie out of its sleeve, turn off the TV and stare out the window, and think about that first night with Sarah, after the city, on the train back to Northhollow. It's because of that train ride she writes what she does on my portfolio. But that's days later. Here, now, we're still on the train, making out, our lips raw with kissing.

My hand slips up her shirt and touches her bare breasts, my thumb circling her hard nipple. I want to do more than touch her, I want to move my mouth there, my tongue, and taste her everywhere. But I shouldn't even be doing this much in public, so I control myself. At least the train is mostly empty.

At some point, the conductor comes to take our tickets and, I swear, we barely stop. Just hand him them, breathless, like we don't even care.

Only when we reach the station before Northhollow do I force myself to stop and sit up. My breath is heavy, and I'm hard as a rock, so if I don't stop, I'm not going to be able to get up and out, and to my car. I need to find a way to calm down.

Sarah sits up, too. Looks at me, amused. "You're a mess," she says, laughing.

She thinks it's funny I'm so out of control, and maybe it is. As if to instigate further, she slips her hand between my thighs and squeezes.

"Wow, you want me bad," she whispers, leaning in.

"I do. But I need to be able to walk soon, too, and if you do that, you're going to make it impossible."

"I have faith in you."

"Don't," I say.

"Okay, fine." She gives another squeeze, then pulls her hand away. "Here. I'll be good."

We sit in silence for a minute, until she says, "Hey, you've got wood, Klee. Get it?"

"I get it," I say, feeling my ears redden, but she leans in and says, "No, I mean it. You've got Wood. As in me. Sarah Wood. Klee has Wood. See?"

She takes my hand and sits back, satisfied. I breathe deeply, wanting to keep it from sinking in. I need to pace myself. Be wary. Be steady. Because, as much as I want to believe her— to trust anything up here in Northhollow—by the time we reach the top of the long gravel driveway to her house, a strange distance has wedged its way between us, and she tells me to drop her there.

No inviting me in.

No plans for hanging out again.

"Here is good. Thanks. Good night, Alden," is all she says, then she heads down through the darkness without another word.

Day 5—Morning

"I was thinking we might talk about your parents today. Your mother, and your father."

Dr. Alvarez looks down, thumbs through the papers on her clipboard. I close my eyes and think about Sarah. More and more things have been coming back to me. That day in the city. The train ride. The piece of tape I found wrapped around my portfolio handle the Monday after.

KLEE HAS WOOD, in her scrawled handwriting, like a salve for any doubt I was feeling.

And, the way she smiled at me when I finally noticed it was there.

"I know it's difficult, Klee," Dr. Alvarez says, "but I think it's important that you try."

I swallow and nod. I like Dr. Alvarez a lot, but I wish she wouldn't keep bringing up my mother. She doesn't know her the way I do. If she did, she'd understand. Talking about my mother isn't going to help me. My mother is the main reason I'm in here.

"I get that you may be angry with her, but she's genuinely worried about you. She calls often, to check in. Even though she understands there isn't much I'm able to tell her. Still, I can see how badly she wants to help. She's on board with doing anything that might."

"A little late for that," I say, trying to stay focused on *Daubigny's Garden*, but the room is starting to reel again.

"Klee?"

"Yeah?"

"*You* are my patient. This needs to be very clear. Your mother and I discussed *nothing* of substance. She just wanted to check in on you. If there is something I should know, please, tell me. And know anything and everything you say in here is confidential."

". . . You'd think . . . confidential . . . are they going to sue . . . ?"

My mother's friend Annette is whispering to her a little too loudly in the corner, while the priest chants up front and sprinkles holy water and waves incense over my father's mahogany casket. My mother responds, but her voice mixes with the priest's and the organ music, so I can only make out every third word.

"Nothing . . . yes . . . insurance . . ."

I don't care. It's not like I want to know.

The priest raises his arms, his white sleeves trailing beneath like angel wings. "Let us sing now the *Song of Farewell*."

We've been standing in the back since we got here. My mother refused to sit. I was happy enough to be back here, too, out of the line of all those prying eyes. The looks of pity, of horror. As if to ask, "How are you all making it through . . . ?"

The wake was brutal, if strangely surreal. I felt disconnected, like I had walked in on someone else's nightmare. At least there wasn't an open casket. They say it can help to see the finality of it all, but the finality was pretty clear last week when I opened the shower door. And, when you've done what my father did, there's no way to fix up the body for viewing.

". . . shall dwell in the land of the living . . ." the priest sings.

". . . do with the letters?" Annette whispers.

My mother nudges her friend and lowers her voice even more. ". . . rid of them."

"Jesus . . . kidding? . . . Whatever you need from me, I'm here for you, Marielle."

The priest and organ finish abruptly allowing that last part of Annette's stage-whispered answer to break through the sudden silence remarkably loud, intact, and clear. Causing Aunt Maggie to turn from the front row and glare. But she should know better. My father wouldn't care. He hated religion. He hated the church. He'd think this whole ceremony was a bogus waste of money just for show. I'm surprised my mother agreed to it. Now, I think both of us just want to be done with it and out of here.

"Ashes to ashes, dust to dust," the priest says, crossing himself.

". . . mustn't ever find out . . ." my mother says.

I press the heel of my hand to my forehead, and Dr. Alvarez watches me, concerned. The headache that's hung consistently in the background spreads sharply from my sinuses to my eyeballs.

"She's a fucking Ice Queen," I say. "An expert at *seeming* concerned."

"Tell me what you mean."

My eyes well with tears. I'm angry. Furious. Because now I know what that stupid conversation must have been about. I saw the letters. I wish I hadn't, but I did. I found out. And this is what I'm sure of: The days of my mother worrying about anyone else, helping anyone but herself, are gone. I grab the water bottle Dr. Alvarez left for me and drink it down.

"Let's just say, if she cares," I finally say, "she has a weird fucking way of showing it."

"So let's talk about that. Can we?" But I shake my head, and Dr. Alvarez writes something. *God, the shit that must be written on that clipboard.*

". . . he can never know, Annette . . ."

I close my eyes to block it all out. I don't want to think about it. About what she's done, or what I've done. Or what my father did.

I want to go back a year, before he shot himself. Before we moved here and my mother ruined everything. But if I can't have that, I want to go back a few months ago. With Sarah.

K EE HA WOO.

When everything was shiny and new.

"Do you know how to swim?" Sarah is smiling mischievously.

"Yeah. Why? You know it's almost November, right?"

It's our second date. At least I think it is. I think we are actually dating now.

"Oh, that," she says. "Just a calendar thing. Come on."

She reaches for my hand and pulls me up from where we're sitting on a high, rocky ledge overlooking the Upper Bank Basin, a quiet eddy off a rushing, swirling portion of the Hudson.

I wouldn't even think about following her, except, after a brief chill, the past two weeks have been unseasonably warm. Still, I'm in jeans, a T-shirt, and sneakers, while Sarah is in a T-shirt and cutoffs and flip-flops. So if we're heading down to the water, I'll have to hang and watch while she wades in.

"Is there a path down?" I ask, looking twenty feet below us to the shore.

"Leave your keys and cell phone," she says evasively. She taps a shallow groove in the rock with her toes, slips off her flip-flops, and peels her shorts down.

"Wait. Sarah . . ."

"Yeah?" She gives me a coy look. "What? You didn't think we were *walking* all the way down?"

"I, um. You're not serious, are you? You're not seriously thinking about jumping in?"

"Define serious."

"Sarah, that's like, what, twenty feet down? Plus, the air may be warm, but I guarantee you, *in* there, it's pretty damned cold."

"Your choice."

She pulls her T-shirt off, so she's just in her panties, no bra, and wraps her arms around me, pressing her body to mine. "If you strip down, I promise I'll warm you up good right after." She kisses me, using her tongue to tell me exactly what she means, which succeeds in waking up pretty much every part of me.

I pull her tighter against me, but she pushes back.

"*After.* You ready?"

I'm not.

"How far down? Do you even know?"

"Sixteen feet, maybe eighteen. I forget. Twenty, tops."

"And the water? You're sure it's deep enough? I doubt you're hanging around to cart me places in my wheelchair."

"Am too," she says, "But, you'll be fine. I've done it before, plenty of times. I promise. All you have to do is close your eyes and let go."

Let go. With Sarah. Suddenly there's nothing more in the whole world I want to do.

I strip off my jeans and T-shirt, leaving my stuff where she points, and she leads me to the edge and takes my hand.

"On three," she says. "Okay?" She counts, and we jump, holding hands.

The air rushes up and over me, freezing my skin, whistling past my ears. My stomach lurches hard, a tickle that almost hurts but in a good way. My eyes tear and I think, *This is it, then. A whole lot less messy than my father.*

My body plummets, strong like a bullet, and then I hit the water, hard, stinging, losing my grip on Sarah's hand. I plunge deeper, and deeper, and deeper.

Everything erases from my brain. The pressure is intense on my ears.

No sound.

No thoughts.

No nothing.

Then, pushback. And lightness. From dark green to pale green to blue, a brilliant and stunning restoration of light as I ascend. I surface, above the water, bobbing like a cork. The sun hits my face and my breath relaxes, and my ears fill with the sound of Sarah laughing.

I spin happily toward it, find her treading water behind me, hair slicked back, eyes shining.

"Awesome, right?" she says, paddling over. She wraps her arms around me and kisses me, and I struggle to keep us afloat but don't even care if we go under.

Because, it *is* awesome.

As long as Sarah is here with me, it finally is.

Day 5—Late Afternoon

Shelly is at the nurses' station. She's the afternoon nurse who usually brings me my meds.

"I need to call my mom," I say. She nods and moves away,

to give me privacy. I don't know why I decide to call my mother. Something Dr. Alvarez said. And yet, I don't want to talk to her. I have no idea what I'll say.

The sound of the ringing gives me heart palpitations. I should hang up. Or maybe she won't answer. She rarely answers her phone, so there's that.

I try to breathe past my panic while it rings again. I know I can't keep avoiding her forever.

On the fifth ring it goes to voice mail.

"You've reached Marielle, please leave a message. I'll get back to you as soon as I'm able." *Creative. Personal. Warm.* The machine beeps in my ear, gratefully cutting off my thoughts.

"Hey, Mom, it's me. I'm doing better. I hear you're asking. So, yeah, when you get this, you can call if you want. Or not. Either/or. I don't have too much to say."

I trudge back to my room and sit in the chair by the window, staring out at the brachiosaurus until the gray of the afternoon turns to dusk, and the purple-pink sunset melts toward darkness.

"Mr. Alden!"

I'm watching *Jeopardy!* when there's a knock on my door, and Sister Agnes Teresa enters, pushing a large metal service cart. She maneuvers it to the far side of the room near the window, then stops and glances up at the television. "Well, I'm glad to see you like a good game show!"

My eyes dart to the shelves of her cart, from which ancient board games jut, frayed boxes of Stratego, Parcheesi, Clue, and some I've never heard of: Masterpiece, Mystery Date, and HiHo! Cherry-O. She must have loaded up the entire game room.

"I think we need a few more players for most of those," I suggest.

"Nonsense," she says, squatting to peruse the shelves. "And, it's good to see *you* in bed right where I left you." I can't help but laugh, because it's hard not to appreciate a wiseass. "So, Mr. Alden." She rummages. "There's one particular box I'm searching for." I get up to help, but she waves me away. "You sit. Relax. I'll wait on you. Part of the perks of the stay in the asylum."

"What is it we're playing?"

She stands with effort, a box clutched under her arm. "We start basic, of course," she says, placing the chosen box on the table. I stare down at its familiar lid.

King Kandy, Mr. Mint, and Queen Frostine.

"Candy Land?"

Sister Agnes Teresa sits across from me, feet sticking straight out, until she moves forward and readjusts herself sufficiently so that her legs bend at the knees, even if her feet don't quite meet the floor.

"Don't scoff, Mr. Alden. I am the undisputed champion of Candy Land. Ask anyone here. And, I won't go easy on you just because you're new, or in an alleged weakened mental state." She winks, then pats the box. "And this is the good version, too, so you know I don't mess around. None of that *Princess* Frostine instead of Queen Frostine, or Gramma Glam over Gramma Nutt makeover crap."

I have no idea what she's talking about. I haven't seen Candy Land since I was five and used to play with my mother.

And then it slams me. This one little moment when I'm sitting with my mother and father, and we're laughing, and my mother is holding up a paper crown.

"The crown moves to our side," she says to my father. "The win goes to me and Klee." Gleefully, she places the crown on my head and kisses my cheek. "See that? Whichever team you're on is the one that wins!"

"Mr. Alden, you're going to have to focus better than that." Sister Agnes Teresa taps on the spot where she's lined up the four plastic gingerbread people in the center of the board on the table between us, its simple snaking path split down the center by a groove deepened from years of play. "I suggested you might want to pick your color first. An advantage of sorts. Choose wisely. And may luck be on your side."

I take the yellow man and place him on the starting square.

"Interesting. Some say the color yellow relates to acquired knowledge, being the color that most stimulates the left or 'logic' side of our brains. I might have pegged you more as a blue, but I'm pleasantly surprised. I'll be purple. A color that stimulates imagination and spirituality. Or, better yet, the color that represents royalty. After all, the first one to reach King Kandy's Candy Castle wins."

We play three games, of which I win none, before she says, "Well, that's probably enough humiliation for one evening."

"From losing, or playing Candy Land?" I ask, and for the first time since I've met her, she laughs.

"Touché, Mr. Alden. That's for me to know, and you to decide."

She slides the men from the board into the box and folds the rainbow path away. I take the box and say, "Let me," and wedge it back onto the cart between HiHo! Cherry-O and Parcheesi. As I get back up, I realize something, and squat back down to study the remaining games.

"Annie, Annie," I say finally, standing and turning to her. "She likes cherry pie but not fruit pie, likes apples but not peaches, and likes Parcheesi and HiHo! Cherry-O but not Monopoly, right? And she wouldn't be caught dead playing

Stratego." I dust my hands off, proud of myself, and wait for her confirmation.

"I believe I underestimated you, Mr. Alden, likely because of all the constant napping. You've got your wits about you. You might be a formidable competitor after all."

Day 6—Morning

Nurse Carole rolls a breakfast cart into my room. The white paper cup is there with my pills, proving I'm not ready to leave here anytime soon.

"What time is it?" I ask, wondering if I've forgotten some appointment or something.

"9 A.M. Your mother is coming soon."

"Excuse me?"

"It's Saturday, hon. Visiting day. She said she'd be here in about an hour. And not to worry, that she won't stay." Nurse Carole gives me a look, though I'm not quite sure what it means. She moves to the far side of my room and opens the shades. Sunlight floods in. "Said she's just dropping more stuff off for you, though I'm sure she wouldn't mind spending some time if you want her to . . . It's supposed to rain later. They say thunderstorms, so maybe you can take a nice walk before it starts."

I roll my gaze to the window. It looks clear and blue outside, making me think of those stories people tell about 9/11. That it was perfectly sunny that day, with a deceptively clear blue sky. Not a single sign of the threat to come. Just like now. No sign of impending disaster. But I know better.

"Or if you're not up for that, you could always head down to the family room," Nurse Carole adds. "At any rate," she says, nodding at the tray with my pill cup, "there's some toast and yogurt with granola in there in case you don't have time to make it to the dining hall. You really shouldn't take all that medication on an empty stomach. I'm here until noon if you need anything."

"Okay, thank you." I swallow the pills down. As she's about to leave, I call, "Hey, can I ask you something?"

She stops and turns. "Sure."

"Do you know the nun . . . the . . . the one that . . ." I stammer, not sure how to describe her. Is she a nurse? A social worker? A volunteer? "The one that works here?"

Nurse Carole tilts her head curiously, then says, "You mean Sister Agnes Teresa? Yes, of course, why?"

"No reason," I say, feeling relieved. When she leaves, I take a bite of toast and stare out the window. My view is unobstructed. The excavator has moved elsewhere.

I close my eyes and picture my mother, the way she was a long time ago. The way I remembered her last night, with Dad and me, playing board games. I had forgotten her that way. *Before*. Because there *was* a before, not just before Dad died, but when she was younger, less serious, less perfect. More East Village walk-up than marble-floored apartment on Madison Avenue. Less material. *Less Ice Queen*. Somewhere in the back of my brain she exists like that still, in some fuzzy recess, scratchy and faded, like she's been put through some filter on Instagram.

But she did. She was. We were. I can see us there. All three of us. Our family. We're in pajamas, sitting together on the pilled green couch in Dad's first apartment on St. Marks Place. The one she moved into after they got married. The apartment we still lived in while Dad finished law school at night. Before he got the suit job at the big white-shoe law firm, and we moved uptown, and the money rolled in . . . and he stopped painting altogether.

I can see us there. My mother, smiling and laughing, and me, too. It makes me want to cry. It makes me want to hate her.

I open my eyes, desperate to see the excavator, its solid, massive self, head nodded down, teeth ready to chomp into soil, raze the earth. Erase and obliterate everything that's come before.

And here's something else I want to erase, something that eats at me because I hadn't seen it until just now: On that shabby green couch in that small apartment (or in the kitchen later that night, or the park six months later, or even in that Madison Avenue apartment when we first moved in), it's not my mother who is unhappy. My mother is warm, and cheerful, and smiling.

I'm smiling, too.

The only one not smiling is my father.

I knock and knock until Dad finally opens the studio door. "I'm ready," I say, slipping in. "Can we go?"

Dad is still in his pajama pants, no shirt. Even when he's sleepy and half dressed, he's fresh and clean and meticulous. The green and white stripes of the pants frame a perfect flat stomach, his ab muscles tightening as he leans to close the door behind us. My father is skinny and in shape. Handsome and strong. He goes to the gym religiously, and, even when he can't, he does at least one hundred crunches every morning. Plus pull-ups on the bar that hangs over their bedroom door. And most mornings he runs by the Reservoir, hours before I even wake up for school.

My mother gets annoyed. "Must you be such a prima donna, Mark?" I once heard her ask, but she's one to talk. She's more obsessed with looking good than he is.

My friends have mothers who wear sweats and jeans. Not mine, though. Not anymore. Lately, she's always fixed up. Like she needs to be perfect. As if she's going on a date. Or a photographer might arrive at our door.

My dad dresses nice for work, but on the weekends, or the rare occasion he doesn't have to work, he's dressed in joggers and a T-shirt, holed up in his studio to paint. It makes me happy when he is, because he seems most happy there. Painting. Just being himself. Plus, sometimes, I get to paint with him.

The studio is small, modest, with white walls, a clutter of paintings and canvases, and a big window with northern exposure. Dad told me that northern exposure is the best kind of light a painter can have.

Paint, brushes, rags, and color-splattered palettes fill every space on the folding tables that line one wall. The room smells like his aftershave mixed with turpentine.

The painting on the easel now, the one he's been working on for months, is dark and gloomy, ugly. I don't like it. I prefer when he does big sunny paintings with sunflowers and fruit trees and wheat blowing in fields. This one shows a wooden table in low light, stretching across a dark, old-fashioned room. There's a big bowl of fruit on the table. Apples, pears, oranges, plums. But the fruit is bruised and half eaten, seeds and meaty cores scattered about. Several pieces have fallen to the floor, as if someone took a bite and rejected them. Flowers are scattered, too, some fresh and bright, but others dead and molting, shedding their brown leaves.

I glance at the table where he has the actual still life set up that he's working from, but the bowl there holds only a few normal-looking red apples and tangerines.

Next to the table on the floor is a tall ceramic vase that reaches the tabletop. It holds giant yellow silk sunflowers, the kind Dad often likes to paint. He loves to paint sunflowers because Van Gogh painted them, and Dad did his thesis on Van Gogh. At the School of Fine Arts Boston, where I want to go one day.

When Dad paints, he tells me stories about Van Gogh and his work, like how, when Van Gogh painted sunflowers, he didn't just paint them yellow, but also used orange, and green, and even some blue, if you look closely enough. And, that the reason he used so much yellow in his paintings to begin with was because he drank a lot of absinthe. The liquor went to his brain and made his vision go yellow, so things looked yellow to him, even when they weren't.

Eventually, the lead in the yellow paint went to his brain, and made him go crazy. After that, he had a nervous breakdown and shot himself in the head.

My mother gets mad when Dad tells me this stuff, but he explained that paints are different now. And besides, Dad doesn't drink, so I don't need to worry about him.

Dad is home this morning instead of work. He's taking a personal day and he told Mom I should take one, too. "We both know he'll get more from the museums than he'll get from a day at that school, Marielle." She doesn't want to, but she lets me. "Maybe we'll hit the galleries," he tells me. "We'll head down to SoHo first." I prefer museums, but Dad loves his galleries, especially the ones where his friends work.

"The galleries are where the new work is, Klee," he says all the time. "You already know all the masters. Who you don't know are the masters in the making! Isn't that exciting? To discover new art?"

It's perfect outside, sunny and cool, so I don't really care where we go. I'm just happy that we have the day together.

One of the galleries he takes me to has an entire exhibit drawn on Etch A Sketches. At the counter, they're selling mini ones, so he buys one for me, and tells me if I get bored I should try to recreate the sketches I see. In all of the galleries, Dad talks too long, in a voice I'm not accustomed to. It's more formal than his usual one, which makes me uncomfortable when he introduces me. "Georges, have you met my son?" "Pekka, this, here, is Klee. He's sure to be a great artist one day, as well."

A lot of the men he introduces me to have foreign accents and odd, girlish names, like Danielle, and Jacques, and whatever Pekka is. It makes me hate my name, all artsy and different like theirs. I wish Dad had named me Mark after him.

In the last gallery, Dad buys a painting from a man he introduces as Armond. I remember because at first I think he says Almond. I don't really care for him. He's one of the flowery ones, tall and thin with white-blond hair and blond eyebrows, and an accent that's hard to understand. Dad talks to him in hushed tones, for a long time.

When we're finally ready to leave, Dad says he's buying a painting from Armond. Even Armond argues—it's an ugly painting called *Icarus's Flight Plan,* in which a naked man with wings falls from the sky over a heavily trafficked city. Dad tells me it's an homage to a famous painting called *Landscape with the Fall of Icarus* that was done by an artist named Bruegel. "Well, *attributed* to Bruegel anyway, yes, Armond?" but I'm not listening anymore. Nothing he tells me would make me like the painting any better. It's gray and grim and makes me feel sad and cold.

While Armond wraps the painting, Dad sits on a bench by the door and tells me the story of Icarus, which comes from Greek mythology.

"Icarus and his father, Daedalus," he begins, "were imprisoned by King Minos of Crete, inside a labyrinth of the father's own making."

"What's a labyrinth?"

"Ah, good question. Like a maze."

I listen, rapt as he talks, back to being content. I love when my father tells me these stories. "Daedelus was a craftsman, you see, and so as not to be held captive, he built wings made of beeswax and feathers. Giving one pair to his son, he warned Icarus: 'Be careful, my child, whatever you do, make sure you don't fly too close to the sun.' But Icarus became drunk with his power to fly, and so he got cocky, and rose higher and higher into the sky. So high that his wings melted, and the feathers slipped off, and Icarus plunged fatefully down into the sea."

When Armond is ready to ring up the painting, Dad tells me to wait on the bench where I can't make out most of what they're saying. Except when Armond raises his voice. They're arguing about money, I think. I hear the number four thousand. He tells my father it's too much.

"You're a saint, Mark," he says, handing the painting to Dad when we're finally ready to leave. But Dad hands it back, asks Armond to hold it at the gallery. Dad leans in, whispers something I can't hear, then promises, "I'll be back for it!" as we leave to head up West Broadway toward the subway.

"Why don't you paint and sell *your* paintings there?" I ask my father. We've been walking for a while in silence. "Yours are way, way better than that Icarus one."

Dad rumples my hair and puts his arm around me. "Because I couldn't afford to buy more paintings if I did."

"But four thousand dollars is a *lot* of money."

He looks surprised, and stops and crouches down to talk to me, eye to eye. "Do me a favor, kid. Don't tell your mother about that. It's a gift for her. And it was a lot. But, just so you understand, that artist, if he is lucky, will sell ten, maybe fifteen, paintings all year. Let's say twenty in a good year. And the gallery takes a cut, and you can't survive in Manhattan very well on that."

"You can't?" I try to do the math, because four thousand times twenty is eighty thousand, and that sounds like a lot of money. But Dad adds, "And if the artist is represented, his agent or manager might take a cut. And I may have paid a bit of a premium on that one."

He winks, like he's joking, but his voice sounds sad. And I know that all of this means he keeps being a lawyer and doesn't keep on painting like he wants. I try to think of something smart to say, something that would convince him we could live on that kind of money, so he can quit being a lawyer. He can go back to painting, like he went to school for. Like I bet he still wants to do.

"We don't have to live in Manhattan," I say suddenly, "Or, we could stay, but we don't need such a big, fancy apartment. We could go back to the old one . . . Mom and me, I bet we'd both agree on that." Dad laughs, even though I'm not trying to be funny.

"I'm not so sure about that. Besides, your mother . . . at a minimum . . . she deserves to live nicely." He turns to me, serious now. "You need to know this, Klee, I went to law school because I wanted to. I chose my work, my life, because I wanted to. Not because anyone told me I had to." He pauses, as if he's carefully picking his words, like they're harder than they should be. "I chose this life, and I'm not unhappy in it. Life is . . . well, sometimes life is different than you plan."

But I shake my head. I don't believe him. I've heard them fighting. I hear Mom complaining about money, about needing to fix things, about the money she says he must spend. About how late he works, and how much he travels, and how, lately, it never seems like he wants to be home.

So, he can say what he wants, but at least I know this: When I grow up, I'm going to be an artist, painting and showing in galleries, and not working in some office doing dumb things I don't care about or understand.

"Sometimes, when you're a grown-up, Klee, your passions need to be a hobby, and you find work—a career—that can bring you stability, and other things . . ."

His voice trails off and he puts his arm around my shoulder and squeezes, guiding me to keep walking toward the subway. When we reach the corner, he stops and looks at me hard, again. "When you're a grown-up," he says, "you see things differently. You count your blessings for all the good, amazing things you do have, not what you can't have. And, you, son, for sure, are a good thing. The best thing. So you plow forward, and you don't look back, regretting all the choices that you made."

And, I want to believe that he means it, but when the light changes and we start to cross, he turns toward the gallery, like his whole body wants to go back there.

I wash my face, splashing water up fast and hard, trying to somehow prepare myself for my mother, and to rinse away the fury that has spread over me, not at my mom for a change, but at my dad. For acting like he was happy when he wasn't. For pretending that everything was okay when it wasn't.

For pretending *he* was okay.

Maybe if he hadn't, maybe if he had trusted me—But I can't finish the thought, can't go there anymore, to the place where I imagine he's still here, still alive, and everything is normal.

I turn off the faucet and stare in the mirror, and see not his face but my mother's. Her light brown hair, and tepid brown eyes, her rounder face with softer cheekbones. His face was narrow and chiseled, his eyes, a deep, dark brown. He looked like a movie star.

"You look like your father . . ." my mother always says, but she's wrong. I don't. I can never see him in me at all.

A new wave of nausea rolls over me. I shouldn't have called her. I shouldn't have told her she could come. It's already turned overcast, the clouds a foreboding gray. Soon it will rain, a downpour, and I'll be stuck in the "family" room with her.

I doze off until the unmistakable jangling of my mother's gold bangles and tennis bracelets wake me.

I hear her out at the nurses' desk, announcing herself. "Yes, that's right. Marielle Alden. Did you need me to sign in?"

"No, you're good. Go ahead in, Mrs. Alden."

There's a quick rap on my door. I sit up. My heart pounds to the steady beat of rain pelting the window.

I feel like I'm going to puke.

"Yeah, come in. It's not even closed," I say, when she knocks again.

I glance at the small Dixie cup on my breakfast tray, but it's empty. I've already taken my day's full allotment of pills.

It's a Saturday morning, the weekend after Sarah and I go to the Upper Bank Basin. The front doorbell rings, and by the time I register it, and my mother calls me to the living room, Sarah is standing in our foyer.

Fuck.

I was avoiding this for so many reasons. And now I'm not even sure what's gone down.

"Oh, hey! Mom," I say, breathless, wiping sleep crust from my eyes, "this is Sarah. Sarah, this is my mom."

"We've met."

It's not even 10 A.M., yet my mother is dressed to the nines like she has an important business meeting to go to, except she doesn't. Slacks, pumpkin-colored sweater set, inevitable heels.

Sarah, on the other hand, wears her now ubiquitous cutoff shorts, her Vans, and a skimpy T-shirt that shows both her lack of a bra and her bare stomach, an outfit that shows no sign of a chill in the air as would be indicated by my mother's selection. She looks beautiful, of course, but it's not exactly the outfit I'd pick for her very first meeting with the Ice Queen.

I should have told her my mother can be kind of judgmental.

"Don't give me that look, Klee. Your father likes it when I pull myself together . . ." My mother's frustrated voice echoes from the depths of some distant memory chamber. She holds a scarf to her chest, shakes her head, tosses it back into her drawer, and chooses another. She wraps that one around her shoulders and neck, and turns to me. I must have some look on my face because she says, "So sue me for wanting to please him."

My mother, the victim. My mother just trying to make everyone *else* happy.

"Klee, you have company," my mother says, bringing me back to our living room. "Might you go put a shirt on?"

I stare down at my unwashed, unbrushed self, in just ratty gym shorts, nothing else, which would be worse only if I were also sporting a pee boner, and wonder if I missed some text from Sarah warning me she was coming over.

I didn't even know she knew our house number.

"Um, yeah."

It's not that I'm not happy to see her, because I am. More than anything. I just could have used some warning. I'm embarrassed about myself, about my mother, about our too-perfect home, the premium model off the pages of some glossy architectural magazine.

"Good! I'll entertain your lovely friend here while you wash up and put clothes on." The disapproval in my mother's voice stings, but there's no way I want to leave Sarah alone with her. God knows what she'll say. *Do.* Maybe offer her some tea to go with a polite-yet-frank chat about my father's suicide, about me being fragile because of it, and how she, Sarah, needs to be careful with me. I wouldn't put it past her. And I need to be the one to tell Sarah about my father.

On the other hand, I can't do much in this condition.

"I'll be right back" I say, adding hopefully, "Or Sarah could come wait in my room."

"I think not," my mother says.

"I'm fine here," Sarah adds quickly.

Her hair is still wet from the shower, so she must have gotten up recently, too. When she reaches to pull it back into a ponytail, her shirt rides up higher, nearly exposing the soft, gentle shadow of her chest. My mother clears her throat, so the best thing I can do now is get washed up and get us both out of here.

"Back in five," I say, racing down the hall, then yank on jeans and a clean T-shirt and head to the bathroom.

I brush my teeth, feeling stupid that I haven't told my mother about Sarah. Or more accurately, told her only the most minimal things. She knows we went to the city. But through my mother's eyes, now, I can see how it looks like more, and, well, it feels like more, and so maybe I should have prepared her. For Sarah's sake, if not hers.

I'm back in the living room fast. Sarah sits across from my mother on one of the Queen Anne chairs. She's saying, ". . . at North Side General. In the neonatal unit," so I figure she's talking about her mother.

"Hey! Okay. Ready! So, you want to go for a ride or something? I ask too anxiously, then to my mother, "Okay if I take the car? Not far. Just down to the river or something."

"Of course," my mother says, but her eyes dart nervously from Sarah to me, as if she has something to say. I give a look to Sarah and she stands.

"Let's go," I say, ushering her to the front door.

Outside, I steer Sarah down the front steps and to the far

side of the driveway, letting her into the passenger side before
I realize, though the car is unlocked, the keys are still in the
house. "Be right back!" I call and rush back to the house to retrieve them.

"Here you go," my mother says, standing at the front door,
the keys dangling from a finger. When I grab at them, she
holds them back, and gives me a long, intense look. "You like
her a lot?"

I roll my eyes. "You can relax, Mom. I barely know her," I
say, even though I'm not sure I believe this myself. Still, I need
to shut her down. I don't have time for this right now. Besides,
I'm not the one who wanted to come live here, so she doesn't get
to dislike the one thing that might actually make it bearable.

"It's just . . . She seems like a lot of girl to handle. And
sometimes, well, Klee, sometimes we choose people for the
wrong reasons, for what we want to see in them, rather than
who they are."

"Great. Noted," I say. *I mean, last I looked, my father killed
himself, so maybe you're not an expert on relationships,* I don't add.
"Can I go now?"

"Yes, sure. You know I just worry about you . . ."

"Well, don't," I say, turning away before her hand reaches
my cheek. "It's a little late for that, anyway."

There is so much stuff in my mother's arms and at her feet
she looks as if she's arriving for a stay at a resort. A Louis Vuit-
ton carry-on. Some weird sort of duffel or laundry bag that
has no strings that I don't recognize. An easel, for God's sake,
but the fat-legged, plastic kind they use in preschools that she
must have gone out and bought because that's what they allow
in here, or something.

I see now, too, that her clothing is wet, her nice sage green suit jacket and beige slacks streaked dark in places from the rain. She looks expectantly at me from the door.

"You carried all that?"

"A nice young orderly helped me," she says. "But you can help me from here."

I move toward her and quickly grab the bag and the easel so I don't have to hug her. I know I should, but I can't. My body feels off and shaky, like I'm about to be light-headed again.

"My dearest M . . ."

"Come in," I say, pushing the suitcase into the room with my foot. I eye it, hoping my laptop is in there, but know better. No social media allowed. No contact with the outside world, except immediate family.

". . . a lot of girl to handle . . ."

"Klee?"

I stop, sudden fury hitting me fast and hard. "Yeah?" I ask, voice sharp. I exhale slowly.

"It has wheels. Please don't do that." She bends and lifts the retractable handle and drags it the rest of the way into the room. The door closes behind her, resting open the last few inches thanks to the rubber stop. "Some of your schoolbooks are in there in case you want to keep up with your work. That's why it's so heavy."

"Got it. Good. Thanks." I haven't thought much about my remaining schoolwork. My grades have already been sent to Boston, so I basically just need to pass my classes. My portfolio is the main thing I need to get done. Hence the easel, I guess.

"I wasn't sure what you might need. It would be wonderful if you could keep up while you're here, for when you go back—"

I nod and walk to the bed, and unzip the duffel bag. There's a plastic box of my brushes, all sizes, and not one but two new sets of Amsterdam Expert Series acrylics, the large tubes, enough to cover a small house with, seriously. *Now I can really be like Van Gogh, painting away in the asylum.*

I give her a look, and she says, "I know, overkill. But I wanted to make sure you had everything you might need. And the staff says the brushes are okay." She shifts uncomfortably. "Anyway, you look good, Klee. You really do. I'm so glad for that." She walks over and moves her hand up as if she's going to stroke my hair, but I pivot away and walk to the window instead. She sits awkwardly on the edge of my bed. "It's a relief to see you . . . You look better than I thought you would."

"My dearest A . . ."

I laugh now—I don't know why I laugh, but I do. Not a funny laugh, but a harsh one, coughed out, and her eyes flash up at me, then land, concerned, on the small bandage that still covers my ear. "You have lost weight, though," she says.

"The food here isn't exactly gourmet."

"Well, for the cost, you'd think it might—" Too late, she checks herself, realizing how she sounds. She looks away, apologetic.

I know I should be nicer. More appreciative or something. It can't be easy for her to be here, to see me in here, like this. Not to mention to have dragged all this shit here in her nice clothes in the rain. But the letters, her typed words, keep infiltrating my brain.

". . . My dear, beautiful man . . ."

"You know," I say, anger now cracking my voice, "you could really use some regular weekend-type clothes. Jeans. Sneakers. Something that says, 'Casual Saturday-morning visit with my son at the mental hospital.'"

"Klee, please! Please don't call it that." She winces and I almost feel bad. "I'm sorry if I brought the wrong things. Wore the wrong things. I've been worried sick . . . I was trying to be helpful. I just thought you might like something to do while you're here. They said no electronics. I figured you must be going crazy—"

She hears it, same as I do, and I can't help myself and say, "Sorry, *went already*. Apparently." It's just too easy to let it slide.

It gets the desired effect, too. She stands and moves toward the door.

"Forgive me for trying, Klee. For the life of me, I don't know what I've done." She sounds so deeply wounded, I'm surprised she stops again at the door. "One more thing, Sarah keeps texting you. I know it's none of my business . . . I'm not snooping. I plugged your phone in to charge. I thought you'd want me to . . . It keeps buzzing, and her name pops up. I can't read the texts, it's locked. I just see her name, so don't worry. But I thought maybe someone should let her know how you are, and that you don't have your phone in here, so she won't keep trying. Maybe she thinks you do."

My throat closes and I look away.

"Would you like me to text her or something?"

"No! I'll deal with it. Do you know when I'm allowed to have it back?" I manage.

"Your phone?"

"Yes, all that stuff. My phone, my laptop."

"How would I . . . ? Hasn't Dr. Gomez told you?"

"It's Alvarez. Jesus, Mom."

I can't stop it any longer. The seawall breaks and Saturday night rushes through like a fucking deluge. *The letters. My mother's stupid emails . . . and the knife.*

Dunn's house in the rain.

The ambulance, and Sarah crying . . .

My phone must have been in my sweatshirt, my sweatshirt covered in blood. My mother must have taken it all home. Thrown one out. Plugged the other in.

"That's what I meant, Klee. Sue me. Alvarez," she says. "Shall I go home? It sounds like you'd like me to go home?"

"Yes," I say. "Please. I'm not feeling too well. I'm sorry."

"Sure." She folds her arms to her chest and shakes her head, tears welling in her eyes. "I'm not sure why you're so angry at me, Klee. I was hoping this wasn't going to be a full-blown thing, that you were going to be okay, that you'd be out of this place by now. That you might . . ." She trails off, swallowing hard. Finally, she says, "But I understand it's best that we wait until you're ready."

"Right. Great. That's what we'll do."

"Okay. Let me know what I can do . . . If I can help." She pulls the door open, then turns to me again. "I want to help, son. I don't want to make things worse. You're all I have."

". . . I shouldn't print them, I know, but I can't bring myself to delete them. Sometimes they're all I have . . ."

I don't look at her, don't respond, and she leaves.

"You should have thought of that fucking sooner!" I finally call out, but not until she's gone, my words rendered impotent against the wall of the mostly closed door.

I drive the two miles to Sarah's house from mine, turning down Old Basin Road. I don't remember what day it is. I can't keep track anymore. Maybe mid-November. It's a weekday, Superintendent's Day, this I remember. And that it's the first time things with her go really bad.

Come over, she texts. Mom at work. Whole house to ourselves. ;)

The past few weekends, we haven't had much time together. There always seems to be a football game, and everyone goes, no question. Northhollow is undefeated, 7–0, and you'd think each game was the Super Bowl. Everyone is there to support Abbott and Dunn. Everyone is there to cheer on Northhollow.

And, of course, there's some party after.

I don't go to the games, can't bring myself to. And, the parties? Yeah. I definitely can't bring myself to go to those.

But in school, at least, I've been trying. Trying to be cool and friendly to Abbott and Dunn.

"Maybe next one," I tell Sarah, making up one lame excuse after another.

I don't fit in. I'm not one of them. So why would I stand around drinking and bullshitting? We have nothing in common. They know it. And I know it. The two of them are like some fucking Tweedledee and Tweedledum.

Okay, maybe that's not fair. But I'm sure they don't give a shit about me either. What do I have to offer them? They already think they're God's gift to Northhollow, simply because they know how to hike a ball. And maybe they are. But it's not like two players from Northhollow are ever going to be making the NFL. They'll never get near the pros, let alone a Division 1 college, any more than I'm going to be the next Van Gogh.

But I care what Sarah thinks, and I know she already has her friends. I'm the new guy here. So I'm not about to stop her from hanging out with them. I'm guessing I'm not going to change her mind about them, either.

Maybe I'm just jealous. Maybe that's why I don't like the way they hang around her. All possessive, like they own her. Abbott, especially.

"We're just friends, Klee," she reassures me. "I told you, we've been friends since kindergarten. He gets me. I'm like a sister. He doesn't ask anything of me. He doesn't want anything from me, either. He just lets me be who I am."

And I don't? Besides, she's being totally naïve. It's obvious that dude would put the moves on her in a hot second if given the opportunity.

"Besides, Klee," Sarah said to me the other day, "you're the one who thinks you're too good for everyone. Because you lived in the city. Because you're an artist. Because you're going to some Ivy League school." All of her sentences are spit out like she has a foul taste in her mouth.

"That's not true, Sarah," I say. "It's not fair. And it's not Ivy League."

"Whatever. Museum school. Same difference. You know what I mean." She'd pulled me in then and kissed me hard, like she wanted me to know she was just joking. But sometimes it's hard to tell. Sometimes, no matter how hard I try, I feel like an outsider. Like I'm competing with them for her affection. "And those guys?" she'd finally added, "I know they can seem like assholes, but they're not. I promise you. It's all they've got. They're not trying to impress anyone but themselves."

But, here, now, rolling Dad's car down her driveway, I want to forget all of that. I just want to spend one whole day alone with Sarah.

In daylight, the house shocks me. A gray clapboard cottage with peeling paint and an overgrown, weed-filled lawn that doesn't look like it's been mowed in over a year. I couldn't really see it that first time in the dark. But now that I can, the windows need fixing, as do the front steps. A freestanding shed or garage has half its door bashed in, a large gaping hole in the side, as if someone didn't see it was down and drove a car through it. We may live only two miles apart, but the houses here might as well be a million miles apart from the new construction water views where I live. It might as well be another country.

By the time I turn off the engine, Sarah is skipping outside.

Seeing her makes everything better. The grin on my face must be huge.

"What are you smiling at, Alden?" She pats the hood of the car.

"You. Got a problem with that?"

"Well, I do love you when you are moody," she teases. "And I always forget you have these fancy wheels. Did you have to leave the Bentley at home?" She laughs and opens the passenger door and slides in, leans across and kisses me, then falls into me, urgent, all mouth and tongue. Underneath her minty-fresh-toothpaste breath, I think I might taste the vaguest hint of alcohol.

"Man, you're so easy," she says, slipping her hand between my legs.

"I am. You should take advantage of it." She throws her head back and laughs, then slinks down in the seat, propping her bare feet up on the dashboard. "So, where should we go?"

"We're going somewhere? I thought you had the house to yourself. Didn't you want me to come in?"

She shakes her head. "I changed my mind. The place smells. And it's a mess. It depresses me. And anyway, it's beautiful out. Let's go somewhere."

"Wherever you want." I give her a sideways glance. "But it is way too cold to be jumping in any water."

"Wuss. But okay. None of that. I swear. Just other things." She kisses my cheek.

"Do you need to get shoes? A jacket or something?"

"Nope, you'll keep me warm, won't you?"

She leans against me, and I drive. She tells me to hook a right, then another at the bottom of Old Basin Road, and then we're driving up a hill, and suddenly I'm pretty sure where we're going and I can't stop smiling. Lookout Ridge at the very top of River Drive. I've heard kids at school talking about it, some unpaved path that takes you through the woods to a secluded spot where all the couples go to hook up.

"Turn left here," she says, pointing out a narrow dirt road without a sign that she says is River Drive. After another few hundred yards, we go from dirt road to pretty much unexcavated pathway covered in low bushes and foliage trampled down from years of cars and all-terrain vehicles plowing through.

Finally, we arrive at a clearing that ends at a rickety old metal rail, and she points and says, "Park there." Off to our left are thick woods, and in front of us, steep cliffs spill down into the Hudson. I must look unsure because she says, "Promise you, it's okay. No one will care. No one comes to this spot, except a few stoners looking to get high."

"And people looking to hook up."

"Nope," she says. "Other direction. Were you hoping?"

I laugh, but maybe my heart sinks a little. Still, I turn off the ignition and start to open my door. But instead of getting out, Sarah crawls into the backseat and says. "I prefer the less-traveled places, and it's too cold out there. Plus, you've got this fancy car to take advantage of. You coming to warm me up, Alden?"

I close my door again and tumble into the back, and we make out like lunatics, and then, she's working at my pants, my fly, her teeth biting my lower lip, her sweet-mint tongue sliding in and rolling around with mine.

"You want me?" she asks, and I do—of course I do—but I don't answer, because I actually need to slow things down.

But she's not waiting for an answer, or for me to find a way to chill. She pulls my hands up under her T-shirt, and says, "Don't be shy. Go ahead. You can."

I cup her perfect breasts in my hands, let my fingers pull softly at her nipples. She moans and undoes her jeans, pushing them down, and letting my hand slip between her pale, soft thighs. I touch her there, over her panties, then follow suit, yanking my jeans off, leaving only my boxers, delirious at the feel of her body.

"Wait, do you take something?" I whisper, realizing what we're about to do, yet unable to stop myself from pressing against her. I feel her pulse against me through our underwear. Or maybe it's me I feel pulsing. Either way, it doesn't matter. I'm done before I ever get my boxers fully down.

There's sticky wet bullshit all over the inside of my legs.

Fuck.

Shit.

Jesus, Klee.

Cant you do anything right?

I can't breathe. I can't think. This has never happened before. Not in the city. Not with either of the other two girls I slept with there. It never happened before fucking North-hollow.

"Shit," I whisper. "I'm sorry."

She sits up and pulls her shirt down, pulls her jeans on.

"Fuck, I'm sorry." I say again. I sit up and stare out the window. "I think it's this car . . . it was my dad's and . . . I can't move around right . . ." I don't finish the thought. It's dumb, a lie, and she knows it. She adjusts her clothes, not looking at me. "I can be ready in a minute, if you give me . . ." My words are idiotic, and my ears burn hot and red. I don't even know what I'm saying.

"Forget it, Alden," she says, climbing back into the front seat. "I'm flattered. Really. It's no big deal." But she doesn't look flattered. And she can't even stand to be next to me.

"Sarah—"

"God! You really need to lighten up, Alden. You're too intense. It's hard to take. I like you a lot. I do. But everything with you feels like such a big deal."

"I know. I'm sorry. It's not. I just . . ."

"Stop apologizing! And stop trying so hard. It's not life or death. Sometimes, you just have to chill." She turns around and makes crazy bug eyes at me like she's being silly to lighten the mood. "You're still hot. It's fine. Take a chill pill."

But isn't it all life and death?

I pull on my jeans and move into the front seat, and turn on the car.

"No, don't. Not yet," she says. "I want to stay here for a bit."

She puts her feet up on the dash and slips a broken cigarette from a pocket somewhere. I didn't even know she smokes. I open my mouth, but before I can protest her lighting up in my father's car, she drags at it unlit, inhaling deeply, and says, "See? Chill. I quit months ago. I'm not an idiot, dude," before blowing invisible smoke out the rolled-down window.

"I didn't say you were, Sarah. I don't think it either."

"I know, Alden. We're good." She takes another fake drag and says, "And, really, don't feel bad. About what happened. It's nothing. Seriously. But you're going to have to learn how to chill. One of these days, you're going to have to learn how to fake it and chill."

Day 6—Late Afternoon

There's the sound of a rolling cart, then a soft knock on my door before it opens. Sister Agnes Teresa appears, the swish of her robes sounding as she makes her way into my room.

"Ah, in bed, I see. How novel! In the middle of a perfectly good Saturday afternoon."

"Well, I don't know about perfectly good. There's sort of a monsoon outside, no?"

"Nonsense," she says, waving me off, then wheels the cart to the far side of my bed. She opens the shades and bends to extract a box from the cart's lower shelf. "A perfectly good day for a board game." I roll my eyes, but I sit up and swing my legs over the side of the bed. "Well at least you're dressed," she says, eyeing my T-shirt and jeans. "You had some plan to conquer this day after all. Has something derailed it?"

"My mother. Bearing gifts." I nod toward the narrow closet, and Sister Agnes Teresa glances at the primary-colored easel stashed off to its side.

"I see. Do you finger-paint?" She chuckles at her own joke.

"That's about my speed right now, isn't it?" I say, joining her in laughing. "So this"—I walk over and tap the lid of the box—"should be right up my alley too, right?" She smiles, so I add, "And, I'm taking your chair. I'm pretty sure that other one is jinxed."

She sits across from me, adjusts her positioning. "Take whatever advantage you feel you might need, Mr. Alden."

She puts the box on the table. Chutes and Ladders, with its gaggle of cavorting cartoon kids sliding down pink slides, stares up at me. I must snort because she says, "Do you have an issue with the offering?"

"No. Of course not."

"Well, good. Because I know it may appear simple, but you'd be surprised. There's a lot to be learned from Chutes and Ladders. People underestimate the lessons that abound within the four cardboard corners of this box. Just like in life itself, we're constantly clawing and stretching and climbing in pursuit of life's sweet and just rewards. Our prizes, you know? Cute cats and cookies and blue ribbons and bouquets. But just when we think we have a foothold, when we've mowed the lawn so we're clearly going to get to go to the circus, we take one step too few or too many, and bam! We hit that chute and go falling, falling, falling, irretrievably down."

"I see what you're doing here—"

She interrupts, holds up a finger, and says, "Or do we?" so I let her continue on with her soliloquy. "And sure, you can forget the cats and the cookies and the circus. We both know I'm not actually talking about those. Go ahead. Sub them out. Cats for love, or cookies for a job or a college acceptance, a circus for whatever kind of success. Because we both know, whether we've yet to experience it or not, that for every ladder to love, there is that inevitable chute to loss. And the ladder to health and happiness eventually meets up with a chute that takes you right back down there to death. No matter what we may do to avoid it.

"For excitement, there is lethargy; for wealth, the risk of losing it all, going bankrupt, you see? But we play the game anyway. What else is there to do? So, we roll the dice and keep hoping."

She unfolds the board, raises an eyebrow, and holds out the dice to me. "Go on. Home-team advantage. I'll let you go first."

"I did get out of bed earlier, so you know," I say, shaking the dice. "I made some big commitment in my head. You know, take a walk, get some fresh air, act human? Don't be a wuss or a loser."

She nods. "Sounds like an ideal start."

I spill the dice onto the board and she chuckles. I've rolled a 1 and a 2, which puts my guy at 3, on a square that has nothing. No chute or ladder, no drawing, no person, no nothing.

"Don't fret. Baby steps, right?" she says, but she smiles like she's more than a little pleased, then shamelessly rolls a 4 and gets a ladder up to square 14.

I roll a 5 and get nothing again, and by the time I'm at square 13, she's at square 84, and I'm full-out laughing. And for every chute I hit after that, and slide down, I laugh harder. I can't help it. The whole thing is hilarious and I can't stop laughing for a change.

Maybe it's because it's a mindless task, some childish board game that takes my mind off everything but silly nothingness. Or maybe it's because of how optimistic and nice and funny she is, this dwarf penguin nun, in the face of all the fucked-up shit that's wrong with her, but for the first time in days I feel hopeful. Because if she can be happy and light, then maybe I can find a way to get back there, too.

On Monday, I'm intentionally late, so Sarah's already at the table working when I get to Tarantoli's room. We haven't spoken all weekend, not since I dropped her off Saturday after our humiliating date.

I keep thinking about what happened, and about Sarah telling me to "fake it and chill." Well, fine. If that's what she wants, I can do that. Pretend I don't give a shit about it all. I haven't called. I haven't texted. And, now I'm purposely late to class, with no time to talk.

This is me, Klee Alden, faking it. Chilling. I'm just here at Northhollow biding my time.

I walk to the back of the room and retrieve my portfolio from the cubbies, and slide it onto our table. The handle with the tape—*KLEE HAS WOOD*—dangles like a sad, pathetic lie.

Sarah keeps her head down, working on some new piece she calls *Waves*. It's pretty basic. For the past week Tarantoli has had us working on tessellations, Escher-like designs that explore the division of a perspective, dimension, and plane. It's not my usual style, but it wouldn't be a bad thing to show SMFA I've got range.

I unzip my portfolio and slide out the piece I started, but it sucks, so I pull out a fresh piece of paper. As soon as I do, Sarah reaches across and writes in the corner:

U MAD?

My eyes meet hers.

NO, I scrawl back. *WHY?*

PLAYING HARD TO GET?

Ha, as if.

NO. BROODING, I write instead.

She cracks a smile at that one, which makes me smile, too.

WHY?

I shrug. *I FEEL DUMB.*

DON'T, she writes. *DON'T.*

WHY NOT?

She bites her pencil like she's thinking hard, then finally writes, *BECAUSE I SAY SO.*

We both look at that, and I roll my eyes, and she whispers, "Okay fine, be that way," and she scratches that out and writes,

BECAUSE YOU ARE THE REAL DEAL.

WEEK TWO

Day 8—Morning

On Monday morning reality hits, and a heavy hopelessness descends in the form of my mother hovering in the doorway of Dr. Alvarez's office.

Her features are in shadows, her blond hair illuminated at the edges like expensive gold thread. Likewise, the threads of her Chanel jacket catch bits of light complementing her hair. Her bracelets jangle. Is she coming from a meeting? Why does it always seem like she's dressed to impress?

"... *My dearest M ... You are perfection ...*"

My stomach roils and bile rises into my throat. Did I say she could come today and forget? I don't know what I was thinking.

Yes, I do. Guilt. When she called again. Or, false hope, maybe. Or it was the medication talking. Or maybe I was still high off my first Chutes and Ladders win.

Dr. Alvarez looks at me for information, her expression changing quickly to concern.

"Your mother said you were expecting her? That you said it was okay if she came in?" She gives me a half smile, half grimace, as if to say, "Now that she's here, how bad can it be?"

Bad, Dr. Alvarez. Bad.

I can't stop the images from coming.

"*My dearest A ... My good man ...*"

"Klee?"

"*I shouldn't print these, but I want to carry your words ...*"

I lift my head from where I've lowered it onto the throw pillow in my lap and stare at my mother in the doorway.

"Do you want me to go? I can leave." I hear the tears in her voice. Her arms hang helplessly at her sides. She looks to Dr. Alvarez, then away.

I want to believe her. I want to believe that her upset isn't an act, but she's lied about so much already.

Dr. Alvarez opens the drawer to her left, rummages around, and tosses a yellow stress ball next to me on the couch. "That's up to Klee," she says.

I sit up, and roll the ball in my fingers. ***The chief danger in life is that we take too many precautions."—Alfred Adler.***

My eyes shift to Dr. Alvarez, and she asks, "What say you, Klee? Do you want to try to discuss some things, or do you need another day?"

I need many more days. I need a century.

"No. Let's get it over with," I say.

"Come in, Mrs. Alden. Sit. We'll talk for a bit. See how we do. If Klee needs more time, we'll adjourn. It's flexible, how we do things in here. Whatever is best for him, you understand?"

My mother nods and steps in. Her features reappear. Her lip trembles and she gives me this apologetic look. No, not apologetic. Expectant. Like she's hoping for something I can't give.

I don't get up. I have nothing to offer at this point.

She sits on the other end of the couch, her leather bag perched on one knee, her thin fingers clutched around it.

"Would you like some water?" Dr. Alvarez asks.

"Yes, please." My mother reaches out, and her gold bracelets jangle. She uncaps the bottle and sips.

Jangle, jangle, jangle.

Every move, every sound is exaggerated.

My mother puts the bottle down, takes off her jacket, folding it perfectly over the arm of the couch.

Jangle. Jangle.

"Forgive me," Dr. Alvarez says, "this office is always warm. It's the forced heat. I keep requesting a humidifier to counter it. If we'd had a warmer week, they'd have turned off the heat altogether. Any day now. It's much more manageable in the spring."

My mother nods, fidgeting, and drinks some more water. Dr. Alvarez seems more uncomfortable than usual. She pulls her clipboard to her lap, waits patiently for my mother to say something.

My mother drinks again. A drop of water from the mouth of the bottle lands on her cream silk blouse and spreads outward in a darkening circle. I wonder vaguely if it will ruin it. A minor chute against her many, many ladders.

She recaps the bottle and twists it in her lap. Finally, she turns and looks at me. I don't know if it's for show or not, but her eyes are filled with tears.

"Klee, honey, it kills me to see you here." I close my eyes, and she says, "Dr. Alvarez, please, I don't know what I've done. I just want to help."

But I don't want her help. I want my father. I want Sarah. I let Sarah crawl toward me on her knees.

Wait! No. Not that day.

That day got messed up.

Not that one. Not now. Not with my mother here.

We're doing it again, but this time I'm lasting.

Sarah feels amazing, and I'm lasting.

I think the condom I bought is actually helping. We move

in rhythm, in sync, until she whispers my name, and squeezes my back before relaxing quietly beneath me.

Only then do I let myself go, too.

She brushes back my hair and kisses my forehead. I feel giddy. Happy. Happy because I made Sarah feel good.

I get up and go flush the condom, grabbing my jeans, to pull them on in case her mother gets home. We're in the basement, and her mother's filling in on someone else's weekend shift.

"Nice abs," she says, lowering herself onto the floor and crawling over. She sits on her knees, looks up at me with her gorgeous blue eyes that I can never get enough of, and runs her hands up the length of my torso. "You're skinny, so I didn't realize how much you must work out." She moves her hands back down my stomach and over the front of my boxers.

If she wants to, I can go again.

"No so much," I say. "I do crunches. But there's a lot you don't know about me, Sarah Wood."

I glance down my thin frame and feel myself disappear. All I can see is my father. In his striped pajama pants. In his sunny studio. Painting.

I have the same build as he did. I'm staring down at myself but keep seeing my father.

"Okay. So tell me."

"Tell you what?" I flinch, reeling, slammed by how badly I'm missing him.

"Never mind." She laughs, goes down on all fours again, and crawls toward me. She's still in just her panties.

She sings softly, words to a vaguely familiar old song I know she likes because she plays it on her phone.

"Every cloud must have a silver lining . . ."

She watches me intently, her long black eyelashes batting up at me, and I'm trying to focus, to concentrate.

"Wait until the sun shines through

Smile my honey dear
While I kiss away each tear . . ."

I'm trying to smile, and I'm sure that I've managed, that I'm smiling, but I can't clear my father from my brain.

"Or else I shall be melancholy too."

"Klee . . . ?"

And I'm crying.

Jesus. For some dumb-ass reason, I'm crying.

I don't mean to. I don't want to be.

I hate myself for letting it happen.

Maybe it's something in her voice, how lilting and beautiful it is, or maybe it's the lyrics, or maybe it's because despite trying not to, I already love her so much. And love is trouble. Love is broken and wrong. The people we love don't stick around.

Whatever the reason, Sarah is naked, and singing, and I'm the motherfucking asshole who is crying.

I hate myself for it.

Sarah sits back and looks at me.

I swipe at my eyes and say, "Don't stop, please. I'm just moved by how pretty your voice is."

But she gets up, pulls on her clothes, and walks back to the couch where she left the remote, and turns on the TV, putting the volume up loud.

I should leave. I should just go home and never come back. But I don't want to leave us like this.

I sit on the couch and pull myself together. Fuck me, but I pull myself together.

We watch *Family Feud*. That's what's on, so we watch it. We watch until the Cutler Family wins. When it's over, I reach out and take Sarah's hand, but she slips her fingers out of mine and says, "I'm sorry, Klee. I told you I like you, and I do. I like you a lot. But, I don't know . . ." She shakes her head, eyes looking so, so sad.

"Are you breaking up with me?"

She turns and stares at me, says, "What? No. God, no." But she shakes her head again and wraps her arms to her chest. "I just think you want more from me than I'm ever going to be able to give."

Day 8—Afternoon

"What about you, Martin?"

Sarah is gone.

My mother is gone.

Dr. Alvarez is gone.

I'm sitting in group therapy with Sabrina and Martin.

I'm not sure how I got myself to come here, but I know this: If I'm going to get better, and get out, I need to step things up around here.

In addition to the group leader, Dr. Howe, there's me, Martin and Sabrina, and one other kid about my age. He looks older, but I'm pretty sure this place only goes to eighteen. Maybe it's the shaved head that makes him seem older. He's big, too, like a weightlifter. A tattoo of a swastika sticks out from his T-shirt's white sleeve.

Great. Just great. These are my people now. These are the assholes I'm here with.

His name tag—there was one waiting for me, too, when Nurse Carole walked me down—reads EUGENE in perfect block letters. He's taken a marker and crossed out EU, leaving just GENE. Hard to blame him. Who gives you a name like Eugene?

Eugene. He must be the one Martin called Euclid. No wonder Martin got it confused.

Gene sits with his chair tipped, teetering on its back two legs, hands clasped behind his head. He wears a look that makes it clear he's not all that interested in talking to anyone. I'm with him, but still.

I move my eyes away when he glares at me, glance down at my own name tag, staring at the stupid way I wrote the phonetic CLAY above the typed KLEE when I walked in. I wonder if it makes me seem like a tool.

Dr. Howe clears her throat, and I think for a second maybe she asked me something when I wasn't paying attention. But she's looking at Martin, not me.

"So, did you want to share anything today?"

Dr. Howe has a soft voice and casual appearance. Short brown hair, no makeup. She looks thirty, at most, maybe younger, wears jeans and a white Henley, and Nike running shoes. If it weren't for the "PhD" after her name, I'd think she was one of us.

"Not really," Martin says, and Dr. Howe shifts. "How come it's always about me in here? How come I'm always the only one who has to talk?"

Sabrina casts me a look. "Maybe because you like to talk?" she says.

"Not true! Not always," Martin protests. "Not when I'm in a crap mood."

"Are you? In a crap mood today, Martin? Do you want to talk about why?"

He does seem different today, sullen. Not like the kid in the dining hall who can't stop chatting about everything. It's weird to see him deflect. Up till now, he always seems like he likes it to be about him.

"You don't have to," Dr. Howe, says, "but Sabrina spoke last during yesterday's session, and Gene led us in the mindfulness portion, and Klee is new here, so I thought we'd give him time to warm up. And, we haven't heard from you yet." My eyes shift to Gene again. I'm stuck on the mindfulness thing. Hard to picture the dude leading that. "It can be something simple. Like, how was your weekend? Did you have any visitors? Whatever you might be willing to share."

Martin stares down at his feet.

"I did," I pipe up. I feel bad for the kid. If he isn't talking, he must really not want to.

"My mother came to see me Saturday morning. I wasn't really that nice. I said she could come back this morning, and that didn't go much better."

Dr. Howe nods, making me feel okay about chiming in. Not that I want to continue now that I've started. She shifts her chair to face me better and says, "I'm glad you spoke up, Klee. Do you want to talk a little more about that?"

"Not really," I say. "I was just trying to help Martin." Martin laughs, and I see the corners of Sabrina's mouth curl up, too. I avoid looking at Gene, finding one of Dr. Alvarez's stress balls in my sweatshirt pocket. I squeeze it hard, the Adler quote coming partly back to me. Something about being too cautious, taking too many precautions in life.

"I know I need to deal with it, talk to her. It's just . . . I'm not ready. Some things have happened and I've been kind of emotional." As soon as I say it, I realize how dumb it sounds. Of course I'm emotional. Why else would I be in here? Still, Dr. Howe nods. I squeeze the stress ball harder. "My mother . . . is not. Not emotional, I mean. She's the opposite. After my father died . . ." I stop. Take a deep breath. "Let's just say she's one of those people who is always glued together. Perfect. Fine. No matter what happens. It's so fucking irritating . . ."

My voice trails off. My mother's coldness isn't the problem, not even the tip of iceberg. But it's all I'm willing to share. Especially with some doctor I don't know and some twelve-year-old. Not to mention a psycho with a Nazi tattoo on his arm.

Besides, my mother is who she is. And from the looks of it, she's way better off how she is, than I am.

"I know it's all for show. I'm not an idiot. I'm sure she's the farthest thing from always perfect and calm. It's the show that I hate. It makes her superior. But it also makes her a liar and a fraud."

All four of them are looking at me now.

Fuck. What made me think I wanted to go there?

I shut up, shove both hands deeper into my pockets, and squeeze the ball. I need to breathe. I need to not get choked up. Not in front of Swastika Gene.

I'm so freaking sick of crying.

Sabrina reaches out and puts her hand on my shoulder. She gives it this sweet little pat and then stops. When I look up again, Dr. Howe is waiting for me.

"Do you want to share more, Klee? It sounds like it might be helpful."

I shake my head. "She's an Ice Queen. Period. End of story."

Martin sits forward. "Like from the fairy tale, right?" It takes me a second, and then I nod. I guess that is where I got it from. "The Ice Queen." I vaguely remember some story like that my mother used to read me when I was little.

"I read that, too!" Martin shudders. "Did any of you? With the witch with her white hooded cape. I hated that story so much."

"You mean 'The Snow Queen,'" Sabrina says softly. "My mom read it to me, too. I loved it." Her voice turns brighter. "It was convoluted and creepy, but I liked it."

Martin laughs now, and I do, too, because loving a creepy story seems so out of character for Sabrina.

"How about you, Gene?" Dr. Howe asks.

"Not on your life," Gene says.

Martin leans forward, more animated now than he was before.

"Remember how the devil makes that mirror that distorts everything and magnifies everyone's bad qualities so none of the good ones shine through?"

"And remember the girl's red shoes?" Sabrina says.

"Yeah, that's the one," I say. "That was 'The Snow Queen' not 'The Ice Queen'?" So, all this time, I've remembered the name wrong. My mother is a Snow Queen, not an Ice Queen. That seems so much less fitting somehow.

"Funny you bring up that particular story, Klee," Dr. Howe says. "It's an interesting tale. I'm glad you did. I actually use it sometimes when I work with my younger kids because the story shows a lot about perception and misperception. For example, the Queen, if you remember, who kidnaps little Kai? She isn't the one who originally holds up the mirror that reflects back the ugly things. In fact, we don't know for sure how that mirror got into her heart. Tragedy? Misfortune? We make assumptions, but we don't ever really know for sure.

"So, the Queen appears to be perfect and beautiful, in her white furs and crown, but we don't know why, or how, she got so cruel. The fact is, somehow, early on, the devil—or whatever your version of evil or sorrow might be—got inside her. But she didn't necessarily start out that way. In essence, she's a victim. And she needs to be set free, too."

Sabrina looks up. "I always felt sorry for her," she says.

"You have a big heart, that's why. One of the things the story illustrates is how those shards of glass can get in everywhere, even if we start out happy and pure. And, looking in from the outside, we don't always know how or when, exactly, they got there. There may be things out of our control."

"And even if they are there," Sabrina whispers, "even when those shards get in? We can still be saved by love."

"Save ourselves," Martin says.

Gene shakes his head, drops his chair in a thud. "Only in fairy tales," he says.

Day 9—Morning

"Well, that went well yesterday," I say when Dr. Alvarez finally walks in the room. "Thanks for getting her to leave. I guess I wasn't ready."

Dr. Alvarez's hands are full: a Starbucks cup of coffee, a large book gripped under her arm, her keys dangling from a finger, and assorted papers clutched in her other hand. I get up to help, but she says, "No worries, I'm good," and drops all but the coffee and the book on her desk before moving to her chair across from me. She sets the book on the table, and I take in its familiar cover.

"Exactly right. You weren't ready. I'm sure your mother understood." I snort and she says, "Baby steps. At any rate, I hear group went well yesterday, and that you made some good connections in there. I like group for that. Just some light chit-chat until you realize it's where the real magic happens."

"Was there magic?"

She laughs. "Well, maybe 'magic' is too strong a word. Funny, though," she says, "how we only recognize huge, seismic breakthroughs when, really, all progress is good progress no matter how small. Sometimes we need to be willing to measure it in millimeters, not feet."

"Is there a stress ball for that?" I ask, and she smiles and pulls her clipboard to her lap.

"Anyway, sorry I'm late. I got all the way here, but forgot this down in my car." She taps on the book. "I just happened to find it last night at my favorite bookstore. On the sale rack, no less."

My eyes go to the book, and I shiver. *Van Gogh's Van Goghs.*
My father kept a copy in his studio. A photo of *Wheatfield with Crows* graces the cover. The book contains most of his masterpieces from the Amsterdam Museum's permanent collection.

I page through it, then rest it on the couch next to me. Just holding it overwhelms me, and I want to feel better, not worse. Of course, if that's all it takes to derail me, maybe Dr. Alvarez is being optimistic thinking I'm progressing. I mean, it's more than a week in, and I don't feel much better than I did. Then again, maybe I have no clue how bad I was feeling back then. Maybe I didn't even realize.

Sure, things with Sarah were stressful, but I was plodding along, getting my portfolio done. I was finally making some good pieces in Tarantoli's class, feeling freer now that most of my pieces were submitted.

I was fine.

I was okay.

Until everything imploded Saturday night.

Or, maybe that's my problem: that signs were there, and I didn't recognize them. Maybe I can't tell when I'm already in the midst of crashing and burning.

Truth is, I still don't know how I got here.

"I think I hate her," I say to Dr. Alvarez out of nowhere.

Dr. Alvarez looks up. Her eyes meet mine. "Your mother, I presume?"

"Yes."

She nods. Puts her pen down. Presses her clipboard to her chest. "Always, or lately?"

I think for a second. "More lately than always. More since. No, not always." That last part catches in my throat, comes out in a choked whisper. Until I say it, I don't realize how true it is. I don't want to hate my mother. I didn't used to.

"When you say since, you mean since your father died?"

"Yes."

"Do you know why?"

"Yes."

I see the brief look of surprise cross her face, but she's patient and waits, fingers clasped, for me to explain. But I don't want to right now. The acknowledgment is enough. The rest is a big, gross can of worms. I've worked hard to keep the lid on it, to keep them from slithering loose around my brain.

"We proceed in millimeters, then," she says. She puts her clipboard back down on her lap and jots some notes on it.

I pick up the Van Gogh book again and thumb through until I find *Starry Night,* and lay it open on the coffee table facing Dr. Alvarez.

"He painted this while he was in the asylum at Saint-Rémy."

"There is truly something remarkable about it, isn't there?" she asks. "A good reason it's his most famous painting?" She pulls the book closer and runs her fingers over Van Gogh's gold and indigo swirls.

"A lot of experts believe he painted this way not because of natural artistry, but because he'd poisoned himself, accidentally. From the lead in the yellow paint he used."

"I've heard that," Dr. Alvarez says.

"Yeah. Common knowledge, I guess. As a kid I always thought it was scary. My dad told me how the lead made Van Gogh's retinas swell, so he literally saw those circles, like halos, around everything he viewed."

"It's fascinating. But it seems like a lot for a young kid to know."

I shrug the comment off, but another memory of my mother flashes by. She's yelling at my father about upsetting me, about sharing his warped views. She's stuffing armfuls of sunflowers in the trash.

"Van Gogh was my dad's favorite," I say, defending him now. "So, he would talk about him, no big deal. He wanted me to know everything about art, about him. How he was great, but tragic in the end. Above all else, that's what he was."

"Your father or Van Gogh?"

I swallow hard but don't answer.

"How about you, Klee? Are you worried that you'll be tragic, too?"

Aren't I already?

"I don't want to be," I say, because it's the truth. But the truth might undo you before it sets you free.

I swipe at my eyes with the back of my hand, and Dr. Alvarez passes a box of tissues to me.

"Some perspective—and, granted, I don't know nearly as much about him as you do, but I have been reading up on him—and I would say that, above all else, Van Gogh was a great artist, given what a lasting impression his art has had on the world."

"Maybe," I say. "But he never even knew. He didn't live to see it. He died penniless, without having sold a single painting . . ." I stop, on the verge of tears again, which is really starting to piss me off. I'm tired of being a pussy. I'm tired of being needy. And for fuck's sake I'm tired of crying. I *should* be more like my mother. Made of ice. *Snow.* Whatever.

If I weren't so weak and pathetic, none of the shit that went down Saturday would have happened. Maybe Sarah wouldn't have done what she did. I was too needy. I drove her there.

My face burns red as I try to push the memories of Saturday night from my brain. Maybe this is who I am. A weak, pathetic coward like my father.

"Klee?"

"Yeah?"

"It was a serious question. Van Gogh or your dad, who are we talking about here? I think it's important that we talk about this."

Jesus.

I put my head between my knees again. Despite my best efforts, I can't choke it back anymore. The floodgates open and I'm weeping.

"It's okay," Dr. Alvarez says, and for the first time since I got here, she walks over and sits on the couch next to me. She puts an arm around my shoulders and says, "Don't feel like you have to keep fighting it, Klee. This is a safe place to let it all go." She nudges the box of tissues toward me. "Maybe what you need at this point is just to give yourself a break. Let yourself feel. I think you've been holding back—trying to hold back—for a long time now. And that's no small feat. You've had a lot on your plate. The kinds of things that might break anyone. Even the toughest person on earth."

She moves back to her chair and waits another few minutes before she speaks again.

"From what I know, your father was a talented, frustrated man. He loved you. You loved him. But, he suffered from . . . what? Clinical depression, likely. Or something like it. For a long time. And if he was undiagnosed . . . well, that means he was also untreated.

"So, he suffered without help, and when he couldn't bear the suffering anymore, he took his own life. In a gruesome, violent, terrible way. Seemingly without regard for the people around him. The people who loved him. Who cared about him. Who needed him most of all."

I hiccup back another sob.

"But, it's not because he didn't care, Klee. You and I both know that. But because the pain of being here got to be too much for him to bear. I don't know why, and neither, it sounds like, do you. But at that moment, the pain of it outweighed anything else for him. And only at that moment.

"But that doesn't help *you*, does it? For you, the consequences are the same. You, his son, who loved him deeply, are left grieving. Your grief is all we can try to heal now."

I nod, her words helping me, somehow.

"So, as long as we're already here at rock bottom," Dr. Alvarez says softly, "digging at the painful stuff, let's just do it, shall we? Let's deal with the big purple elephant in the room. Let's go the rest of the way. That's what I'm paid for, right? I might as well earn my keep."

I can hear the smile in her voice when she says that, and so, even though I don't want to, I nod again anyway.

"Okay, good. So, Van Gogh breaks your heart, partly because he's his own tragic figure, and partly because he reminds you of your father, and, now, maybe yourself. Because your father was talented, but also depressed, and ultimately couldn't bear his own life. He gave up painting—what he really loved—for you and your mother, perhaps, and eventually, that made him suffer so deeply that it all became too much for him. And ultimately, that's on you, or so you think. Because if you had done better, or tried harder, or some other story we all tell ourselves, you could have stopped him, right? Helped him. Is that the story you've been telling yourself?"

I swallow hard and nod some more, and she says, "So, of course that's hard for you because how could it not be? You were a part of that life, maybe the most important part. You were the part that should have made him want to live, and should have been enough to save him. You think you should have saved him, and, in turn, you blame yourself."

I press my fingers to my eyes to block it all out. Everything she's saying is the truth.

When I finally can, I sit back up and face her.

She tilts her head and smiles sadly, and says, "I understand how painful that must be, Klee, how you might choose to blame yourself. Except that you already know that's not the truth. Because you're a smart kid. A smart almost-adult. We can only make ourselves happy. We can't save others. We can love others. But we can only save ourselves."

"You're right about that," I say, finally "but wrong about something else."

"What's that?"

"We haven't hit rock bottom. There are still more elephants. And I blame my mother more than myself."

Day 9—Afternoon

When I walk into the GT room, Gene is the only one there. I'm tempted to turn and bolt, wait till the others have joined us, but he's already seen me, and that would only make things awkward, so I walk over and sit across from him.

"Hey," he says, dropping his tipped-back chair down to all four legs. "Early bird—worm, all that."

"Yeah." I miss my cell phone. Without it, I've lost all track of time in this place.

Gene watches me, rocks back onto the rear legs of his chair again. I try not to stare at him, or to look for the swastika tattoo.

"You ever fall?" I ask stupidly instead, indicating his chair. "I did that once in fourth grade. Fell flat on my back. Embarrassed the crap out of myself. Never did it again."

He laughs, but rocks his chair forward again. I glance around for a wall clock, willing Sabrina or Martin or even Dr. Howe to get here, but there is none. I have no idea what else to say to this guy.

"So what do you think?" he says finally. He motions around the room, then leans forward, hands clasped under his chin, like he's suddenly, intensely, interested in me. I shift nervously.

"About what?" *Being in here?* He can't possibly mean that, because how many ways can one feel about being in here?

He shrugs and rocks back farther, precariously this time, arms folded behind his head. And then I realize. From this angle, I can see the tattoo on his biceps isn't a swastika. It's the number 55, that's all.

"You looking at this?" He indicates his arm and I redden. I can't believe I thought what I thought.

"Your tattoo," I say. "What does it stand for?"

"It was my grandfather's number. He played in the NFL in the sixties. '66 to '68, with the Browns. He's the one who raised me. I got it last year when he died."

"I'm sorry," I say. "But, that's cool. About him playing for the Browns, I mean. The part about him dying obviously sucks." I want to say more, ask more, like where his mother is. And his father. Like, who's raising him now? "The tat is cool, too," is all I manage.

"Yeah, I guess." He drops his chair again and looks down. "I miss him. I miss him a lot," he says.

"So, who do you live with now?"

"No one. I mean, it's my dad's house, but he don't live there anymore. Not for years. Guy's a piece of shit and the bank is about to take it anyway, so I mostly hang out with friends. Or, I guess, for now, I live here."

"Oh," I say, wondering what landed him here. Not that it's any of my business, but it's the Ape Can, not a hotel or a homeless shelter, right? So he must have done something crazy to be here. Because that's what we all have in common.

Gene's eyes shift to mine, and something in them is so sad, or maybe mad, like he thinks I don't get it, or don't care. Like whatever I've suffered isn't half as bad. And maybe it isn't. Or maybe the only thing worse than your own father abandoning you, is your own father shooting himself in the head. Deciding you're not even a good enough reason to live.

"My father left, too," I say. "Didn't stick around."

Gene nods, and his face softens. It's enough what I've told him, if only a fraction of the truth.

"How come you keep lying, Alden . . . ?" Sarah's voice, calling me on it like she did that day in my room.

I don't know why I lied. I don't know why I continue to.

I close my eyes and grip my hands in my lap, feeling dizzy and off-kilter again. Dr. Howe's voice drifts in from down the hall, then Martin's. I'm relieved the others are here.

Sabrina follows, and they sit. Dr. Howe looks from me to Gene and back to me again.

"Nice to see you both here," she says. "Ready and eager to get to work."

But I'm not really here, am I? I'm back with Sarah, instead. Lost in the sound of her voice, the feel of her body. Lost in an early morning a few months ago, and the magical way she had of making me forget everything, of making the pain disappear.

"Hey, wake up, Alden."

I nearly have a heart attack. Sarah stands next to my bed, hair hanging down, a mischievous smile on her face.

I prop myself up, confused, and wipe drool from the corners of my mouth.

Did I sleep through Tarantoli? Did she show up here to rescue me?

I reach out to grab my phone, but Sarah covers it with her hand and says, "Don't bother. It's Sunday. Ten thirty. I've been up for hours. Texted you three times, then got bored, so I walked my ass over here."

My eyes dart past my half-open bedroom door, trying to hear my mother, trying to sort out what kind of disaster might have already gone down before Sarah made her way to my room.

"She's not here," Sarah says, walking to my door and pulling it open fully. She gestures into the empty hallway like a

Price Is Right model showing off a new car, and adds, "I got here just in time to see her leave. Dressed up all neat and pretty, like she has a meeting with a CEO. So, I figure it's safe to assume she's not coming back anytime soon?" I wrack my brain to remember if my mother told me where she was going. "I let myself in. The door wasn't locked. We have the whole fancy place to ourselves. Apparently your mom is under the delusion that you don't need to lock your doors up here in the sticks."

She laughs, and I sit up, overwhelmingly happy that she's here. Especially given how tense things were the last time I hung out with her. I wasn't even sure we were dating anymore.

"My mother is always dressed up," I say, trying to remember where she went. *Bereavement group? Fund-raiser? Lunch with a friend?* "She could just be headed to the convenience store. Anyway, I'm glad you're here, but you scared the crap out of me. I thought you were an intruder. I thought I was being attacked."

"You wish." She lifts the blanket, slips into bed, and crawls on top of me. "Or, maybe you are." I feel self-conscious, though, about my breath, and more, about the piss boner I'm acutely aware of.

"Can you give me a minute?" I nudge her off me. "I really have to brush and take a leak."

"Gross, yeah, you do." She waves her hand in front of her face, and I get up, taking the sheet with me. "Anyway, I'm starving," she calls. "I'm going to find us some breakfast while you're gone."

"Help yourself to whatever."

When I return, washed and brushed, she's taken me up on my offer. In one hand she holds two slightly crispy toasted waffles, and in the other, a bottle of maple syrup. Wedged under her arm is a bottle of expensive vodka.

"Sunday brunch!" she says, setting the waffles and syrup on my night table. She holds the vodka bottle up in a toast.

"It's a little early for Grey Goose, no?"

"Maybe." She smiles coyly. "But, we need something to wash those down."

"Breakfast of champions," I say, as she uncaps the bottle and takes a swig. "So, you're serious then? At ten A.M. No glasses even?"

"Ten thirty. Lighten up, Alden. Or if you can't, this will help."

She presses the bottle forward, so I take it, though there's not a chance I feel like drinking straight vodka first thing in the morning. Maybe I should explain that this bottle probably cost a hundred dollars or more, which is the only reason my mother hauled it up here. She doesn't drink vodka, only highbrow shit like Prosecco or a fine French wine. But then I decide, fuck it, maybe she's right. Maybe for once I should loosen up, and since my mother doesn't drink it, she won't notice. No sense in it going to waste.

I drink, feeling the liquid burn a bitter, hot trail down my throat, but I force another sip anyway, then a third, before putting the bottle back on my nightstand. A warm surge rushes me like melted caramel.

"There. You happy? Now you owe me," I say, closing my door just in case. I fall back onto my bed, pulling Sarah down with me. "God, you feel good. I want you so bad, all the time."

"I know you do, Alden. I know it." She kisses my forehead and whispers, "It's okay. I want you, too."

I roll her off me and onto her back, simultaneously reaching toward my nightstand drawer, trying to remember if I have any protection in there. But I can't reach, and when I get up to search, she gets up, too, taking the Grey Goose bottle with her.

She roams, sipping and touching and looking at everything, when all I want is for her to come back, to let me touch her again. Instead, I watch from this distance, dumbfounded by how beautiful she is. Her body. Her hair. Her way of being. How wound up tight I am compared to how fucking free she is.

At my closet, she turns and gives me a mischievous smile, and pulls the door open.

It's disappointing, I'm sure. No skeletons to be found. Only a few button-downs and a lone pair of khakis echoing on hangers. Everything else I own is either folded in my dresser drawers or still tucked away in boxes in the guest room or garage. There's no old sports equipment, no boxes of books or toys giving clues into little me. No stashes of Bob the Builder Legos, or even a mess of dirty laundry. This isn't my home and never will be, so why would I have bothered to unpack?

"Impressive," she says, her voice turning somber. "I've never seen such a neat and empty closet. Hey, tell the truth, Klee, how come you never invite me over? Are you ashamed of me?"

"What? No!" I get up, but she holds a hand out, takes another sip of vodka and brings the bottle over.

"I believe you. It's no big deal. Drink. And eat your waffle. Today I get to the bottom of who Klee Alden, International Man of Mystery, really is. I could have done this without even waking you. I thought about it, too."

She walks to my desk, and opens and closes its drawers. She won't find much in there either.

Except she does. Because I've forgotten the album. If I had remembered, I may have tried to stop her. I don't want to look at that now. Maybe not ever.

"Eureka," she says, pulling it from the back of the bottom drawer.

My heart aches. It's not mine, but my father's. From a long, long time ago. When we were packing up the apartment, I'd found it and shoved it in my backpack for safekeeping.

She walks to the bed, sits, and opens to the first page. "So, tell me, Alden," she says.

Tell you what? Nearly all the air leaves my lungs.

My father's young face looks up at me. Handsome. Hopeful. His hair shorter and darker than I remembered. No gray. Almost a crew cut. His eyes crinkle with his smile. He sits on a park bench with his arm around my mother. She looks young, too, and happy, which makes me feel sorry for her. For everything. When did she grow so cold and bitter?

"You're wasting your time if you want dirt on me," I say to Sarah, who keeps flipping. "This was my father's. From before they were married, and I was born."

"Not exactly," she says when she gets near the end. She stops and holds out a photo of my father holding a baby. Me. Wrapped in a white blanket with blue stars. Asleep on his shoulder.

Sarah looks at me.

"Me, obviously," I say.

She touches her finger to my newborn face and says, "You were pretty then, too," but I'm not listening. I'm lost in my father's eyes, trying to see if they look happy or sad. To see if he was glad that he brought me into the world. He looks like he is, but who can tell?

I study his face some more. When did he get so unhappy? Unhappy enough that none of this mattered anymore?

"So, you never told me," Sarah says, closing the album. She walks to my desk and puts it back where it came from. When she turns, she says, "How did he die, again? Cancer, right?"

"Yes," I say. "Cancer." I should tell her the truth. Blurt it out. Get it over with. But I don't. I can't. I don't know why. I've never even spoken the word "suicide" aloud. I'm not even sure I know how to. Anyway, it doesn't seem true. As if, in my head, I've substituted a whole other story. Cancer. Or a car crash. Something more glamorous, or at least nobler. Something that doesn't mean I didn't matter.

Because, if I tell her that—the truth—then she'll know, too. I. Don't. Matter. Enough. Not to her, or my mother, or to anyone. How can I, if I didn't matter enough to him?

"It was awful," I add, "but he went fast."

She stares at me, then sits on the bed and says, "How come you keep lying to me, Alden? Why don't you trust me?"

I pick up the bottle of vodka and drink some more, but the room is already spinning. I search for my waffle, but I put it down somewhere. Or maybe I ate it already.

"I don't know," I say. "The fast part is true." She touches my hair, looks in my eyes, and waits for more. I need to tell her. I owe her that. "He killed himself with . . ." My voice hitches. "He killed himself."

I watch her face, waiting for the words to undo me, waiting for them to send her running from my room. But they don't do either. We just sit there, the words still ringing in my ears.

Finally, she says, "Oh my God, that's awful, Klee." She touches my arm. The look on her face, it's brutal. She pities me. It's exactly what I didn't want to see.

I shake my head. "I don't want to talk about it anymore. I only want to be with you now. That's the only thing I want in the whole world."

"You should have told me . . ."

"I know. But now I did. And, I don't want to talk about it anymore. Please. I just want to be with you."

I stand and pull off my boxers, tug at her shirt, until she lifts her arms and lets me peel it off over her head. Her breasts are beautiful. Her body is beautiful. She smells like cinnamon and apples and falling leaves. The feel of her skin erases everything.

She slips off her jeans, and I climb on top of her, not waiting, or kissing, just needing to be fully immersed with her now. Then I remember, and pull out, and fumble at my nightstand drawer.

"It's okay," she whispers, "I've got protection," and she guides me back in, and we move together, delirious, and sweaty in our vodka-soaked haze.

Drunk or not, I don't last long, but she doesn't seem to care—not this time—and when we're finished, we lie there, quiet and breathless, if not the smallest bit free.

Day 9—Evening

"Do you swim, Mr. Alden?"

Sister Agnes Teresa stands by my bed, holding a pair of yellow swim trunks.

It's late, after ten, because the lights in the hall have been dimmed for quiet hours.

I press the remote that turns off the television and swing my legs over the side of the bed.

"Um, yeah, I guess I do. Why?"

"Good," she says, tossing them onto my bed. "Go change. I'll wait. I can rescue you, if need be. I'm a certified lifeguard," she adds.

"Klee?"

"Yeah?"

I stare at my phone, at Sarah's number, then press it again to my ear.

"You there?"

It's 2 A.M. I'm probably dreaming. I'm not even sure if I'm awake.

"Yeah," I say anyway. "Is everything okay?"

"Yes. Sure. But I need a favor, okay?"

"Of course. Anything."

"I need you to rescue me. Tomorrow ten A.M." I hear the tears in her voice now. "My dad is coming. I thought . . . I need you to come with me into the city."

Sarah calls me early the next morning and says to meet her at the Northhollow train station. "Don't pick me up. I want to walk," she says.

The only other information she gives is that we need to be at the Midtown Hilton by noon.

When I get there, she's already up on the platform. She's wearing a black wool peacoat with a baby blue scarf slung around her neck, and black leggings with Timberlands beneath that. At least she's dressed warmer than I thought she'd be.

"Hey," I say, wrapping my arms around her, but she wriggles free.

"This weather sucks, sorry. They're predicting a blizzard." She blows on her bare hands. "Thanks for agreeing to come."

The train is delayed, and the stationhouse is locked, and my hands are already numbing through my gloves. Two weeks before Christmas, and it's downright frigid out. Thick, wet snowflakes have begun to spiral down through the gray air.

"Want mine?" I ask, pulling off my gloves and holding them out to her. She shakes her head. "So, what are we doing again? Midtown Hilton, I know. But the rest was kind of vague this morning."

"Yeah, I know. Sorry. My dad is in. With Tyler and Stephanie. I learned this late last night. Apparently they got tickets to something."

"Stephanie?"

"My stepmom. Whatever."

"Well, you like her. So, that's fun, no? I'd think you'd be happy. Why do you want me to come?"

Her eyes dart away. "Not for me," she says. "Just them. The tickets are for her and my dad. They want me to watch Tyler while *they* go."

The train finally comes, but it's slow going because of the weather. The city, however, is going to be packed with the holiday shoppers no matter what. Tourists flooding in from everywhere. My dad used to have a rule: No museums or shows or even mildly trendy restaurants from the day after Thanksgiving through the New Year. So, anywhere we'd take an eight-year-old is going to be hell on earth.

Still, I've come up with some ideas and I'm going to brave them, because Sarah seems miserable, and I want her to have a good day with her brother.

She barely talks on the train, or on the subway up to 53rd Street. And, when we enter the lobby of the Hilton, the first thing she mutters is, "Stupid fucking asshole" under her breath. At first I'm not sure why, but then I am. There's a small boy alone at the concierge desk. He looks like her, with dark brown hair, a round face, and the same wide-set blue eyes. A bellman stands next to him, tapping away on his cell phone.

"Sarah!" The boy exclaims, and she lets go of my hand to run to him.

"Where are Steph and Dad?" she asks, but only after they've hugged.

"They paid him to watch me," Tyler says, indicating the bellman. "Roberto." The bellman nods at us, then goes back to whatever is on his phone. "They were going to be late because you were supposed to be here by noon."

He makes a face, and Sarah says, "Jesus, it's only twelve

thirty. I can't help it if the train was delayed because of the weather."

"Don't worry," he says. "I didn't mind. Roberto is nice. He watched me. Oh, and they said to tell you they weren't planning this. So, no dinner. Cuz we have to be back home tonight. But that they'll see you when you visit longer in two weeks."

"Okay," Sarah says, trying to keep her voice cheerful. "By the way, this is Klee. He's going to hang out with us."

"Klee, yeah. Your boyfriend," he says, making his voice singsong on the last word. I smile. She told him about me, then.

"No, *your* boyfriend, brat," she says, swatting him playfully, then she helps him bundle up in his coat and mittens and hat, before we head back out into the city.

Despite their repeated pleas, I won't tell them where we're going, just head us up six blocks, then east on 59th Street. The snow is downright blizzardish, and Tyler doesn't walk very fast, but he doesn't complain either, and we finally make it to Dylan's Candy Bar on the corner of 3rd Avenue and 60th Street.

"Voilà," I say, crossing us and planting my hands on Tyler's shoulders to stop him in front of the main window. "My dad used to take me here on my birthdays. Even the most jaded New Yorker can't refuse an hour inside Dylan's."

The window is set up as Santa's workshop. Gears made out of larger-than-life red-and-white peppermints spin and drop platter-sized spice drops and Mike and Ikes onto a conveyer belt that moves past rotating elves.

The place is a sugar-coated heaven.

"Holy cow!" Tyler says, mustering his first real show of enthusiasm, and we push in and through the insane sea of shoppers to get to the ceiling-high M&M bar in the back. Columns of graduating rainbow-colored M&M's reach floor to ceiling, taking up an entire wall. Red to orange to yellow to green to purple, with multiple shades and gradations in between.

Sarah looks at me with an odd look of concern.

"Total tourist trap, for sure," I say. "And overpriced. But there's no kid on the planet who doesn't love it here, trust me."

"Yeah, except, it's going to cost a fortune, Klee—"

"Don't worry," I say. "I don't mind. I've got this."

"You can't."

"I want to," I say. "Consider it part of your Christmas present, okay?"

"Okay," she says, then, "Whoa, Cowboy!" and she moves quickly toward Tyler to stop him from unloading an entire metal scoop of pale blue M&Ms into his bag.

By the time we cover all three floors of the store, the kid's bag is filled with more than $30 of seriously overpriced candy that will clearly send him into a sugar coma. But when I pay and hand the bag back to him, it's worth it just to see his goofy smile.

"Come on," I say, when we're outside again. "We're just picking up steam. Stop number two on the Klee Alden Christmas tour of Manhattan."

"Let's not," Sarah says, shivering. "It's cold and I'm spent. Let's just go back to the hotel and hang there."

"No can do," I say, pulling her close to me. "It's only two thirty, and Tyler here has a whole lot of city to see, right, Tyler?"

"Right," Tyler says, dangling a curl of red shoestring licorice into his mouth.

"Besides," I add, "your parents won't be back at the hotel until after five."

"They're not my parents," Sarah says. "You mean my jackass father and his wife."

The good thing about a snowy day in December is that it's already twilight by 3 P.M.

I'm holding Sarah's hand and she's holding Tyler's as I pull us across Madison toward Rockefeller Center.

"A tree is a tree, Klee," Sarah whines. "It's really cold. I don't even get what the big deal is."

My nose runs and I swipe at it with frozen fingers. I'm cold, too, and Sarah has finally taken me up on my offer of gloves. But it's worth it. I know it is.

"You will," I say. "And we're here, anyway. So you might as well enjoy it now."

As we move through the thickening crowds, I hold tighter to her hand, and grab Tyler's, too. If I lose him here, I'll never find him again. He lets me take it, and the feel of his small hand in mine makes my heart ache with thoughts of my dad. It occurs to me how needy a thing like love is, or can be, to care about someone so deeply. To simply want to hold on to them. It feels that way with Sarah. Like the harder I try, the more she only ever backs away.

But maybe that's not right. Last night she called *me*, so maybe she's just looking to me to be the one to hold on.

All I know is, standing here now, holding Tyler's hand with the snow spinning down through the city, I long for my father and wonder whether I tried hard enough. If I had tried harder, maybe I could have done something to hold on to him.

"Okay, I hate to admit it, but you're right, Alden." Sarah has stopped in her tracks, slowed by the bodies and the spectacle before us. "Oh my God, it's beautiful," she says. Against the dusty gray sky, the tree is magical, aglow with a million dots of red, blue, and green.

"It looks like a giant Christmas cookie," Tyler says happily. His eyes are huge, his cheeks a deep, rosy red.

I smile, pleased with myself, as I maneuver us expertly

through the crowds. The closer we get, the clearer the carol-
ers grow. Their voices rise in harmony, above the rat-a-tat-tat
of tin drums, together on the melancholy rumpum pum pums.

Camera flashes pop, tiny light explosions illuminating the
snowflakes that tumble steadily down.

When we finally get close enough, I stop and let Sarah and
Tyler move the remaining few feet ahead of me toward the
tree. Still within sight, but able to truly take the magnitude of
all of it in. I can hear them singing, Tyler on tippy-toes, head
turned up to the sky, his rumpum pum pum louder and more
joyful than all the other voices.

And when Sarah finally turns back to find me again, her
black hair shimmering with colors that reflect off the melted
snow, the look on her face is so sad and lost, even though
she sees me, even though her brother holds fast to her arm,
that it makes my chest squeeze tight and my breath disappear.

She's right there, I think. *She's right there.*

So why does she feel so far away?

It's weird to walk the floor at this hour, with the skeletal night
staff, and nursing stations all but empty, in a pair of yellow
swim trunks that don't belong to me. As we pass through the
main lobby, one nurse sits with her back to us, staring up at a
wall-mounted television.

"She loves her old movies," Sister Agnes Teresa whispers,
indicating the sepia glow of the screen.

An orderly I don't recognize drags a bucket, swabbing a
mop across the floor, unconcerned.

When we reach the stairwell, Sister Agnes Teresa wraps her
short fingers around the door handle and works to pull the
weight of it open. I don't know if I should help or not, if offering

would somehow insult her. She's probably stronger than I am anyway.

Watching her maneuver the stairs is equally uncomfortable. She grabs hold of the railing and tilts slightly as she drops herself step to step. The other hand holds up her robe so she doesn't trip on it.

We go down a flight, stopping at a door marked L1. I reach out to open it, but she says, "Wait, we need a special key," and she extracts the magic set from her pocket.

The door opens into a dark hallway, and I follow her until we reach a windowed stretch of wall beyond which I can make out the hulking silhouettes of gym equipment. Elliptical machines, treadmills, and weight stations. Past that, at the next bank of windows, a dark, rectangular abyss of water.

"Here we are," Sister Agnes Teresa says, opening the door. The sharp smell of chlorine enters my nose. "I always love it best at this hour when we don't have to contend with the therapy crowd."

"Yeah," I say, soothed by the gentle waffle of water that comes with the shift of air as the door closes again.

Sister Agnes Teresa moves to the wall and switches on a rear bank of lights. "How about just those? We leave it ambient, is that okay?"

I don't answer, stand lost in the play of light across the water's surface, reticulated patterns that shimmer and dance like it's a night sky, and we've disappeared from this room.

"It's beautiful up here."

We're on the observation deck of the Empire State Building, where Sarah clasps her fingers around the guardrails and stares out across the building tops of Manhattan to the shimmering Hudson River in the distance. Her breath puffs out like cigarette smoke.

"I'm glad we came," she says, reassuring herself, or maybe me. "I'm glad to be with you." Things have been weird and distant between us, so it fills me with hope to hear her say this. Especially since it's Valentine's Day. "You're a hopeless romantic, you know that, Alden?"

I lean in against her and close my fingers around hers, feeling, as always, the rush of electricity that glues me to her. "I hope not," I say, wishing things could feel easier between us. *Be* easier. Be clearer.

"I just mean you're good at this," she says. "I'm not. And you are." She twists toward me for a second and says, "Good at all this stuff. Good at being good, you know? I'm not sure I really deserve that."

"Of course you do," I say, and I want to say more, but her words choke me up, and I'm hyperaware these days of seeming too weak, or saying too much, of wanting more from her than she's willing or wanting to give. I need to be strong if I want to hold on to her.

Or maybe I'm trying too hard, overthinking everything. If she wanted to, she would have broken up with me. But she hasn't. Like with a cat, the more I stay back, the more she seems to gravitate toward me. Maybe that's the secret of Sarah. That I need to let her come to me when she wants to. In her own time. Still, I want to pull her to me now and kiss her, kiss her the way we used to always kiss. It's been weeks since we've kissed like that, since before she went to her father's for the holidays.

"That's good, right? That you get to spend time with him?" I had asked when she first told me she was spending Christmas Day through New Year's at his house. As much as I hadn't wanted her to go, wanted her to be here to celebrate with me, I was happy for her, too. A chance to get away from her mom, and have real quality time with her father. "You'll get to see your brother, too, right?" I'd asked, trying to be supportive and muster genuine enthusiasm.

She had only shrugged, and said, "Not worth the price I have to pay when I get home. Let's just say the record is three weeks straight of trying to drag my mother back up from the Pit of Despair."

"What do you mean?"

"You know, the you-betrayed-and-deserted-me Pit of Despair."

"So then don't go."

"I have to. It's in their Agreement," she'd answered.

And she was right about afterward. For the first few weeks of January, I barely saw her outside of school. She was always helping her mom around the house, or going places with her. Part of me wondered if she was just making excuses not to be with me, but then she'd call or text and tell me how she wanted me and missed me.

You looked hot in T's today. Away this weekend. Keep it up & I may have to do you in janitor's closet.

I pull her to me now, and kiss her. She responds halfheartedly, so I stop and peer into her eyes. She stares off past me, until I raise my brows in question.

"Nothing. What? You know how the holidays get to me, Klee."

"Old news. It's February. I was hoping we could fully enjoy the evening. *Enjoy* enjoy." I waggle my eyebrows.

"We are. I am," she says, punching me playfully in the chest. "It's just not that easy. To switch gears. I wish she'd meet someone, get over him already."

"Me, too," I say. "Hey, I know," I add without thinking,

"come with me to Boston next year." The minute I say it, I'm panicked. It's exactly what I shouldn't be saying.

"You don't even know if you're going," she answers, though I'm not sure how she means it. A challenge? A dig? Something else?

"Formalities," I offer, trying to sound casual, though I don't even come close. I like her too much. Jesus, I'm in *love* with her. "I won't have trouble getting in. At least I don't think so. And there are lots of schools up there. Northeastern, BU, a whole bunch of them."

"Can't afford it . . . we've had this conversation before."

"What about your dad?"

"He's not paying either."

"Okay, fine, but how do you know? Did you ask—?"

"Klee!" she interrupts, fury in her eyes. "I told you to stop! I'm not going! I'm not leaving her. She'd fall apart. She'd fucking kill herself if I did that! You want me to have that on my head?"

I shoot her a look, the words cutting the darkness, echoing in my ears. She realizes too late what she's said, how it sounds. Not that she meant anything by it. But she's right. Maybe there was something I could have done. Something I didn't do that would have changed things. Maybe I'm selfish because I couldn't see the problem, didn't even realize I needed to help him.

Tears sting my eyes. Sarah looks at me and says, "I'm sorry, Klee. Really. I didn't mean anything by that. But, see, that's the difference between you and me. You have options and I don't. You don't even get that there's a difference."

"I do. I mean, I don't know if I do, but you have choices . . ."

She whirls on me. "See? You don't! With your nice house and your fancy car and the whole stupid world at your fingertips. I'm stuck here, forever, in Northhollow. If not because of money, then taking care of her. So get over it. Stop trying to fix things. And stop trying to make me something I'm not!"

"Sarah—"

"What?"

You're being ridiculous, I want to say. *And unfair. Besides, she's a grown woman. A nurse. She cares for people. She doesn't expect you to care for her.* But I don't. Because I know better. If my dad had needed me—had asked—I would have stayed, too. If only he had asked.

"Hey, Klee?"

"Yeah?"

"I'm sorry." She takes my hands and presses them to her cheeks, which are pink with cold, or maybe pink in the glow of the spire lit up for Valentine's Day. "I am. I know you mean well, and I don't want to fight. This isn't your fault. I came here because I wanted to. I want to be here with you."

She leans into me now, and pulls my arms around her, and we're kissing again, but this time her body gives, and folds completely into mine, and all I can think about is that, somehow, we're going to be okay.

When we stop kissing, we both turn and look out over the sparkling city together, this city I love, that now Sarah loves as much as I do.

"See that mist?" I ask, nodding at where the sky is shrouded with fog.

"Yeah?"

"Reach out and see if you can touch it with your fingers." She presses her body to the guardrails and extends her arm out through the grating, stretching her fingers just far enough to touch the tip of the patch in front of us. "That's actually a cloud," I tell her. "We're actually standing in the clouds. You're touching a cloud."

"That's amazing," she says.

"You're amazing," I say, moving behind her, and pressing into her again. "Every time I'm with you, it's like I get to touch a cloud."

"Don't do that." She shrugs me off and closes her eyes. "I hate when you do that. You're too nice . . . I can't return it . . . Don't make me be mean to you." She wraps her arms to her chest and starts walking again.

I follow silently, wishing I didn't always seem to say the wrong thing. Halfway around the perimeter, she finally stops to take in the opposite side of the city. The winking PepsiCo sign. The shimmering green-black of the East River. The steady lines of traffic to the north and south of us, even at this hour, alternating streams of white and tangerine, crawling toward us in one direction, snaking off into infinity in the other.

"I'm sorry," she says finally. "I don't mean to be like this. I know you were only trying to help. It's just sometimes . . ." She turns away from me again, stares out through the grating for a while. "Do you ever wish you could fly, Klee? I don't mean jump, I don't mean kill yourself, but fly. Really fly, like a bird. Like in my dreams." She puts her arms out, closes her eyes, and tilts almost imperceptibly from side to side. Like a kid pretending to be an airplane. "Even for a few minutes, just let loose and forget everything. Everything but soaring weightless through the sky. I think even if you crashed and burned at the end, it would still be worth it. Just to have those few minutes to fly free."

"No," I say, "I don't." And that's the truth. I don't think about it and I don't want to try. Because the fact is, she's wrong. And, that's something that *she* doesn't get. She's lucky enough not to have to get it. To know it. It's all a hypothetical to her. But I've lived it, so I know. It's not worth it. Not one iota. I've thought about this a hundred times since my father died. Because after the freedom is the nothingness.

Nothingness.

If not for you, then for everyone else left behind.

"What are you thinking about?" Sister Agnes Teresa leans forward and swishes her hands through the water.

She doesn't wait for my answer, though, just stands and pulls her robe off to reveal a navy one-piece. "Yeah, I know it's not pretty, and yes, even nuns own bathing suits," she says, draping the habit over a chair. "I told you *we* were swimming. You think I was going to send you in alone?" She waddles to the steps, and I try not to stare. "You coming, or you just going to sit there enjoying the view?"

I shake off the thoughts of Sarah and follow her down, wading tentatively into the cool water.

Once in, I lie back and let my body relax, my arms and legs drifting outward, my body floating weightlessly, the hollow echo of nothingness temporarily displaced by the water in my ears.

"I'm bored. Come swim with me." I tap Dad's shoulder, then tug at it. "Please? We could race."

He opens his eyes and squints up at me, says, "In a minute," then rolls over and pulls the towel over his head. The back of his neck is burnt, so I adjust the towel downward to cover it and the rest of his reddening shoulders.

We're on vacation at some fancy resort in Fort Lauderdale, Florida. The hotel pool has been crowded all day, but it's nearly dinnertime so the other guests have begun to depart, finally leaving enough room on the far side so we could do it, race, he and I, if he wanted.

"Play with the other kids. Let him rest, Klee." Mom glances over from the chaise lounge next to him, a book splayed open on her chest.

"They all have brothers or sisters to play with. Plus, now they went to dinner. They don't want to play with me."

She picks up the book again and turns the page. "Don't be silly. Play alone, then."

"I've been playing alone all day."

Dad rolls over and sits up. "It's okay, Mari. I'll do it. Let's go, kiddo. I bet you can't beat me." He gets out of the chair and bolts toward the pool.

"No diving, it says!" I call after him. Dad doesn't listen, plunges into the deep end, but no one left around the pool seems to care. I lower myself in from the side and take off after him to the deep end.

I might be scrawny, but I'm fast. We race five times and I beat him twice, though one of those times is mostly a tie. By then, we're both tired and panting, so we quit and float on our backs. Just me and Dad, side by side. Palm trees line the edge of the pool, and brown coconuts dot the high fronds. That song comes to me, the silly one Dad sings sometimes about the lime in the coconut and the doctor mixing it all up, which makes me smile.

"I like it here. Don't you?" I say, but my voice through the water sounds far away and distorted, so I'm not even sure he can hear me. I stand, letting the water leave my ears, and hold to Dad's swim trunks so he doesn't float away. "I wish we could stay longer."

Dad rolls his head to the side to look at me, the waterline covering his bottom eye. "If wishes were fishes," he says.

"If fishes were wishes," I say.

"If only . . . That reminds me . . ." He rights himself and moves toward the steps, so I follow. He sits and pats the step above him for me, and I smile again and brace myself, because I'm pretty sure I know what this means.

"There was a great Taoist master," Dad says, "named Chuang Tzo. And one day—well, one evening, the great Chuang Tzo dreamt he was a small silver fish darting through the waves."

"What kind of fish?" I ask, swishing my hands through the water while he thinks on this.

"I don't know. It doesn't really matter."

"It does."

"Okay, a mackerel. Let's say a mackerel, then."

"Are they silver?" He nods. "Okay. A mackerel, then."

I cup my fingers like a hand fish and move it through the water, arcing up into the air, then diving down beneath the surface.

"Good work," Dad says. "You act out the words best you can. So, in the dream, Chuang Tzo had no awareness of himself as a person. Only as a fish."

"The silver mackerel," I say, making my hand swish along the edge of the steps.

"But when he awoke, Chuang Tzo found himself lying there, dry—on land, of course—a human again."

"And?" I ask, my hand flopping over to land belly up on the edge of the pool.

"And, as he looked around, he thought to himself, 'Was I before a man who dreamt about being a fish, or am I now a fish who dreams about being a man?'"

I stare up past the coconuts to the sky. An airplane is going by, a silver fish gliding through clouds. When my father doesn't say more, I ask, "And, which was he, the man or the mackerel?"

My father looks at me and nods, then starts out of the pool again, taking my hand.

"I don't know. Good question, son. Which was he?"

Day 10—Morning

Dr. Alvarez's door is open when I get there. She sits at her desk doing paperwork. "If you do this type of work," she says, "it's not the patients that will kill you, but the forms."

She nods at the couch and I sit. There's a green stress ball on the table, and I take it, thinking of Sister Agnes Teresa, of our late-night swim, wondering if my hair still smells of chlorine.

"Give me a moment. I'm just finishing up," she says. I turn the stress ball in my hand: ***When we are no longer able to change a situation, we are challenged to change ourselves."—Viktor Frankl.***

"I found that this morning, thought it had your name on it," she says without turning around. After another minute or so, she shoves the stack of papers in a drawer. "So, I was thinking," she says, standing, "it's beautiful outside this morning, and as far as I know, you haven't been out in days."

It hits me when she says this. I haven't been outside since I got here.

"Of course, if you were recovering from appendicitis or some sort of surgery or whatever, you might stay indoors for a while. Wait till you felt strong enough to venture outside. Mental illness is no different. Sometimes we need to stay inside, sort of cocooned up where we feel safe. But I'm guessing you're ready to go out now. You're doing much better, Klee. I hope you feel that. So, I'm thinking the fresh air will do you a world of good."

The phrase "mental illness" sticks in my head. It sounds

awful and permanent. Or maybe I'm thinking about it wrong since most illnesses get better with time. Maybe it doesn't matter what you call it, though, only figuring out what you need. And, Dr. Alvarez says I'm doing better, so maybe I am, though suddenly being anywhere but in here—inside the safety of the Ape Can—seems more than a little intimidating. Maybe because it means they'll be sending me home soon.

"What if I'm not ready?" I blurt. Dr. Alvarez's eyes meet mine. "What I mean is, how can I be ready, if I still don't know how I got here? Metaphorically speaking, I mean, 'cause I know how I got here literally."

Dr. Alvarez smiles and smoothes her slacks. "Baby steps, Klee. You'll be ready. How about we start with a walk, though? The grounds are quite lovely this time of year, despite all the construction, and I sprung for my comfortable shoes." She holds up a foot, revealing sockless brown loafers. "Some of the spring bulbs are starting to bloom, and the honeysuckle is divine. That's the upside of all the recent rain. April showers and all that, right? You could even bring a canvas and some paints?"

I shrug but get up. The thought of going outside is appealing, if not the part about trying to paint. Despite all of Dr. Alvarez's prodding, and my mother's fiercely heroic efforts to cart all that stuff up here in her Chanel suit and high heels last week, I've not yet cracked open a thing.

"My patient after you has graduated to something less intensive, like you'll be doing soon," Dr. Alvarez adds, "and no one new has been put in her time slot yet, so I have some extra time today. I thought we might take a leisurely walk. I won't know what to do with myself otherwise." She smiles, then catches something else in my expression. "That's right, Klee. People do graduate out of therapy, all the time. They go from in here to out there. From every day to weekly, to not at all in some cases. People get better and go home. They resume their real life, though often with some therapy in place, as I would recommend in your case. Not yet, of course. But soon. You don't need to be in a place like this much longer. This is more than most of you kids really need."

"If you say so," I say.

"I do. I say so. Now, about that walk. I'll wait down here. You go up to your room and get your things."

I head down the sterile hallway, past the god-awful fish mural to the stairs, and pull open the heavy steel door.

The smell of chlorine drifts up.

Maybe the pool door is open. Maybe there's therapy going on like Sister Agnes Teresa says. How come I never noticed the smell before?

I want to go down and explore, but we're not supposed to wander the halls. "There are only two places you should be while you're here: somewhere specific, or on your way there," a nurse had told me the day Dr. Ram first came in to see me. "It's important you follow the rules."

Dr. Ram stopped in again yesterday to check my vitals. He even removed my bandage and said I was looking good. "Not much more than a notch, really," he had said. My hand moves reflexively to my ear. Only a regular Band-Aid there now.

Progress, then, right? So, maybe Dr. Alvarez is correct. Maybe when I go home it won't have to be a big ordeal.

I head up the stairs to get my things. A canvas and some paints. I'm reluctant, but Dr. Alvarez is waiting for me.

Soon, she had said about me going home, but the thought— the possibility—makes me dizzy. Of course, I have to leave here at some point. I need to catch up in school. Get on with my life. But soon? I don't feel ready. Not yet. Not at all. I'm not ready to face Sarah. To face school. Or Keith Abbott or Scott Dunn.

Fuck.

I grip the railing and race up the rest of the stairs, and lie down for a minute on my bed. The whole freaking room is spinning.

I focus on the ceiling, then look out the window, at the edge of the excavator glinting yellow-orange in the sun. *Better. I'm still safe here.* This place, this room, feel as much like home to me as anywhere lately. Certainly, as much as our new house does.

When I feel steadier, I walk to the bathroom, splash cold water on my face, and stare at myself in the mirror. If nothing else, I've got the most impressive stubble I've ever grown. Not that it's saying much. I'm not a fan of it so much as taken by surprise. Maybe that's what I should do: Grow a beard, put on a hat, and return to school incognito. I doubt I can shave anyway. It's not like they're handing out razors in here.

"Dude, you are a world-class fuck-up," I say aloud to myself, then head back into the room to gather my supplies.

"Everything okay?" Dr. Alvarez asks, concerned. "I was worried you decided not to come."

"Yes. I was just looking for some things." I pat my backpack, which is jammed with two 5×8 canvases, a choice of brushes, and a box of acrylics. "I'll need some water, though. If I'm going to paint."

She pulls two bottles of Poland Spring from her purse. "Will this do?" I nod. "Good. We'll make it work somehow, make a bowl out of bark or something." She laughs and adds, "Now, what say you we blow this popsicle stand?"

One blast of sunshine and, at least momentarily, everything feels lighter. I inhale deeply, and Dr. Alvarez smiles. "Keep up," she says, walking briskly. "Amazing what some fresh air can do for the soul."

We cross the courtyard where the excavator is in full motion. I shove my hands in my sweatshirt pockets and follow, wondering all sorts of personal things about her I don't know. Like her age, and why she works in the Ape Can. I mean, who wants to deal with a whole bunch of kids who have gone psycho? When we clear the noise, I ask. "It's probably none of my business, but I was wondering how old you are?"

"Funny you should ask. I'm about to turn forty. In two weeks. It's a big one, I suppose. Why?"

"No reason," I say. "Just, you know pretty much everything about me."

She laughs. "Fair enough. Did you think I was older or younger?"

"Both," I say, and she laughs more heartily now.

At the far end of the courtyard there's a gazebo surrounded by mostly barren gardens. When we reach it, she says, "Let's sit for a moment," and we move toward a circular bench and sit facing out toward the Ape Can.

"They keep talking about expanding the property to include more amenities, put some tennis courts in, maybe an outdoor dining patio. But so far all I see is pointless digging. It would be nice, though, wouldn't it?"

I nod. "How long have you been here? Working, I mean."

"Thirteen years."

"Wow. Long."

"It is, isn't it?" She stretches her legs and clasps her hands behind her head. "I got a residency here right after grad school and have stayed ever since."

"Do you hate it?"

She laughs again and shakes her head. "God no, does it seem like I do?"

"No, not at all. I just wondered. It seems hard."

"Hard, yes. I guess it is. But, I love it, too, actually. It's just difficult to believe I've been here so long—anywhere that long. I was just your age a blink of an eye ago, on the verge of everything, and now, well, I'm here, on the verge of old." She smiles, but she seems a little sad when she says it.

"You're not that old," I offer.

"Well, when you put it that way . . ."

I laugh realizing how it came out.

"This birthday . . . forty . . . It's a little tough to swallow, I suppose. But I try not to think of it that way. I've accomplished a lot, or enough to be at peace with myself. And, I'm always getting better at what I do. Or trying to get better, at least," she adds. "I'll probably never be quite as good as I want to be."

"But, doesn't it get depressing?"

"The work? No. I wouldn't call it that. Hard. At times, frustrating. I can't tell you the amount of times I've wished I had a magic wand." I smile at that, and she knocks off her shoes, wiggles her red-painted toenails around. "But, depressing, no. The opposite of that."

"Really?"

She puts her hand over mine, squeezes, then lets go. "We *all* need some help at one time or another, Klee, it's as simple as that. No shame in needing it." I nod, wondering if it can really be that simple. "Now, *not* trying to help?" she says after a pause. "I think *that* would depress me. Although life is not always easy, and, like I said, having a magic wand would be good."

I turn and squint at her. "To be honest, sometimes it seems like you do."

"Well, *that* is a compliment, isn't it? So, thank you. That means a whole lot to me. But let's hold that thought, see how I do at getting you out of here. And, anyway, I'd like to take vast amounts of credit, but the truth is, mostly all I do is listen. It's amazing how listening helps. Or at any rate, it rarely makes anything worse." She slips her shoes back on. "I'm okay with that. Not making anything worse."

She seems like she's going to get up, but then she changes her mind, spreads her arms out on the bench, tilts her head back, and closes her eyes.

"I love it out here. So very peaceful," she says. "You know, Voltaire said, 'The art of medicine consists in amusing the patient while nature cures the disease.' I often think that's true, that, for most people, time will cure what ails them." She chuckles and sits up. "Or maybe I just want to believe that because it takes the pressure off of me."

"Is there a ball for that? The Voltaire quote?"

"Ha, no," she says, resting her head back again. "But there should be."

I want to laugh, too, to trust that time and distance will heal things, but I'm thinking of Sarah, of my mother, of the party and Abbott, of all the humps I have to get over if I want to be well again.

After Valentine's Day, things are better for a few weeks, but by March, Sarah has pulled back again.

"What's the difference?" she says when I try to talk about it. "You're leaving for Boston soon."

"I can stay if you want me to, go to Pratt in the city instead."

"Don't say that, Klee! It's ridiculous!"

"Sarah—"

"I swear! Don't say it again."

So, I try to hang on but not push her too hard, even when doing the first seems impossible without doing the second. But I have to. Sarah's the only thing worth anything here in North-hollow.

In school, she's constantly with her friends, casting me aside for Abbott and Dunn and a few of the girls they hang out with. I realize that, beyond their first names, I don't really know them at all, haven't made much of an effort. There's probably no point in making one now. Less than three months left of school and I'm out of here. The city or Boston, pick one. I won't stay here in fucking Northhollow. Maybe Sarah's right. Maybe I do think I'm too good for here.

Still, I try to find balance. The few times I try to make plans with her, Sarah says she has plans already, but I'm welcome to come hang out with them.

Them.

It's always felt like that, hasn't it? Either just us or just them. I decide I'm going to try harder to fix it, for her sake. Which is what happens on Friday when I ask Sarah about her weekend plans.

I find her at her locker. Talking to Abbott.

Asshole.

I put my arm around her and make small talk, before finally asking what's up for the weekend. Sarah flinches at my arm so I pull it back, worried I seem like a possessive douche-bag.

"Hey," I say, "listen. I have to work on my portfolio tonight. You want to head into the city tomorrow and walk the High Line?" I turn to Abbott now. "Hey, Keith, how about you get a date and come with?"

"Klee . . . he doesn't want to—" She sounds mad. I don't get it. I thought she would like that I invited him.

"No can do, Alden. No fancy museums for this dude. Besides, party at Dunn's house tomorrow night. Didn't you hear?

We're celebrating. Porter got accepted to Michigan. A D1 school and all that. It's a big deal." He smiles disingenuously. It makes my stomach roil. "It's pretty huge news around here."

"I hadn't," I say. "And the High Line isn't a museum. It's a park. A linear one. You know what linear is?" Sarah gives me a look. "Maybe a rain check, then."

"Maybe, yeah," Keith says. What he doesn't do is reciprocate. What he doesn't say is, "You should come to Dunn's."

Fine by me. I wouldn't go if he asked. A little late to be making friends after all.

Dr. Alvarez stands. "Hold that thought. Let's walk for a bit." I look up, surprised. "We'll walk and talk some more. Maybe we can find a spot to paint," she adds.

I shoulder my backpack and get up. I'm sweating for some reason. I wipe my damp palms on my jeans.

"Okay, yeah, that'd be good," I say. "That'd be better, I think."

She doesn't wait, but walks ahead of me, close enough to hear me talk but far enough ahead to give me space to gather my courage.

"Saturday, I don't call Sarah. I spend the afternoon working on portfolio pieces. Maybe I want to make her sweat some," I say, laughing a little at the admission, "or maybe I'm panicked about how far behind I am. I should be. I have to get this last piece in pretty soon or I'm going to be doomed. They're waiting on me and I've been slacking. There are no more extensions they'll give me due to 'circumstances.'

"Late afternoon, Sarah texts. Something like, 'You should

come, Alden. If you want to.' It doesn't read like she means it. More like she feels sorry for me, and obligated. The truth is, she's never really wanted me to blend with her Northhollow friends, which, as I said, was fine by me."

"Until it wasn't," Dr. Alvarez says.

"Yeah. Maybe. I guess. Anyway, at some point later that afternoon, or maybe early evening, another text comes: '44 Pine. L past 7-11. Trees section off Main if you do want to come . . .'"

I wince at the sound of the address that's now burned into my brain at the thought of Dunn's house, the pouring rain. But I manage to plow forward.

"Sarah doesn't usually work that hard to convince me, so I'm thinking, okay, maybe she does want me to come. I guess I felt confused," I say to Dr. Alvarez.

"I get that," she answers. "Maybe Sarah did, too."

I nod, and swallow hard. I'm not sure which parts of the story are important and which parts aren't. But suddenly, I get it. Sarah did feel something for me, maybe even loved me, through it all. At least, I'm pretty sure she did.

"I didn't want to be a pity project. I didn't want her to feel sorry for me. So, I convince myself I'm not in the mood to go to a party, to hang out with those assholes, even if I should try for Sarah's sake. Maybe she sees something in them I don't, but the fact is, I don't, and unlike them, I'm not a phony, so I'm not going to be an asshole and pretend.

"It's funny, because I remember thinking then how badly I missed Cleto and Dan. Especially Cleto. He's more like a brother than a friend. If I had called Cleto that night, then maybe none of this would have happened."

"Maybe not," Dr. Alvarez says, "or maybe he wouldn't have been home. Or maybe that wouldn't have gone well, and something else would have gone wrong. We can't go back.

You can't change what's behind you. Only what's waiting ahead."

I squeeze the stress ball in my pocket. "I guess," I finally say. "But I keep wishing I wasn't the one who dropped the ball."

"You don't have to be. You can still pick it up," she says. "But, first, take me back there."

"It's so stupid," I say. "Stupid and awful and dumb. So, Sarah texts me with the address, and for a second I think about going, but instead I think about texting Cleto and Dan. Heading into the city to see my friends, you know? But it's already after seven, and starting to pour. And, even if they were around, by the time we got our shit together and I made it into the city, it would be close to ten."

"So you went to the party instead?"

I shudder. "Not at first. Not like you think," I say. "I ignore the text, turn on the television, because, like I said, I decide I should make her sweat. But even with nine thousand channels, there's not a single thing on. I'm feeling anxious and bored, so I wander to the front of the house, but my mother is out—again, like always—not that I'd even want her there if she was.

"At like eight o'clock, I text Sarah back—'I'm gonna stay here. Headache. Portfolio. Talk tomorrow'—and I walk to the spare bedroom.

"I don't know what I'm planning to do in there. Go through some things, maybe. There's so much we haven't unpacked. We still haven't touched most of my father's things since he died.

"The room is a mess, a sea of unpacked crates and cartons. Our apartment in the city wasn't small. All of Dad's stuff, still in boxes, on the floor, on the dresser, on the perfectly made-up guest bed. Like guests will ever come. Several of my father's larger canvases that couldn't fit in boxes are propped against walls, some wrapped in brown paper, others not. It makes me sad to see them there like that, uncared for.

"I walk around looking through them, like I'm in some sort of morbid museum. They move me to tears. Honestly, I'd forgotten how beautiful they are. Sunflowers and seascapes and still lifes. Each one worthy of a gallery wall. In the back corner, I come across a large wrapped one and peel back the corner of the paper. Not his. Ugly. It's *Icarus's Flight Plan*. I remember."

"Icarus falling," Dr. Alvarez says. I think she just wants me to know that she's listening.

"I start to feel dizzy, off balance. I can't catch my breath. I remember wondering if someone my age can have a heart attack. I swear I thought that," I say, turning to her. 'Maybe I'm having a heart attack.' Anyway, I know I need to stop the thoughts from coming because they're making me angry. Filling me with rage: *He stopped painting for Mom, because of money. If he hadn't stopped painting, he'd still be alive.*

"I pull boxes down from the stacks, rifling through my father's worldly possessions. I'm looking for something—a clue. Maybe some message he's left for me. Honestly, I don't know what I'm looking for. When I spot the box marked MARI/PERSONAL I open it. I know it's not right, but I do.

"Fuck her, right? Because maybe there's something of his I want in there.

"I sit on the bed and work to peel off the tape, but I swear she's got it hermetically sealed. There must be five layers of packing tape running around it. So, I run to my room and grab an X-ACTO knife from my drawer, returning to the guest room with purpose. And when I have the box open, I shove the X-ACTO knife in my sweatshirt pocket and sit with her stuff on the floor."

Dr. Alvarez makes a sound, something sympathetic and

pained that comes from the back of her throat, but I can't stop now. She's the one who wanted to hear.

"The crap inside the box is mostly disappointing. A bunch of file folders, envelopes. A few of Dad's red-brown legal folders. Not even hers, so I don't get why they're in her personal box. I page through them but have no interest in the stuff. Legal notices. Tax returns. One folder taped shut again, marked GRIEVANCE COMMITTEE V. ALDEN, ESQ. Not her handwriting. Someone else's."

"No curiosity?" Dr. Alvarez interrupts gently.

"Not really. I'd hear my Dad talking to my Mom about stuff like that all the time. 'Some disgruntled client,' he'd explain. 'A frivolous claim to get out of paying the firm's bill.' I know one had made them fight, a few months before he died. My mother had bitched about losing their shirts. 'My shirt, not yours, Marielle,' he had snapped at her. She was always worrying about money, but it's not like she was the one working."

"I see. So then what happened?" she prods.

"There's another folder, this one clearly in my mother's handwriting, marked PERSONAL & CONFIDENTIAL. More tape, but slimmer." My heart wrenches. "There are photographs in there, birthday cards, letters. From her to him—*"My dearest Mark"*—and him to her—*"My darling Marielle."* Gushy stuff. Cards dating back from before they were married. College photos, and all sorts of emails, from back before we even had Gmail."

My throat constricts, knowing what's next.

"And then I come to another envelope inside that one, plain, filled with more emails. These are weird, different, newer. You can tell because of the paper. Crisp and white. But, the tops are cut off, so you can't see who sent them, or when: *'My dear, beautiful man, I can't stop thinking about you, your face, your body . . . I never thought I would feel this way again . . .'*

"Shit like that. I can't even think about it now. But it all makes sense suddenly. My mother's obsession with always looking good, fixing herself up, like she's going on a fucking date . . ."

I let my voice rise higher, mocking her. I know I sound childish doing it, but I want Dr. Alvarez to understand. "*'My dearest man, It won't be Christmas without you. I know you're scared and overwhelmed, but soon it's going to be okay. Give me some time . . . Maneuvering is needed to protect people . . .'*

"'Maneuvering.' Can you believe that? And it must have been Christmas, right before my father killed himself." I barely get the words out. Even now, I feel like I'm going to throw up.

I wait for my words to re-form, for the air to stop squeezing in on me. "Anyway, I shoved the papers back and threw the box in the closet."

Now, like then, bile rises in my throat. All those nights she was out. All those afternoons? While he was working, doing shit he hated to keep her in her fancy clothes, and fancy apartment, with fancy things, she was in some hotel room in the city. And now, maybe he's here, up in Northhollow. Maybe that's why she was so anxious to drag us up here!

"I couldn't think, I couldn't breathe," I say to Dr. Alvarez. "I just needed to get out of there."

"And that's when you went to Dunn's house."

"Yes," I say quietly. "To find Sarah. I thought Sarah would help me. I thought she would understand."

"Klee?" I've gone cold, clammy. I'm doubled over on the cool dirt of the path. Trees tower overhead, sunlight streaming through onto Dr. Alvarez's brown loafers. "Klee, are you all right?" She squats down next to me, puts a gentle hand on my back. "It's okay. I'm glad you told me. It's going to be okay."

I turn and look behind us. It feels like we've walked so far. But in the distance, through the trees, I can make out the solid outline of the Ape Can.

I slow my breath, am able because she takes breaths with me, showing me how. Slow in, slow out. Holding it for counts in between.

"Square breathing," she says. "It works pretty much every time."

I do as she says, and after another minute I feel more stable. Like the cold has left me and the spinning has stopped again.

I sit down on my ass in the dirt, knees up, head rested on them. The cool quiet helps.

Jesus," I finally say. "That's what I thought, Dr. Alvarez. That if I just found Sarah, everything would be okay."

"But it wasn't?" she asks.

"No." I say. "It wasn't okay at all."

It's raining so hard by the time I get in the car, I can barely see out through the windshield. I drive anyway, navigating back roads I still don't know all that well. Especially when I get to the Trees section.

Aspen, to Oakwood, to Ash.

The roads are dark, with only intermittent street lamps. I squint, frantic, trying to keep my mother's words, the awful disgusting images, from prying their way in.

Dunn's house is in the polar opposite direction from where I live. Past where Sarah lives, past where we go to River's Edge.

They call this neighborhood "the Trees" for obvious reasons. Ash, to Dogwood. Dogwood, to Poplar, to Pine.

Where's Pine?

I turn on my wipers, but the rain streams down harder and faster than they help. My headlights bounce back at me off the sheet of rain, blurring things, making it harder and harder to see. Worse, these back roads are pitted from the winter's ice and snow, filling with rainwater that splashes up as my father's Mercedes bumps through.

At the end of what seems like a dead end, I turn back, squint down the length of Dogwood again.

I see a sign I missed, but when I reach it, it reads Maple, not Pine.

A crazy thought pops into my head: *What if there is no Pine? What if it's a setup because Sarah didn't want me to come?*

But she wouldn't do that. Sarah loves me. She told me she does.

"My dearest man . . ."

Something I see now: *People lie all the time.*

By the time I pass Ash again, I'm having a hard time breathing at all.

I should turn around and go home, but instead I turn the wipers higher. Their useless *shum-shum* does nothing to clear my vision.

Calm down, Klee. It's not a highway. You're not being tricked. Stop being such a baby.

Stop being a pathetic little wuss.

My eyes scan frantically, squinting as they land on the street signs. Poplar again, and now tears are making it hard to see.

Shit! Are you kidding me?

I pull the car over and swipe at my face with my sleeve, then look up and see it: *Pine Street. Right in front of my nose.*

No tricks. No lies.

Find 44 Pine. Where Sarah is.

Before I reach the house, I hear the music. The curbs and the lawn are thick with cars, the house lit up like a fucking Christmas tree.

I pass one parked car after another, looking for a spot, looking for Sarah's mother's car. But none of them look like hers. *No big deal. Maybe she got a ride.*

The music intensifies. I slow Dad's car to a crawl.

What if she's not here? I'm never going to find a place to park. I'm going to have to circle around again.

A high-pitched double beep, and I stop. A black car's lights flash twice, and two kids come stumbling out into the rain. They climb in, close the doors, and its backup lights go on.

At least I won't have to walk too far.

The car backs out after several drunken maneuvers, and I ease my father's Mercedes in.

Find Sarah, and everything will be okay.

I shove it in Park, pull up my hood, and duck out into the torrential rain.

By the time I reach the door, I'm drenched. The door is open, though, so I won't have to ring.

I push it wider and step inside.

The music is deafening. The place is crawling with people. Smoke, body odor, alcohol. The air is sweaty and oppressive. Beer cans, whisky bottles everywhere. The cloyingly sweet smell of weed.

"Alden is here!" someone says, and there's laughter. I push my way past. I don't even care. I'm shivering because of how soaked I am.

I make my way down the hall, my eyes scanning frantically for Sarah. She's not here in the hall or in the kitchen.

As I push through the living room, someone yells, "Dude!" and I nearly trip over a guy on the floor on his girlfriend. In the corner, I spot Anna Morrissey from Tarantoli's class. I yell, "Hey! Have you seen Sarah?" but she simply shrugs, and the girl next to her says, "Oh, shit!" then covers her mouth and leans into Anna.

Doesn't matter.

Head down.

Find Sarah.

"Try the basement," someone says, pulling my shoulder, so I make my way down through the crowd.

But she's not there either, so I make my way back upstairs.

There's a second flight up, to the bedrooms.

I take those stairs two at a time.

In the first room, there's a bed, at least four bodies writhing and necking, the mess of jackets and bags kicked to the floor.

I close the door and open another one. It's like a *Price Is Right* I don't want to win.

Another bedroom. Another couple. No Sarah.

I'm almost relieved.

Maybe she left. Maybe she left and went home.

I stagger down the hall, dizzy and buzzed from the smoke and the din. I just need to check the rest of the rooms and get out of here.

I pass a bathroom. The lights are off except for a nightlight, and the door is ajar.

Someone is moving in there.

I push the door open, then close it quickly. Mortified.

A girl is on the toilet.

Then I hear it: A moan. A guy's voice, then her's.

Sarah's.

She isn't peeing. She is sitting on the toilet. Backward.

I push the door open again, a migraine pulsing in my eyes.

She's straddling someone.

Abbott.

He turns, annoyed, and sees me.

"Shit!" He nudges her, and she turns now.

"*Klee?*" Her face is horrified. Scared.

She has no shirt on.

"Holy shit, Klee."

She gets up, off the toilet—off Abbott—and walks toward me, arms folded to cover her chest.

But I can't bear it.

I can't speak. I can't stay.

I start to back away.

You don't matter. No one will ever love you enough, Klee.

"Klee!"

I can't breathe.

Sarah reaches out to grab hold of me.

"No! Please, don't touch me," I say.

I back against the door.

Who closed it?

"Klee . . ."

I need to get away.

"Let him go," Abbott says, moving toward me.

"What he says," I say.

I jam my hands in my pockets, trying to process, but everything's a blur. Everything is waffling in front of me.

Abbott reaches out as my fingers strike metal. I pull the X-ACTO from my pocket, and wave it in front of me.

"Fuck! He's got a knife, Keith! Jesus, Klee! Please . . ." But I'm not going to use it. I just want him to stay away from me.

He backs off, but my body is trembling. I feel as if I can't hold on to myself. I'm breaking apart, shattering. I'm a building made of glass in an earthquake.

My father. My mother. Now Sarah.

I need to steady myself. I need to stop things.

"Klee . . . ?"

I reach up.

"Klee . . . ?"

I need to stop it all from shattering.

"Klee!"

I slice, and they both reel away. One swift slice and I'm free again.

The pain . . . the pain is all I feel.

The blood flows and I grow dizzy, so I lower myself onto the floor.

Now I can stop trembling and think.

Relief.

Relief.

I close my eyes.

Relief.

"I wasn't trying to hurt myself," I say softly. "I wasn't thinking."

I just want someone to understand this.

Dr. Alvarez nods, and I sit down next to her. Shoulders hunched, I stare at my feet.

The air echoes.

"I just wanted to stop feeling the pain," I finally say.

"I get it," she says. "Replace one pain with another, right?" I nod, grateful. "I understand. And now?"

"And now." I look up. Around. We're in a beautiful clearing. Sun streams down through the green lace of trees. "Now I just want to be okay."

We don't speak for a while, just sit, and when I do look around again and take in our surroundings, I notice things I hadn't at first.

A matching white stone bench across from the one we sit

on, its legs carved with ornate fruits and birds. A small shrine of sorts in the center of the clearing.

I get up and walk over. It's a low, flat tree stump, upon which three stone Buddhas, a few assorted crystals and beach rocks, and several metal bowls filled with water and floating flower petals are perched. A few stems of silk flowers faded from the sun.

I give Dr. Alvarez a quizzical look and she says, "No, I didn't put most of that here, if you're wondering. Just one of the Buddhas, and some beach rocks. The others were already here when I found this spot."

"Oh. Wow. Weird. I mean, cool, I guess. But weird."

"Agree," she says. "For what it's worth, I'm not particularly religious. But I find it pretty and soothing. Years after I discovered it, I found that one Buddha, the small one in the center, at a garage sale. And, I love how the rainwater fills the bowls."

Dr. Alvarez walks over and adjusts one of the bowls and picks an acorn from the ground and drops it in. I peer up through the canopy of branches, tracing the beams of sunlight down. They fall almost perfectly mid-altar.

"Comforting, right?" she asks. "I can't tell you how often that happens. As if it's all truly meant to be here. The woman who sold me the Buddha said her name is Green Tara. I looked her up once. She's the Goddess of Universal Compassion. The story goes that she was born from the tears of a bodhisattva who saw the world suffering and wept. His tears formed a lake from which a lotus flower sprang. When the lotus flower opened, Green Tara was revealed." I nod, reminded of the stories my father would tell. "Who knows if it's true, but it's a lovely thought, don't you think?"

"Yes," I say, scavenging a small bud of some sort from the ground and placing it in one of the bowls. I want to add something, leave some sort of contribution here.

I take a step closer and study Green Tara's face. Something

about how tranquil she appears fills me with a desire to paint. I could pull out my brushes and canvas, but I'm tired, too, so maybe tomorrow. Maybe tomorrow I'll ask if we can come back so I can paint.

Dr. Alvarez sits on the opposite bench and stretches her legs. She's taken off her shoes again and wiggles her red-polished toes. The soles of her feet are brown with dirt. I smile, thinking of the first day I sat with her, and how comfortable I am, how very much I like her now. I trust her completely. Has it really only been a week and a half?

"So," she says, smiling at me, "the worst of it is out, yes? And here you are, in the sunshine, still standing."

Day 10—Afternoon

When I get back to my room, Martin is waiting at my door.

I'm so not in the mood. It's not that I mind the kid, but I don't feel like talking. And seriously, he's way too young to think he should be hanging out with me.

"What's up, Martin?" I ask, still feeling the weight of the morning. I feel heavy and churned up, like my insides are the contents of a cement mixer. I want to lie down, take a nap, or find some mindless rerun on television.

"Want to hang in the game room? There's a Ping-Pong table in the back."

"There is?" I think of Sister Agnes Teresa, going in there and loading up her cart with board games from the past several decades, and find myself wondering if she's good at Ping-Pong, too. Because, that I could beat her at, though the thought is unfair. She can probably barely reach above the table.

"Do you know Sister Agnes Teresa?" I ask.

"Who?"

"Sister Agnes Teresa. The nun who volunteers here."

"The short one?" Martin asks, which makes me laugh a little, because it's seriously the understatement of the year.

"Yeah, her."

"Oh, yeah. I've seen her around. Why? What about her?"

"No. Nothing. I don't know. I like her. She comes in and plays games with me sometimes."

"She does?" Martin sounds hurt. So I guess she doesn't do the same with him.

"Dumb games," I say, not wanting him to feel bad. "Seriously. Like Checkers and Candy Land." I laugh and Martin laughs, too. But the truth is, I do feel a little special now. Like Sister Agnes Teresa picked me, saw some reason to annoy and enlist me. "Anyway," I tell him, "sure, why not? Ping-Pong it is."

"Okay, but I'm going to whip your butt," Martin warns.

"I'm used to that." I follow him the few doors down the hall. "Hey, where's Sabrina?"

"I don't know," he says, pushing the game room door open and switching on the lights. "We're not really friends, or hadn't you noticed?"

"I hadn't," I say. "And, I'm sure you are," but the insightfulness of his statement kind of surprises me. The kid is smart, clearly, but he doesn't always seem aware.

Martin shrugs and says, "No, we're not. Why would we be? Anyway, none of us stick around long, if we're lucky. So no one is actually friends inside here."

"I get that," I say. "But I also think we are. Maybe there are different kinds of friends. People who support you." I want to rumple his hair, do something. I'm suddenly feeling pretty sorry for the kid.

"Maybe." He shrugs again. "Then again, what do I know? It's not like I'm some sort of an expert."

"Really?" I want to say, "Aren't you?" because he always acts like one. But he sounds so defeated, so instead I ask, "So, do you have many friends at home?"

"Not exactly. You?" Martin finds the rubber stop from behind the door and wedges it in the crack so the door won't close. "House rules," he says, walking to the shelves. He retrieves a clear plastic bin filled with white Ping-Pong balls and padded paddles. "Follow me." He heads back to a second room. "So, do you?"

"Do I what?"

"Have a lot of friends."

"Me, nah. Same as you. Not too many. But, I only came to Northhollow this year."

I figure he'll ask me why, and I'll have to explain about my father and why my mother moved us up here my senior year. Explain about Cleto and Dan, and what good friends we were. But all he says is, "Yeah, figures. Most of us in here rarely have many good friends."

I stop walking, my mind going to Cleto again. "Is that true?"

"Of course it's true. We're loners. We isolate from others. We mess up relationships. There are plenty of signs before we end up in here. You're pretty new at this, aren't you? This isn't, like, step number one."

Jesus. I think about Sarah and how adamant I was about not hanging out with her friends. Then again, Abbott and Dunn, well, can you blame me about them? But still. And Cleto and Dan, I never reached out to them . . .

"We're all guilty of it," Martin says, shaking his head. "I hear everyone's stories. None of us ever think we play a part. But we do. We refuse to connect. We withdraw. Or at least we don't reach out to anyone for help. We can do it alone, we think. We don't need anyone else."

He stops at the small green table, the kind that converts to a card table or bumper pool.

"I know, I know, not regulation size. Better than nothing. You serve," he says, tossing a paddle and two balls at me.

We volley back and forth, my game off given the odd size of the table, until Martin slams the ball hard, making contact with the very edge of my side of the table, before it whips past my head and into a window.

"Nice shot," I say. "You didn't tell me you were a prodigy at this, too."

Martin shrugs. The last few days he's lacked his original enthusiasm. "Dumb luck is all," he says. "Besides, it's a pointless thing to be good at. Anyway, I envy you. Being in college soon and all. I wish I were you." He retrieves the ball and takes his serve.

"Hey, Martin, you're a cool kid," I say. "And smart, too. I know you know that. But not just smart. Not how you think, but in other ways too. You have a whole lot going for you."

"You think?" Martin asks, giving me an eye, trying to figure out if I'm pulling his leg. But I'm not. I put my paddle down, walk over, and put an arm around him, give his hair a brotherly ruffle.

"Yeah, no kidding. I do."

After Martin goes back to his room, I head to the nurses' station. There's something I need to do.

"Could I make a call, please?" I ask. "To an outside line. A friend, in the city."

"Go ahead," the nurse says. "Dial one first, to get out. You can sit over there." She motions to an empty cluster of chairs across from the desk.

It's weird to use a landline, been forever since I've had to, and suddenly, I'm not even sure I know his cell number. It takes me three false starts before I think I have the sequence right.

The minute it starts ringing, I panic. It's a weekday. I didn't even look at the time. He's probably still in school. My eyes dart to the clock above the nurses' station: 2:36 P.M. They just got out. But maybe he has some club and stayed after. Maybe he's with Dan. Maybe he has a girlfriend.

It rings four times and I'm about to hang up, when I hear his familiar "Hey yo." I don't talk. I can't get words out of my mouth. "Who is this?" Obviously he's confused. I'm calling him from the fucking Ape Can. How might that come up on his caller ID?

I should hang up.

"Asshole," he says.

"Cleto?" I say, fast.

"Klee? Hey! What up, man?"

Not much. I'm calling from the loony bin.

I had a bad day and went off the deep end.

"Klee? You there? Where you calling from, man?"

"Yeah, hey. I am. It's been awhile. I just wanted to say hello."

"Good to hear from you. Me and Dan, we were just talking about you this afternoon. No shit. Maybe your ears were burning, bro."

I feel sick. I feel like I could actually throw up. I don't know what made me think it was a good idea to call Cleto from in here.

"You all right, man? Whose number is this? You around this weekend? Want to come in? Melting Snow is playing at the Copper Penny, and Dan and I thought you might come in."

Melting Snow is a band we follow. *Used* to follow. And, the Copper Penny is a dive bar down in the Village where Dan's uncle works and lets us in. As long as we stay away from the bar.

"I wish," I say. "Yeah. If I could, I would totally come in. But not this weekend. That's what I'm calling you about, man."

"Okay, sure." I hear the disappointment in his voice, and it hits me again that he tried. *He* tried. Even after I moved up here to Northhollow. He and Dan would both call, and we'd make plans, but inevitably I'd find a way to blow them off. *We're loners. We isolate. We mess up relationships. There are plenty of signs before we end up in here.* "But not because I don't want to, Cleto. I do. I'm going to. I had a little accident . . ." I say.

"Are you okay?"

"Yeah. Thanks. Well, not an accident, exactly. It's been a little hairy around here."

"Sorry to hear that. Can I help?"

"No. I'm okay. I mean, I think I am, now."

"Do you want to talk?"

And, suddenly, I do. I really want to talk to Cleto. To my friend. Tell him everything. So I do. Whispered with my back turned so the nurse won't hear. The whole ugly saga. About Sarah and my mom and her dumb letters—her affair—and how things got fucked-up long before that. "I didn't deal with my dad when it happened, I don't think," I say, "and it all piled up, and I kind of went crazy, I guess."

"Wow," Cleto says. "I had no idea."

"I know. I lost it, dude. I mean, seriously lost it. But I think I'm getting better in here."

"Shit," he says, after a few seconds of dead silence. "That's fucked-up. I feel bad. I don't know what to say."

"It's okay."

"Yeah." He's quiet for a few seconds, then says, "So, you think you're getting out soon?"

"Yeah. I mean, I hope so. I'll have to stay in therapy and shit, stay on medication."

"That makes sense," Cleto says.

"Yeah. Anyway, I figured I should tell you. Reach out.

You're my best friend, Cleto. Always were. And I sure don't have any friends up here. And I didn't want you hearing through social media or some crazy shit like that."

"Okay, man. I'm glad you did. Feel better, Klee. Holy shit. You'd better get better," he says.

Day 11—Morning

Dr. Alvarez has her back to me, looks out her office window at the drizzle.

Yesterday, in the sunshine, talking to Dr. Alvarez, to Cleto, everything felt more hopeful, more doable. But today I'm back to worried again. What if I never feel well enough to get out of here?

When I walk in, she turns and smiles. Dr. Alvarez's smile can almost make me believe what she believes. That I will get better. That I have. That soon I'll be ready to go home.

"Klee," she says, nodding at the couch, so I sit. "Have I told you how much I like your name?" I don't say anything because I'm not sure what to say. "Clay," she says, then, "Clay," again. "Simple and solid, and appealing."

I shift uncomfortably. I don't give much thought to my name. I mean, I do, but not that way. It's a burden at times. And I was never a fan of Paul Klee.

"My mother liked him," I say. "My father and I preferred the Impressionists and Postimpressionists, obviously. Manet, Gauguin, Van Gogh. But my mother, she likes the Bauhaus painters, and abstracts, too, Kandinsky, Klee, and more modern ones."

"I can imagine why you wouldn't love it, then, but it's a great strong name they chose for you. Though I imagine the mispronunciation drives you crazy."

"I guess," I say. "I'm used to it." I twist and look out the window. The rain has intensified. A spring storm, thunder and all.

"Believe me, I get it. It's strange, you probably don't know this yet—or maybe you do?—but my first name is Ailîn, circumflex over the second *i*."

She's right, I didn't know her first name. Never even thought about it. In fact, her having a first name never really occurred to me. I just think of her as Dr. Alvarez.

"So, see? I do get it, which is why I felt so bad when I realized I'd been mispronouncing your name. Although, no one really calls me Ailîn anymore. Not for a long time. My close friends and family all call me Lynnie or Lynn, and my mother passed away two years ago . . . She was the only one who called me by my proper name." Her voice turns sad, and I realize we have more in common than I knew. She lost a parent recently, too. Though I'm guessing from something more normal than mine. "Anyway, as far as I've ever been able to tell, my name means 'transparent' or 'clear,' which makes me like it better than I might. It's a Mapudungun name, a language isolate spoken in south-central Chile. Don't ask me what any of that means."

She winks at me and moves around the coffee table to sit in her chair. "My mother was Chilean," she says, "but I've seen Gaelic derivations, too. My father, now he . . ." She laughs at some funny thing I'm not privy to. "He was from San Salvador."

"Oh, wow," I say, twisting back to look out the window again. A low rumble of thunder is followed by a quick succession of lightning flashes.

"Boring, more like it." She laughs softly. "I guess my point is, I like names. I'm interested in them. I often wonder if and how they shape us. I've tried to do some research on what our names may have to do with who we are—who we become—if anything." Another crack and rumble of thunder, this one louder and closer, and the rain opens up, stretching down in an almost deafening sheet.

"Anyway, I looked up your name, because I was curious. I mean, it sounds like Clay, but I was curious if I could find an exact reference. Besides Paul Klee in particular. I wondered if it had a distinct meaning.

"As you can imagine, you don't find a lot of references for the version with your spelling, and most do, in fact, relate to the painter. There seems to be a Greek reference, too, to clover, or someone who lives near a field of clover. I like that a lot, because if you think of clover you might immediately think of good luck. But I wasn't satisfied. That wasn't the thing that I was looking for.

"So, I went with the English translation, Clay, which is how you pronounce it, after all. And, well, do you have any idea of the meaning?"

I try to focus over the din of the storm. I'm agitated; it conjures up Dunn's house, and all I want to know at this point is how I get from here, to better, to home.

"Some kind of dirt or mineral or earth, I would think?" I ask halfheartedly.

"Aha, see? Right, you would think. And there is that version, short for Clayton, derived from Old English. But there's another meaning altogether that I found in my search."

She pulls out a folded piece of paper from her sweater pocket, and presses it onto her lap. "I couldn't find the origin. But it's the spelling with the *k*, and they say it means 'He who is immortal.'" She pushes the piece of paper across the table to me. My eyes go to hers. "Not a bad choice, all things considered, right?" I nod, swallowing down the lump in my throat. "So, now that we've talked about all that other stuff, what happened with Sarah, what happened with your mom, perhaps it's time we talk about your dad."

So we do. With the rain and the thunder pounding in the background, and the paper with the word "immortal" squeezed in my hand.

We talk about him before, and we talk about after. And we talk about the afternoon I found him. And when we're finished, Dr. Alvarez says, "That's a lot to handle, a lot to take in, stuff that very few of us could process on our own. We should and will talk more about it. Talk about tools, ways you might handle it, and let go. Ways you can truly allow yourself to heal.

"But before all that," she says, "I want to tell you that I'm sorry. I'm sorry for this tragic thing that happened to you. And I'm sorry for your pain. I can only imagine how awful it must have been."

Her words sit there between us, kind and gentle and true. The rain has stopped. The room has grown quiet. My eyes shift to the wall, above Dr. Alvarez's head, where *Daubigney's Garden* hangs, constant.

If only I could disappear into it.

I close my eyes and pretend I am the missing cat, slipping beyond the matted edges, skirting along the cool grass. I imagine that inside the white house with the blue roof is my father. My mother and my father. From before. All of us laughing and whole.

But the truth is, even then, before, the picture doesn't look normal and whole. Something is off, something deeper that is trying to horn in.

"What are you thinking?" Dr. Alvarez asks.

"I'm thinking of trying to see the world the way it really is," I say. "Or was. Instead of how I remember it, or want it to have been. It makes me think of this picture book I used to love as a kid that my mother read to me. It was called *Zoom*, I think, and each page, each picture, was a smaller scene from within a bigger scene on the previous page. So that, when you turned the page, the town in the picture on the first page, with its roads and houses and cars and all of the life going on, turns out by the end to not be a real town at all but only a picture on a postage stamp, stuck to a envelope—a letter—in the hand of some kid. And the kid walks down a street with the whole wide universe around him."

"Fascinating," she says. "I'd like to see that."

"A part of me feels that small sometimes. That inconsequential. Like my life is nothing more than a postage stamp. Like nothing I do will ever matter enough . . ."

"Enough for what?" she says.

"I'm not sure. Enough to hold on to the people I love."

"Enough to hold on to yourself, maybe?" she asks.

I nod, feeling the tears well up, but also feeling more in control, feeling able, this time, to hold them back if I want to.

"But, now, see, I'm thinking that maybe that's wrong," I say. "Maybe I'm looking at it all the wrong way. Maybe it's good if the little moments don't matter, and the only thing that matters is what adds up to the whole. Because, that way, that night with Sarah at Dunn's house, my mother's letters that I found, and whatever she did or didn't do . . . well, those moments just become postage stamps, but they don't define the whole wide world around me. They don't define him, or her, or me. And Saturday night, what I did? That's not me either. It was a moment. A postage stamp. It doesn't have to mean I'm like him."

"Like your father?" she says. "Doomed to be him."

"Right," I say. "Maybe I'm not him at all. He's the postage stamp, but I'm the kid with the letter in his hand."

Dr. Alvarez smiles, but she doesn't say anything. She waits for me to go on.

"Sarah's been texting me," I say, not expecting to. "My mother told me. She's texted me several times."

"Is that good or bad?" Dr. Alvarez asks.

I look back at where the small black cat should be, and will myself there. Home. Inside that soothing white house. Will myself back a year, maybe more. Will myself back to that shabby couch, with the three of us laughing in the Village. But now I get that I have to stop looking back and look forward. Forward to Boston and to college. Forward to the whole rest of my life. Because this week, this month, this year, they don't have to be the big picture. They're just the postage stamp on one single letter.

And even though I'm not sure exactly what all this means, or if the math of it even adds up at all, it sits squarely in my chest like an answer.

Day 11—Evening

Sister Agnes Teresa stands over me with a box in her hand. Smaller than a board game. Yahtzee. No, not Yahtzee. It reads Boggle on the box.

Never heard of it. I roll my eyes but in a teasing way. The truth is, I'm happy to see her regardless of what kid game torture she plans to put me through.

"I'm sorry to find you sleeping," she says in her froggish voice. "I thought we were making some progress here."

"We were. I mean, I am. I mean, we are." I sit up and push the sheets off my still clothed legs. "In case you don't know it," I say, "progress can be pretty exhausting."

She laughs and walks to the window to lift the shade. The sky is deepening, but it still holds its full grasp on day. It must be well after six. It's staying lighter and lighter these days. "That was quite a storm earlier. It's cleared up nicely," she says. "Anyway, I thought we might play a few rounds, then go for a swim."

I move to the table and sit in her chair. "So, what is that?" I ask.

"Boggle. Any good?"

"Probably not," I say, smiling.

She puts a small blank pad and a mini pencil in front of each of us, then takes out the cube with the clear lid, shakes and shimmies it until the letter dice fall into their squares, and places it in front of me with her hand placed over the top.

"No head starts," she says, "and words must be at least four letters long. This isn't amateur hour. No using a letter twice unless it appears twice on the board. No backtracking over a letter once you've used it already. Got it? It isn't brain surgery." She holds out a sand timer. "You ready?" I nod, trying not to give her the satisfaction of knowing I'm still totally unclear on the rules. "Good." She takes the lid off and places the timer down, then quickly flips it back again to stop the grains. She squints at me.

"What?"

"They took the bandage off."

My hand goes to my ear. "Oh, yeah." She *tsks*. "What?"

"To tell you the truth, I'm disappointed." She smiles. "It's not so bad, you know. All that fuss, and there's nothing but a glorified nick. Nothing you'll even get stared at for. No one will even notice that. Grow your hair out a bit. No one will even care."

I make my way to the deep end and dive.

The smell of chlorine is a salve.

I swim five laps without stopping, then stroke back to the shallow end without coming up for a breath. Sister Agnes Teresa sits on the edge, dangling her short, heavy legs.

"You coming in?"

"I might," she says. "You swim for a bit. I don't want to show you up here, too."

I laugh a little. "Suit yourself." I push off again and swim several more laps until I'm winded and tired, then float on my back, staring at the ceiling above me. With the water in my ears, everything grows quiet and calm.

Eventually, I hear Sister Agnes Teresa wade in. She makes her way toward me in an awkward half walk, half dog paddle, her short limbs moving faster than they should to keep her head above water. Watching her, it's hard to believe that she's a certified lifeguard.

"How do you do it?" I ask, when she finally reaches me.

"Do what?" she asks, short limbs treading in place.

"Everything. All of it. Go about life like it's normal and fine. I mean, you always seem happy and content. But it must be hard, right? I mean, with all the . . ." I search for an acceptable word and settle on "challenges."

With a flail of her arms, she positions herself upright to standing, her chin barely bobbing above the waterline.

"Whatever do you mean, Mr. Alden?" she asks, then she takes off, easily swimming the length of the pool.

Day 12—Morning

So, I'm doing it, then.

Walking down to Dr. Alvarez's office where, in a few short minutes, my mother will be joining us, and I will confront her. Tell her what I know, and how I feel.

"Ask questions without fearing the answers," Dr. Alvarez told me. Tell her I found the letters and ask whether my father knew, too. Whether that had something to do with what happened to him.

"Knowing is better than imagining most of the time," Dr. Alvarez had said yesterday, "and, besides, I hate to break it to you, Klee, but married people cheat all the time. Get

cheated *on*. It doesn't make it right, and for sure it is awful
and upsetting, but it is rarely a basis for suicide. So, maybe it
contributed to your father's deep unhappiness, but there were
more likely other compounding issues, and an underlying di-
agnosis of depression. So, you can be angry at your mother
all you want, that is fair. But I don't know that you can blame
her for his actions."

I take a deep breath and plow forward past the god-awful
fish mural. Either way, I will confront her. Get this off my
chest before I get out of here.

So that I *can* get out of here.

Even if it means letting my anger free fall, letting my
mother see how very much I hate her.

Even if she ends up hating me.

"I doubt that will happen, and you can't keep walking
around with it, Klee. You see that now. You need to get your
anger out in the open. I can tell you from experience: It's never as
bad as you think it will be."

But what if she's wrong? What if it's way, way worse?

I hover in the doorway and breathe a little easier. No sign, yet,
of my mother.

Dr. Alvarez has the Van Gogh book on her lap. When I
walk in, she turns back a few pages and taps at it with her finger. On the glossy page, a swirling lavender sky meets a sturdy
green tree in a stretch of golden grasses.

"*Wheat Field with Cypresses,*" I say, sitting. "One of my favorites of his."

"It's a very hopeful one, don't you think? You can almost
smell the trees and feel the sun on your face, hear the wheat
rustling in the wind. I'd like to find a print and add it to my

wall." I nod. "And this one?" She points to one with a chartreuse sky and bold yellow sun, a man in blue gathering something in his arms beside a knotty tree limb. "I flagged a few of the ones I liked best, but what interests me, too, is how very different they all are, some so free and almost whimsical, and others so much heavier and dark.

"*The Sower*," I say. "And that one," I add, pointing to the opposite page, "is *The Potato Eaters*." I shudder for effect. "I never liked that one. At all."

"*The Potato Eaters*," she repeats, running her finger along the center of a dark, bleak painting of a peasants sitting at a wooden kitchen table.

"*Les Mangeurs de Pommes de Terre* is the actual title, which translates to 'Potato Eaters.' It's one of the few I actually hate. My dad had a print of it hanging in his studio. I used to pretend it wasn't a Van Gogh."

Dr. Alvarez chuckles. "Well, I can certainly see why you weren't a fan. It isn't an easy painting to take in."

"My dad loved it, though. He was taken by its skill. He would try to explain to me—to show me how Van Gogh could make the viewer *feel* the peasants' dirt and grime and unhappiness. 'To feel austerity through paint, to smell the loam of the earth,' he would say. 'It's as if the peasants are painted not from oils but from the very dirt they sowed.'"

"He made a good point. It's incredible. You must miss sharing art with him."

"I do," I say. "I miss lots of things."

"Yes." She closes the book and says, "Yes. I do love how the commentary, the extra information, makes me like the painting better. Or at least helps me to appreciate it more. I also love how we can learn so much about a person by the art that moves them. Not just paintings, but the books they read, the movies they watch over and over again. And, the inverse,

too: how we presume to know so much about something—
someone—by those external factors, when so often we know
very little. But it seems notable that your father was drawn to
this painting and you are not. Perhaps that speaks to some dif-
ferences in your nature. Either way, I'm grateful you've shown
me how to look at Van Gogh's work more closely, in a different
way, and that comes from you, through him. So, in some small
way, I feel like I knew him, too. You've taught me something
here, something that seems very much worth knowing."

I open my mouth to respond when a knock sounds at the
door. I swallow hard. Dr. Alvarez's eyes flash to mine, and I
say, "Speaking of learning things that may—or may not—be
worth knowing."

My mother perches on the edge of the couch in a green sweater
set, jeans, and dress loafers with a fat heel, trying to appear
more casual. She looks especially uncomfortable in the jeans.
I didn't even know she still owned a pair.

Her eyes dart nervously from Dr. Alvarez to me, back to
Dr. Alvarez. Finally she turns back to me and says, "How are
you doing, Klee? Any better?"

"Actually, a little. Yes. Hanging in pretty well, I guess."

"That's good!" She turns to Dr. Alvarez. "Right? That's
very promising?"

Dr. Alvarez smiles. "Yes, Mrs. Alden, very."

My mother nods and wrings her hands as if she can sense
the shitstorm coming, then twists to look out the window. "Finally nice out again. Enough already with all the rain!"

Maybe it's because I'm feeling better, stronger, but my
mother seems kind of fragile right now. Weak and frail, like
some of her usual Ice Queen exterior has melted. Or maybe

it's just that I know I need to confront her, and the guilt has settled in my bones.

But she's the one who should feel guilty here, not me.

"So, Klee has been working hard in here," Dr. Alvarez says, shifting her feet under the table. My mother seems to make Dr. Alvarez uncomfortable, too, and her words feel careful and measured. "Really good work. And, I think he has been making solid progress. But there are some things we agree might help to get off his chest, and out in the open, so we might try to work through them all together." She studies my mother to assess her participation, but my mother's face is placid and unreadable. She has located and put up her ice shield.

"Yes, fine, of course," she says, smoothing an imaginary wrinkle in her jeans.

"Klee, would you like to start?"

Already? I'm not prepared yet. My heart bangs so hard I think it might break through my ribs. I shift my weight away from my mother and stare out Dr. Alvarez's office door into the waiting area. I could leave now and not do this. Get up and walk out the door. I only have to spend a few more months with her and I'm gone. Off to Boston, or if I've fucked that up already, then wherever. I don't need to do this. I don't need to have a relationship with my mother.

Dr. Alvarez says, "Klee, would you like my help broaching what we spoke about?"

"No," I say, turning back. "I'll do it." My heart drums over my words, the rhythm of my pulse rushing into my ears. I turn to face my mother squarely.

"Who is A?" I ask, my voice breaking.

"Who?"

" 'A.' Your 'dearest man.' " I spit the words, making air quotes to help jog her memory. Her face stays a mask of confusion.

She can do this, my mother: make you believe she's innocent, that you're the one who doesn't know what's going on.

"In your emails," I clarify. "In the box in the guest room. 'My Darling M . . . How I miss you . . .'" My voice rises singsong and sarcastic. "I heard you talking about him, at the funeral. 'He shouldn't ever find out. He can never know.' That he would be me, I assume? Of course, I was standing right there!"

Her face goes white with recognition. Her lower lip starts to tremble. "Jesus, Klee. That's what this is about? Dear God, now I understand. Now I—Oh, God . . ." She turns to Dr. Alvarez. "I tried to save him from all this."

"I'm sure you did. But you didn't save Dad, now, did you?" My rage propels me off the couch. I need to move away from her or I might lash out. Break something.

Dr. Alvarez moves toward me, catches my arm, and tries to calm me. But I don't want to be calmed. I want to say my piece. I don't give a shit anymore who hears it.

"You acted like you were broken up when Dad died, but you didn't care at all, did you? You were happy to move on! You were cheating on him. *You* did this to him! You were probably *happy* he was gone!"

"Klee, my God, please don't say that!"

My mother stands now, too, but Dr. Alvarez nods for her to sit again, so she does, not able to stop the tears from streaming down her face.

"How could you do that to him?" I shout. "To us? How could you hurt him like that?"

"Klee, please, I hear you, and I'll answer, but you're not going to like the answer. You're going to have to listen anyway. Please. You don't know what you're talking about . . . There are things you don't understand . . ."

Dr. Alvarez hands my mother a tissue, but she doesn't take it, waves it off. Her lip trembles worse, and her voice is barely more than a whisper now. "I'm sorry. I should have told you. It wasn't like that. Your father was, that is . . . those emails weren't mine."

She leans forward, reaching for my arm, but I whirl away from her.

"Please, don't touch me. Not ever again."

"Klee, please. Jesus, you have it *all* wrong." My mother looks to Dr. Alvarez, helpless. But she's got *that* wrong. Dr. Alvarez is *my* ally, not hers. She's here for *me*, and she knows the truth. So the Ice Queen thing isn't going to work anymore.

"He did everything for you," I say. "Gave up everything! His painting . . . his *art* . . ." My voice shakes, but the solidity of my alliance with Dr. Alvarez—with what she knows—gives me courage to keep going. I'm finally saying what I've wanted to for years. "His art, our old apartment, everything *he* loved and cared about. For you. So you could have your fancy shit, your expensive apartment, your nice clothes. But even that wasn't enough. You had to cheat on him. You betrayed him. You might as well have held the gun to his head—"

"Klee! Stop!"

"No, you stop—"

"Klee!" My mother shouts loudly this time, enough to make my name echo and reverberate, and me listen. "Those weren't mine! The A was a man named Armond," she says, more softly now. "Those letters were your father's . . ."

The silence is swift and deafening.

Finally, I manage, "What?" Because, that second part . . . I'm not even sure I've understood. What she just implied about my father.

Armond.

"What?" I say again, but now I get it. It's starting to solidify. I don't know how it can be, but I'm trying to.

I look to Dr. Alvarez for help.

"Hear her out, Klee," she says.

I sit and wait, if I still can't look at my mother.

"The letters you found, Klee," my mother says, 'those were between your father and a man."

I hear what she's saying, but none of it makes any sense in my brain.

"Bullshit," I say weakly. I say it, but I know that it's not. She's not lying. I don't know why I couldn't see it before.

The growing distance between my mother and father . . . her coldness . . . The weird way my father acted that day in the gallery with Armond all those years ago . . .

All those years.

"Jesus." I put my head in my hands. "How long—?"

"I'm so sorry, Klee. I should have told you—"

But, of course, if I just looked back myself, I would know.

Of course I would.

Anyone looking in would see.

I slide down off the couch and onto the floor, lie back on the rug, and stare at the ceiling. Down here out of the swirl of the blizzard.

"Are you okay?" My mother reaches down, but I wave her hand away. I wait for the crow, for the red-bearded man, while I breathe. Neither appears. Just an odd, hollow ringing in my ears.

Dr. Alvarez gets up and moves toward me, but I say, "Actually, I'm okay. I think I'm okay. I just want to be down here for a minute. Go ahead, Mom, you can talk if you want. I'm listening."

My mother slides over on the couch so she can reach down and touch my bent knee. I fight the impulse to stop her from keeping her hand there.

"I'm so sorry, Klee. I kept things from you . . . not to lie, but to protect you. To protect your memories of him.

Maybe I was wrong, and I shouldn't have. But they weren't your problems, they were our problems. Grown-up problems, that it didn't seem fair for you to have to know. I thought it would be better if—" Her voice stops. A hiccup escapes and her hand disappears from my leg. She pulls a tissue from the box and blows her nose. "I thought wrong, I guess, and I'm sorry. Because without knowing, how could you possibly understand?"

I sit up, pull my knees to my chest, and study her face, so broken and apologetic, it almost hurts to look at her.

"I am so sorry, Klee. I'd known for a while, well before his death, but there were other issues . . . I didn't want to involve you in them. He was hurting, I knew that. But I was hurting, too. He made so many mistakes, but I loved him. It's hard to explain, but I did."

The room is quiet. I close my eyes, glad to feel the floor under me, solid and sure.

"So, my father was gay, is what you are telling me," I finally say. "And Armond was his boyfriend. Or whatever."

"Yes," she says. "For several years."

She smiles sadly and I nod again, and push a fist to my forehead and bang it there. Because I'm an idiot, because I didn't see it, because I didn't want to see what I probably should have known.

My mother leans down toward me. "I'm sorry," she says again, touching my cheek. "I was trying to protect you."

"Yeah. I know."

"He was many wonderful things, your father. But he did things wrong, too, and lying to us wasn't the worst of it. He wasn't honest with me, or with you. But worse, he wasn't honest with himself. Not for a long time. And it led to bigger problems. Deceitful behavior. Problems with money. I'll explain if you want. But first, you need to know this and understand: know that I loved him. Even after I knew, and none of this changes how very much we both loved you."

Dad and I are in his studio painting a huge canvas of sunflowers together. I always feel important when he lets me help.

"Everyone thinks objects are just one color, that sunflowers are yellow, say, and limes are green, but if you look carefully, you'll see it's not true," he says. "Limes have hints of blue and yellow, and sunflowers are gray and blue and green and orange, because color is like that, more than you see at a first glance."

I stare at the sunflowers and squint, but try as I might, I mostly see yellow and orange. Still, I nod so he thinks I can see, because I don't want to disappoint him.

"Well, good. Remember that, Klee. That there's always more to life than you can see with your own two eyes."

After that we paint, and I make sure to load all different colors on my brush, and Dad says, "Good, see? Just like that," or, "Maybe not so much blue in that one."

As we paint, Dad talks to me about art and "technique," and he tells me about different famous artists like he always does. Van Gogh and Gauguin, Pissarro, Degas, and Toulouse-Lautrec, but mostly Van Gogh.

He tells me Van Gogh was brilliant but crazy, and he got in a fight with Gauguin once, and the next thing you know, Van Gogh is chopping off his own ear and chasing Gauguin down the street with it.

"Wait, why did he want to give him his ear, again?" I ask, because he's told me this story before but it never makes sense.

"He didn't. It wasn't a thoughtful act, but a desperate one. He wrapped it up, and tried to give it as a gift."

"To who?"

"Some say a girl. A woman."

"Why would she want it?"

Dad laughs. "Oh, I doubt she did. He wasn't thinking straight by then. He'd gone mad. After that, they sent him to the asylum at Saint-Rémy."

"Was he angry because he was sick?"

Dad looks over at me confused, then adds, "Oh, mad as in crazy, not angry. They sent him to a mental institution is what I meant."

"Did he stop painting then?"

"No. He painted more than ever, and better than ever. Sometimes we must be crazy for our art."

"Then what happened?"

"He painted magnificent paintings, sometimes a hundred or more in a year. He painted *Starry Night* while he was there."

"Did he get famous?"

Dad laughs, but the sound has lost some of its joy. He walks to the sink to wash his brushes and add more paint to the palette. "No, he was never famous, Klee. Not while he was alive. Not until long after he died."

"That's sad," I say. "How did he die?"

"Shot himself in a wheat field."

"Why?"

"Because he was crazy, I told you."

There's a knock at the door, and Mom comes in. She's smiling. She's made us her "fancy" sandwiches with little ruffled toothpicks poked into them.

Mom puts the tray on the worktable near the door and doesn't say anything, just stands watching us as we paint. The look on her face is happy, angelic. Like there's nowhere she'd rather be.

After a while Dad says, "Why don't you sit, Marielle, or better yet, grab a brush and come help?"

She laughs but shakes her head. "You know I have two left hands."

"It's just for fun. There are no mistakes. We're doing an abstract of sunflowers." He winks at her. "Our homage to Van Gogh."

Her face changes.

I see it now, how her face changed. Every time he talked to me about Van Gogh. I never saw it back then.

"Of course, who else?" she says.

I want her to go back to being happy, like she was when she first walked in. If I tell her how smart I am, how much Dad has taught me, maybe she'll smile again.

"Did you know he cut off his ear to give it to a girl? But he didn't die from that. He went mad. Which means crazy. But, when he went to the hospital, he still painted. He painted hundreds of paintings. But then he got sicker and shot himself."

"Jesus, Mark!" Mom's eyes flash with fury. She walks to the vase and pulls the sunflowers out, jamming them into the garbage. "Why do you have to do this to him? He's just a little boy . . ."

"It's life, Mari. You can't shelter him." He dips his brush and keeps working.

"It's not life, it's death! And it's not okay. He's eight years old, for Christ's sake. Let him be eight. Let him be carefree. Don't teach him this morbid stuff you keep in your head, just because you're not happy with your life! You think it's cute, to turn him into you, into the crazy artist you want to be. Well, it's not! So knock it off. Seriously. Keep your morbid, inappropriate bullshit to yourself!"

She storms out, leaving the studio broken and quiet. After another moment, Dad says, "That's your mother for you. She'll get over it. If you're going to paint, well, you're not a baby. We can't protect you from the world."

Right. Because, I'm not a baby. I'm an artist like Dad is. Like Van Gogh was.

"We artists stick together," I say, "because there's more to life than we can see with our eyes."

"You got it, kid," my father says.

Day 12—Afternoon

I skip Group, which Dr. Alvarez says is okay. I think about looking for Sabrina and Martin after, to see how they are, but I don't want to talk to anyone. I just need some more time to process.

I'm not ashamed of what my father was. It's not like that at all. I'm mad at him for lying to us. For faking things. For being an imposter. For thinking he needed to be.

I'm mad because I don't know *who* he was.

I stare out my window, down onto the courtyard where the brachiosaurus is in motion, loud and rumbling, chomping up sections of earth.

Memory after memory seeps in, with my parents in role reversal, a personal Freaky Friday where Dad is moody and absent, and my mother is the one trying to be cheerful, the one trying to hold everything together.

Why did I make *her* out to be the villain, sticking up for him over her, over and over again?

Did I think he needed protecting?

My chest constricts.

If those were Dad's letters, how could he live that way, and not tell us? Tell *me*.

Didn't he think I deserved to know?

Day 12—Evening

"You awake?" Sister Agnes Teresa's familiar voice asks after a soft knock.

I'm already dressed in the swim trunks, hoping she might drop in.

"Rough day?" she asks, when she sees me.

"You don't know the half of it," I say.

I wade forward, letting the cool water envelop me. When I turn back, Sister Agnes Teresa is folding her habit over the side of a chair. She wears the same serviceable navy one-piece she had on the other night.

I dive under and swim the length of the pool and back without coming up for air, letting it wash away the images from the past few days that play on a loop in my head.

"My dearest man, I could breathe in your deep, musky scent forever . . ."

I try not to imagine anything. Try not to think beyond the words.

I wouldn't have cared. Not one iota if it meant him sticking around.

Still, Jesus, I should have known.

I resurface in the shallow end, gasping for breath.

"You okay?" Sister Agnes Teresa asks, looking down with concern.

"Yeah, better now," I say. "I just need to swim."

"Then swim we shall," she says.

She wades in next to me and swims a lap of breast stroke, far more gracefully than I could have imagined a few short days ago. After several more laps in silence, we meet in the deep end, where I float on my back and she paddles around until she's close enough to flip over and float next to me

"Tell me everything," she says. "If you want to."

And I do, and it's not as hard to tell as I thought it would be. The more I repeat the details, the more they lose their power, become a story of my past, a piece of history. Words dissolving away in the water.

"So that's it," I finally say, righting myself so I can see her. "Though my mom tells me there's more. She says my father wasn't depressed because of that, that he was lying about a lot of things. Money. I don't know what."

Sister Agnes Teresa rights herself, too. The look she gives me is full of grief and of understanding.

We swim together to the shallow end, and she climbs up the steps ahead of me.

"So now what, Mr. Alden?" she says. "What are you going to do about all of this?"

That's the question of the hour, isn't it? I mean, what am I supposed to do? Everything is fucked-up and my father is gone. How can I tell him now that it would have been okay? How does he give me that chance? How do we see that we could have figured it out, together? That we would have still loved him, even if we couldn't be the same kind of family anymore?

I make my way toward Sister Agnes Teresa, but I'm not quite ready to get out. Maybe I'll swim a few more laps before going back to my room for bed.

"You know, Klee, we all have hardships," she says, calling me by my first name for the first time that I can remember. She grabs her towel and dries off. When she's done, she holds a second one out to me. I reluctantly haul myself out, sit on a chair, and dry my hair. "We get what we're dealt in this life, that's what I've learned. So, the way I see it, there are only two choices in the end: Pity yourself and shut down, or put a smile on your face and keep going. I suggest the latter. It works better. You're only seventeen. As they say, you have your whole future ahead of you. And, there's a whole wide world of tragedy and heartbreak ahead. But there's adventure, too. There's love and joy and discovery. And plenty of good living still to be done."

Day 13—Morning

"Mom?" I stand at the nurses' station. Shelly, the weekend nurse, is dispensing colored pills into paper cups.

"Klee? I'm so glad you called. It's . . . just really good to hear your voice."

"Yeah . . . so, listen. When can I come home? I think I'm ready to come home."

Silence on the other end, then the sound of my mother hiccupping back tears.

"We'll talk to Dr. Alvarez. We'll see if we can get you checked out this weekend."

"No rush," I say. "Another day or two won't kill me. Plus, I want to say goodbye, and Dr. Alvarez doesn't come back in until Monday."

Day 13—Evening

I sit on the edge of the pool and swirl my legs, making waves while I wait for Sister Agnes Teresa.

She's in the corner, draping pieces of clothing over a chair. Tonight, she's left the room lights off altogether, leaving only the pool light on.

"So peaceful this way, don't you think?" she asks, but tonight it agitates me.

I'm melancholy and filled with despair.

I miss my father.

I miss all the things I never got to say. The things that he needed to hear.

"It wouldn't have mattered to us," I whisper aloud to him, swishing the water once more. Blue-green ripples journey outward, bouncing the light, and casting illusive ghosts about, which flit and dance across the dark tile walls.

"Many years ago," my father begins, "there were two boys, named Liu Ch'en and Yuan Chao. They were cousins."

I roll my eyes. Of all the stories my father tells, Liu Ch'en and Yuan Chao is his favorite. I like his stories, but I don't get this one. I don't get what he wants me to understand.

It's presunrise. We're on vacation again, maybe somewhere in Mexico. He's taking me fishing. We've left Mom in the hotel room to sleep.

Dad leads me down a dock to the edge of the water. There are big rocks, slick with moss that we have to cross over, so he holds my hand tightly as he pulls me forward.

"It's important to be careful," he says, looking back at me, "but not too careful. If you're too careful, you'll never do anything."

Eventually, we reach the large flat rock the concierge told us is a fishing spot called Fisherman's Boulder. Dad sits and nods at me to do the same. His long, bony legs are bent up in front of him. I sit, folding my knees the same way.

"Isn't this heaven?" he says. "I'd like to paint it."

"It is," I say. "We should have brought our paints."

"We'll fish instead. And paint in our heads."

"Okay," I say. "So tell me the story. About Liu Ch'en and Yuan Chao."

"They were cousins," my father says.

Whenever Dad tells stories, the kids are always cousins or "only" children like me, never siblings, so I wonder if Liu

Ch'en and Yuan Chao were really brothers, and Dad just says they were cousins so I don't feel sad.

"Yep, I know that part," I say.

"So one day Liu Ch'en and Yuan Chao go into the hills to fetch water, a chore their mothers have asked of them. The walk to the stream is a joyous one. The hills are lush with springtime. Flowers everywhere."

"The stream is in the hillside?" I ask.

"Yes," he says. "Well, through the hills to a clearing. Anyway, the cousins are overcome by the beauty of it all. They put their pails down and set off for a walk. They walk and they walk, and the countryside grows more sparse with each step, until the path they're on ends, and they find themselves at the entrance to a cave." Dad nods across from where we sit, as if there is a cave there, but all I see are boats and water.

"They want to go into the cave, but a blue fairy sits on either side of the entrance, each on a large stone, like this one." He pats the rock under us. "Only there, it is dry. The stream is gone."

I lean my head against his shoulder, not caring if we fish at all, just happy to be here with him.

"At the fairies' feet is a white rabbit," my father says, stroking a hand through my hair. "The rabbit keeps hopping up and down. Up and down. Up. Down. Each time it jumps, the flowers at the mouth of the cave blossom, opening into full bloom. And, each time the rabbit sits, the flowers wilt and close.

"For many minutes, the fairies watch the rabbit like a game. The cousins, Liu Ch'en, and Yuan Chao, are mesmerized.

"After a while, the fairies ask them, 'When did you arrive?'

"'A few minutes ago,' Liu Ch'en answers, looking to Yuan Chao. 'Not more than that,' Yuan Chao confirms. Broken from the rabbit's spell, they turn to leave. But the fairies say, 'No, you cannot go now. You must stay here in our grotto. If you go home now, no one will recognize you.'

"The boys don't understand what the fairies mean and cry out in protest. 'No! No! We must go home.' Seeing that they can't persuade the cousins to stay, the fairies give them each a reed, and say, 'If you find everything changed at home, return here and the reed will open this cave.'

"So, Liu Ch'en and Yuan Chao take the reeds and return to their stream to collect their buckets. But when they get there, the stream has dried up and the terrain is unfamiliar. Perplexed, the boys flee to their village, but they find no trace of their home."

"Where is the house of Liu Ch'en and Yuan Chao?" I jump in, remembering this part from when he's told it before.

"This is the same question they ask of two white-haired old men who sit in a meadow where the house of Ch'en-Chao used to stand. The old men reply, 'Liu Ch'en and Yuan Chao were our ancestors. We are their descendants in the seventh generation.' "

He stops, and I say, "Dad . . . there's more. I know that's not the end of the story." My lip quivers, something about the story always unsettles me. Dad says, "No, don't worry." He holds a finger to his lips and continues.

"The cousins, too, are terribly confused about how they— barely young men—can have descendants in the seventh generation. It means, of course, that they would have to be very old.

" 'Perhaps,' Liu Ch'en says to Yuan Chao sadly, 'the white rabbit at the grotto represented the changing seasons, and each time it jumped, another year had passed by. It jumped hundreds of times, which would mean our day at the cave lasted four hundred years.'

"Fearful, they cry out to the old men, 'But we are Liu Ch'en and Yuan Chao!' " My father cups his hand to his mouth and calls out across the water, as if he, too, is calling to the old men. "The old men shake their heads, their long beards swishing at their chins. They summon the other people of the village, who come and beat Yuan Chao and Liu Ch'en. 'Young rascals,' the villagers cry, 'How dare you come bother old men!'"

"But why were the villagers mean?" I ask. "Why didn't they care about the cousins?"

My father picks up a pebble and rolls it between his fingers. "They didn't recognize them."

"That's sad," I say, and he agrees.

"The boys flee back to the cave, reeds in hand—remember the reeds the cave fairies gave them?—but the entrance is closed up tight. And when they open their hands, the reeds are gone, and they can't remember where they've left them. They knock and knock at the cave door, but there's no answer. In their grief, they bang their heads against the stone until they die.

"But the ruler of heaven takes pity on their sad fate and grants them favor, appointing Liu Ch'en the God of Good Luck and Yuan Chao the God of Bad Luck." Dad tosses the pebble into the river and it quickly disappears. "The end," he says, standing and grabbing his fishing rod. He nods for me to get mine, too.

"That's it?" I ask, disappointed yet again. "I still don't get it." But I don't push because my father has tears in his eyes.

"You will one day, Klee," he says, clearing his throat, "I don't feel like fishing anymore, okay?" Then he takes my hand and leads me back in the direction we came, toward my mother.

Day 13 into 14—Overnight into Morning

It's daybreak, but dark out, pouring rain. I'm walking down West Broadway toward Spring Street.

Thunder booms in the distance and lightning flashes in jagged streaks between the tall buildings, momentarily lighting up the entire sky.

Dad engulfs my small hand with his so I feel safe, looks down and smiles at me.

"Tell me what it all means," I say, but all he says is, "Nothing to be afraid of now, Klee."

Another clap of thunder and he's gone. The sky undulates and darkens and the cold rain streams down, drenching me.

I run and I run, but I'm not little anymore. I'm me now, eighteen.

As I run, and the rain pelts down, people move out of my way, rush off the streets, under awnings, huddle in doorways, umbrellas snapping in the wind, newspapers held over their heads. I try to wedge myself between bodies in an open doorway to stay dry, but no one seems willing to let me in.

Then Martin is waving from a doorway. "Come on in, Alden. *Mi casa es su casa,*" he says. I move past him into the building. A doorbell chimes. "Are you coming?" I call back, but he shakes his head and says, "It's not my thing, you go in."

The door clicks shut behind me.

The room I find myself in is dimly lit, musty, quiet. "We've been waiting for you, Klee," a voice says.

A girl with wild fuchsia hair and multiple piercings looks down on me from behind a tall counter where she sits in a white lifeguard chair. The counter is covered with art books and brochures. *Van Gogh's Van Goghs* stands open, on display.

I look up at her, and she asks, "Are you going in for a swim?" She nods toward the end of the room.

At first I don't know what she's talking about. This is an art gallery. There's no pool here. Then I see it. A huge painting of a lake. Suddenly, the gallery seems familiar, and I realize it's the one where I went with my dad, where he bought *Icarus's Flight Plan.*

My father will be here, then! I search and search but don't see him anywhere.

The girl with the wild hair coughs. "Look closer," she calls down. "You're not paying attention." She motions me toward the painting of the lake.

I walk toward it and squint, the lake coming alive before my eyes, with fish jumping and people splashing and swimming and diving in.

"Remarkable, right?" she asks. And some of it is, but some of it isn't. Some of it is master quality, and some just seems juvenile, painted like the fish in the mural at the Ape Can.

"Who painted those?" I ask. "Those fish are bad. They don't belong in a gallery."

The girl shrugs. "It can't all be good, right?" she says.

"No," I say. "I guess it can't. But I wish it could."

I move closer to the lake, and she says, "You can touch it if you want. You can go in: make it better. I don't get why the whole world thinks you shouldn't touch art."

I do as she says, reaching out to touch the people in the lake, one after another. Some of them are familiar: Sarah, and Abbott and Scott Dunn.

Sarah reels when I touch her, then dives, disappearing like a mermaid, under the surface. Sister Agnes Teresa and Martin are there. Sabrina, too. I scan the water for Dr. Alvarez, but the girl says, "Don't look for everyone. Not everyone can be where you want them. So, are you going to buy it?" she asks.

"Me? No. I don't like it."

"You don't have the money," she says.

I feel nauseous and panicky, and turn to leave.

"It's okay, son, stay." A man, lanky, with white-blond hair and eyebrows, has appeared and holds tightly to my arm. "I think you're looking for me," he says.

"I am. I was. I need to talk to you," I say.

"Of course you do. Follow me."

I follow him down a long, dark hall to a narrow tunnel that slopes downward, leading us underground. Water drips from the ceiling, and our footsteps echo, wet and hollow, as we proceed. When we reach an open space, he puts a hand on my shoulder. "Don't feel sorry for yourself," he says. "Take this reed." He moves away, revealing the entrance to a cave. Sitting before it is Sister Agnes Teresa.

"I've been waiting for you," she says.

I follow her into the cave, strewn with paintings, framed and unframed, small ones and huge canvases that take up the length of a bedroom wall. "Hold on," she says. "I'll find the one that is yours."

"I didn't paint one," I say, but she disappears through a door, and returns, dragging a large canvas.

"I know," she says. "You didn't. He did. He asked me to give it to you." She switches on an overhead light to illuminate it, revealing Van Gogh's potato eaters, *Les Mangeurs de Pommes de Terre.*

Five gaunt, ugly peasants sit at a wooden table, their faces bleak and tired. Grotesque. A lack of hope permeates the painting. One peasant is unseen, her back to the viewer. But from under her cap, I see her long black hair.

"I don't want it," I say. "He knows it's the one painting of his I never liked."

"That's because you're looking at it wrong," Sister Agnes Teresa says. "You're looking at it upside down." She waddles around the front, turning each corner with effort until she makes a full rotation with the painting, then steps away again. "There. Try now."

This time I see it. The painting is so much different than I thought. The same bleak peasants sit at the table, their gnarled fingers thick with dirt. But their faces are no longer grotesque, they're familiar and happy and warm. Dad's face, Mom's, and mine. And, next to my father, sits Armond.

"And, look here," Sister Agnes Teresa says, pointing. "Look how many sunflowers! And none of them simply plain yellow. But you have to look carefully to see all the colors."

Beneath the table, I see them. Sunflowers. Van Gogh's sunflowers. The floor is covered in them. And as she turns the painting again, the sunflowers multiply and come to life, spilling out of the painting and into the room.

"You see, Klee," Dad says, turning from the table where he sits between Mom and Armond. "I wanted to accomplish what Millet said I could. To paint people so they'd appear to arise from the very same soil they've sowed."

"And?"

"Don't you understand? I wanted you to understand."

I nod, but I don't understand at all.

"We're sown from dirt, and sorrow, and flower petals. You and me. Your mother, Sarah, Armond. Do you understand, Klee? I need you to. It's important that you understand."

I nod again, reaching out to touch the smear of dirt on his nose. But, I can't find him through the blur of my tears.

"Please, understand, Klee," he says.

I keep nodding until he disappears.

I awaken, drenched in sweat. It's still dark out, but that weird slate gray before the sun rises.

Quiet.

Still.

The clock reads 4:42 A.M.

I'm still here, in the Ape Can. But in a few short hours, my mother will pick me up and bring me home.

I throw on sweats and a T-shirt, and walk to the closet,

sliding out the duffel she dropped off over a week ago. I pull out the large sets of acrylics and the biggest brushes, add those to the small set of brushes and second acrylic set still in my backpack, and head out into the hall.

The hallways are desolate, the lights still dimmed for sleep hours. A male orderly sits dozing at a desk on the far end of the hall. I hear a nurse talking in someone's room. Maybe Sabrina woke up. Maybe Martin had a nightmare.

I slip past, go quietly into the stairwell, and walk the long corridor that leads to the hall I take to Dr. Alvarez's office. Halfway down, another lone nurse sits at a desk. She's got her head down, a blue light bouncing off her face. Probably playing Candy Crush on her iPad.

I continue down the hall to the fish mural. Across from it, there's a bathroom. I duck in and fill a paper cup with water. I'm going to need more, but this will get me started. On my way out, I nudge the small wooden wedge with my toe, to hold the door open. It spills light out onto the wall.

I unzip my bag and pull out the paints, using the empty box as a palette. I don't touch any of the finished work, but rather start at the far end, blending the blues from the earlier section of ocean so that there's a seamless flow between the existing mural and my new work. As I move down the wall, I deepen the blues to near black, light to dark, from sky down to the deepest abyssal zone.

I paint slowly, methodically making my way across the wall, blending the blues with reds into violets and purples, choosing larger brushes as the mural expands. By the time it's 5:30, I have a decently large section covered. A magnificent swirling sky melting into a cobalt sea of erupting waves. And beneath that, the ocean bottom, deep as black space.

I return to the bathroom for clean water, biting the ends of tubes to squeeze out the last bits of paint, opening new tubes, adding layer upon layer upon layer.

By 6 A.M., the early staff is arriving. They stand and watch, silent, but no one stops me. The sea is now filling with vibrant color, silvery fish and neon anemones awash in pinks and oranges and greens. And, at the bottom, one sleek magenta squid, his inky, watchful eye focused up to the sunburst sky.

By 6:30, I'm almost done. Almost out of paint, anyway.

I stand back and study it; the staff watching breaks into an admiring, if embarrassing, round of applause. Considering my lack of supplies, it's not bad. You can definitely see Van Gogh's influence.

You can definitely see my father's.

I return to my bag and retrieve one last tube each of cobalt, black, silver, and titanium white. I'll have just enough to do what I am hoping to do.

I run my brush through the paints and begin to blend the light of the top of the sky with the darks, so the sky near the ceiling doubles back on itself, returning to midnight again. Deep ocean into daylight into night sky into deep ocean or night sky again.

When that is finished, I take a finer-tipped brush and dip it into the white alternating with silver, and work my way across, dotting the sky, where the squid's gaze falls, with a hundred shimmering pinprick stars.

Finally, I kneel at the base, and I write, *For Dr. Alvarez, A sky full of stars. In honor of my father, who lost sight of them.*

MONDAY MORNING

My mother wears jeans with heels, less makeup than usual, and her hair pulled back in a natural sweep that seems as if she put just a bit too much effort into not putting effort into it. Still, she manages to look younger this morning, softer, yet somehow also more solid. She stands at Dr. Alvarez's door afraid to fully come in.

"Hey, Mom." I walk to the door, and awkwardly hug her. She pats my back, then drops her arms to the side, making me realize how long it's been since we hugged. We're out of practice, but it's a start. Something to work on, I guess.

"Dr. Alvarez says the checkout is relatively quick," she says, studying my face. "They require me to sign you out, and if you're willing, they want you—us—to agree that you'll continue to do outpatient therapy."

"Here," I say, "right? I'd like that." I turn to Dr. Alvarez. "I'd like to continue with Dr. Alvarez if I can."

Dr. Alvarez smiles. "That works for me," she says.

My mother moves into the room, the gold bracelets jangling on her wrists. "Whatever you both feel is best. So long as you're coming home."

Even though I've tried to prepare myself, my stomach lurches at the word "home," at the thought of going back there, back to school.

At the thought of facing Sarah.

What if I'm not ready? It was never easy being there in the first place.

"If you'll excuse me for a moment," Dr. Alvarez says,

getting up, "I just need to get some paperwork from the administrative office," and she slips quietly out the door.

My mother and I sit. She turns her body toward me on the couch. "I want you to know that I loved him, Klee," she says, picking at a thread on her jeans. "Even after he told me, I still loved him."

"I know. I get that now," I say.

"We were so young when we met, when we married. Maybe I should have known. I felt so stupid when I found out. Looking back, I should have seen . . . I had my suspicions, of course, but I don't think even he knew. Not at first. Not fully. Not for a long time. He was raised a certain way—his parents, well, you didn't know them very well. They were of a time, wanted certain things for him. He wanted those things, too. Or thought he did. Everything else he put out of his mind. He was good at that, your father. From the time I met him, he had a vision about what his life would be. About what it *should* be. And he worked hard to get it there. And anything that got in the way . . . that's how he was. Single-minded. He got what he wanted and avoided what he didn't want to see. He wanted to be successful. And he wanted a family. And, for sure, he wanted you."

I shift uncomfortably, swallow back tears.

"And he loved us always, Klee," she says. "He did. No matter what happened, I always knew that. The rest, he couldn't help . . . You were the best thing that ever happened to him. I know this. And you need to know it, too. He was very proud of you. He always told me you were braver than he ever was."

"When did you find out . . . What happened?" I manage, but it comes out as little more than a croak.

"A few years ago, but not the full extent. He said it was something on the side . . . compartmentalized. That's what he called it. I didn't realize there was anyone in particular. Someone who meant that much, that he was supporting . . ." She breaks down here, then regains herself. "I didn't know specifically about Armond."

"Armond," I say aloud. "I met him once. He owns a gallery downtown." My mother looks alarmed, but I'm stuck on something else. "Wait, what do you mean, 'he was supporting'?"

"He was supporting him, too," she says, choking back a sob. "Completely." She pulls a rumpled napkin from her bag and uses it to dab at the corner of her eyes. I pick up a box of tissues from the table and hold it out to her. "And, *that*—he, the whole mess—was the way bigger problem we had. Because, apparently, your father, in his infinite wisdom, was trying to keep both Armond *and* the gallery afloat. In addition to us, our family. He made a good living, Klee, but there wasn't enough money to go around. Not for two families. That's why he—"

She takes a moment to collect herself before she's able to speak again. "Really, this isn't stuff you needed to know, shouldn't have had to handle. I tried to spare you the whole nightmare. But you're not a kid anymore, are you? And I don't want you thinking your father did what he did just because he loved someone else, because he was gay. That was hard, that was devastating for us, but it wasn't . . . it would never be . . ."

She shakes her head, unable to talk anymore. But I need to know. I need to understand.

"That wasn't what?" I ask. "What are you talking about, Mom?"

"He was depressed," she says. "And he had loaned out lots of money. He created all sorts of problems I didn't know about. And then he borrowed—well, they say stole—escrow money. From his firm. He must have felt desperate . . . From some big client's account. When they found out about it, well, there's a zero-tolerance policy when a lawyer does that . . ." I raise my eyebrows, and she quickly adds, "He was going to pay it all back."

"Jesus," I say. "Are you kidding?"

She shakes her head again. "I wish. He was a good man. He got caught up trying to hold it all together. Trying to help everyone. And they found out. He lost his job. They were bringing him up on charges in front of the grievance committee."

I look at her in disbelief, not wanting to believe it's true. "They would have disbarred him," I say.

She nods. "They were going to. That was clear. I didn't know all of this, Klee. Not soon enough. Only right before he died. If I had, I would have done something. Made different choices. I would have stopped him. I would have found a way to help. He was so ashamed . . ."

"Jesus," I say again, because I don't know how else to respond. "Wait," I add, something else occurring to me. "Are we in money trouble, then?"

"Yes and no," she says, staring down. "Not completely. The apartment sold for twice what the house up here cost, and your father left a sizable insurance policy. Of all the things we have to worry about, at least here, now, money probably isn't one of them. We'll be okay."

So that's why we came up here.

"I don't need to go to Fine Arts Boston," I say. "I can stay here or something."

"Don't be silly. There are accounts already set up for that. And, he'd want you to go. Getting you better and there is our only concern now." She smiles weakly. "I should have told you all of this sooner, but after your father died, I figured there was no reason for you to know. I didn't know you'd seen the letters. I should never have kept them. I didn't realize just how much you were suffering."

"It's okay," I say. "I'm okay now. I'm going to be okay."

I stare out the window. The day is bright and warm, Dr. Alvarez's office awash in sunshine. I think of all the times Sister Agnes Teresa came in to open my shades. To let the outside in. "It's a good reminder," she had said.

"Are we ready?" Dr. Alvarez asks, breezing into the room with a handful of papers.

"Almost," I say. "Yeah. There are a few things I'd still like to do. Can I have another hour?"

My mother nods, says she has some errands to run, kisses my forehead, and says she'll be back to get me then.

Sister Agnes Teresa sits on the chair by the window. A small white box rests in the center of my bed, next to a pack of Hostess Sno Balls in all their coconut-coated, pink glory. Somehow, I knew she'd be here.

I hold up the Sno Balls. "Nobody eats these," I say. "Nobody."

She smiles. "Nonsense, Mr. Alden. Though they may be an acquired taste."

"Right," I say. "I haven't acquired it. But I'll keep them to remember you by."

"That'd be nice," she says.

"And this?" I hold up the small white box.

"Open it. I hear your mother is here. That she's ready to take you home."

"Yeah, she is," I say. "I might have misjudged her. I mean, I did. I misjudged her."

"Well, it happens," Sister Agnes Teresa says, after I tell her the rest of the story. "We sometimes judge. And when we do, we often judge incorrectly. On the other hand, you don't seem like a truly judgmental person. So if you did, maybe there was a pretty good reason why."

"I don't know," I say. "My mother, she tried . . . she was only trying to protect me . . . And, I was hard on her. I blamed her." I stop there, wondering how I'm ever going to do this: go home and just go about business as usual.

Maybe I need more time.

Maybe I'm not ready.

"Sometimes," Sister Agnes Teresa says, "we get angry at those who are the safest to be angry with."

"I guess," I say. "But that doesn't make it fair."

"Who says life is fair, Mr. Alden? Life is rarely fair."

"That's it?" I say. "Life isn't fair? I was hoping for something more profound. Something I might hang on to, that might let me know I'm ready to go home."

She's quiet for a moment, then looks at me thoughtfully. "I'm a nun, Mr. Alden, not a magician."

"I know," I say. "But still. I was counting on you. How am I supposed to just pick up my life and go on? Especially here, in Northhollow? I mean, how do I do that? How do I go back and face everyone?"

Sister Agnes Teresa walks over and holds out her hand to me. I take it, and she squeezes, then she pulls me in for a seriously awkward hug. When she loosens her embrace, she holds fast to my hand and gives it a firm shake.

"With wisdom and bravery, Mr. Alden. The same way the rest of us do."

"Your mother's not back yet. Let me get a sweater and we'll take a quick walk."

Dr. Alvarez leaves me at the nurses' station with my pile of bags. On top of the bags is the small white box from Sister Agnes Teresa. I've left the easel in the game room next to the art supplies. They'll find use for it there.

While I wait for her, I lift the lid off the box and pull the note from it again. A yellow Post-it, and under that a key chain with a small metal ladder, maybe two inches tall. Probably for a dollhouse or something.

For when you hit those chutes.
With bravery and love,
Sister Agnes Teresa

I slip the keychain and note in my pocket and wait for Dr. Alvarez by the main door.

The air is chilly, still raw from the recent rain. I pull my sweatshirt tightly around me.

We walk silently until we reach the white stone benches in the clearing, the Buddhas with their bowls of water overflowing. Dr. Alvarez sits and pats the bench for me to sit, too.

"The mural is beautiful," she says. "What a gift. I'm sure we'll all cherish it, but me, most of all."

"I'm glad it was okay." I toe at some sort of seedpod that has half buried itself under the mud.

"You know, Klee, people have been grappling with the same basic problems for thousands and thousands of years. Whether they've turned to God or spiritual leaders or psychologists or mentors, you're not alone in finding it overwhelming to make peace with it all."

"I see that now. I thought I was okay. I didn't realize how badly I needed someone to help. I didn't realize how much of the burden I put on Sarah." My throat catches when I say her name. I need to get over it, cope with whatever happens when I see her at school. I don't know if she'll even talk to me. "I don't know what I'm going to say, how I'm going to go back and face her now, after what I did." I raise my hand to my ear, and run my finger along the small notched scab. "I'm embarrassed," I say. "I humiliated myself."

Dr. Alvarez's eyes follow my finger, and she says, "You got lucky it wasn't worse. The thought was more destructive than the damage you did. In a few weeks, it will barely be noticeable."

"In a few weeks . . ."

"To be clear," Dr. Alvarez says, "I'm not making light of your actions in any regard, and for the time being, you should remain on antidepressants and continue therapy, so we can make sure you never feel that desperate again. But I guess what I want you to know is that you'll get through it. This is the stamp on the envelope, remember? You won't be defined forever by these actions. And, honestly, Klee, people, kids your age, do all sorts of stupid and impulsive things. Sane people. Normal people. If only that *weren't* the norm. So, I'm guessing they'll be hard-pressed to judge you."

"But they will."

"Maybe," she says. "I guess you'll have to breathe through it. I'm confident you will." She nods up at something, and I peer up through the trees. A hint of sunlight seems to be breaking through again. "Remember, Klee, any of us, under enough pressure, without enough support, are in danger that the next bad thing can send us spiraling. It's why we must pay attention, and be mindful. Act from what we know and not from what we fear. And seek out help when we need it. From family. From friends. But also learn to trust yourself."

I shrug and glance past her. I know there are some things I'm going to have to solve on my own.

"Here. You think I'm lying, but I'll show you," she says. She gets up from the bench and turns to face me, rolling up her sleeves. "I have a PhD and a double master's. I have a loving husband and a good career. I've had friends and partners, successes and failures, and so far I've made it through. But there was a time—a brief moment in my early twenties—when I didn't think I could."

She holds her wrists out to me, undersides up, to show me where, on each, a faint pink scar runs vertically along the tender skin.

"You?" I ask. "But why?"

"For the same reasons many of us do. We feel hopeless or helpless or alone. The thing we learn if we make it through is that we're not."

My eyes fill with tears. They're not sad tears, just grateful. Dr. Alvarez reaches into her pocket and hands a tissue to me, but I shake my head. I'm okay.

"Anyway, what you need to know," she says, rolling her sleeves back down and buttoning them, "is that my life is happy, my days are good. Very good. Unbelievably lucky and good. But not all of them. Bad things happen, now and again, and some days are impossibly hard. And others still, mildly hard. But even on the worst days, I'm not in danger anymore." She smiles gently, sitting beside me again on the white stone bench. "But all in all, if I had to average it out, most of them are happy, fulfilling, and good. Those far outweigh the bad days, and they do make it all worthwhile."

I don't know how to respond. It both surprises and comforts me to know that even Dr. Alvarez wasn't always as sure and clear as she is now.

She gets up again and walks to the stump with the Buddhas resting on it, puts her hand on Green Tara, and says some mantra.

"It's Green Tara's," she says. "I like the sound of it, even if I don't fully know what it means or believe in it. I like the feel of it on my tongue, the lilt of it, you know? And sometimes it's just good to have a mantra. Something to say when you're anxious. Yours can be anything. A quote that you like, or a song lyric. Something you say to remind yourself. We can work on that."

"Okay," I say.

"Oh, and one more thing, Klee. This?" She holds her wrists out but doesn't uncover the scars again. "It was a long time ago. I've lived a whole lifetime since then. Honestly, I barely remember what set me off back then. What made me feel so broken. But it seemed so very important at the time."

"Like a postage stamp," I say.

"Exactly."

I look at my own hands, studying my fingers which held a paintbrush again this morning, feeling good and right when they did. It made me feel normal again, like me. Klee. Just that alone makes me feel all sorts of things I can't fully express to Dr. Alvarez. I feel sad, and quiet, and grateful all at the same time.

"'For my part, I know nothing with any certainty,'" she says, walking again. "'Except that the sight of the stars makes me dream.' It's Van Gogh, right? The quote you left for me."

"Yes."

"You've really given me a whole new appreciation for him," she continues. "What a gift it is to always be learning. There truly was no other artist like him. How sad that it wasn't a life fully appreciated while he lived it." I nod and she says, "But your father's life, Klee, your father's life wasn't his. Nor is yours. And the sight of stars," she says, reaching up to point through the trees, "is always right there. Right in your line of vision. Even on the cloudiest day. They don't disappear, you know, just because the clouds are obscuring them. They're always still there. Waiting."

HOME

It's weird to walk into the house after so many days gone.

It feels unfamiliar. But this place always has.

I wonder if it will ever feel like home.

Still, my mother is trying. I can even smell home-baked cookies.

In the hallway, I turn and give her a suspicious look.

"Don't get excited. They're slice and bake," she says.

My room is just how I left it, except for a stack of clean laundry folded on my bed.

I drop my bags by my closet, pick up my cell phone, and stare at it. I have twenty-two missed messages.

I pile my books on my desk and put the rest of my clothing and supplies away. Finally, I sit at my desk and pull the folded sheet of paper from my pocket and add Martin's and Sabrina's numbers to my contacts. Only then do I press the message icon to read through all of the texts.

The most recent is from Cleto, saying he means it, that he's there for me if I need him, and to let him know when I'm home again and can get to the city to see him. "Or we can come to you, Revenant. No problem. Who doesn't want to waste a day trekking up to the boonies?"

I smile a little and decide to call. At least Cleto won't treat me any different.

It rings through to voice mail.

"Hey, Cleto, it's me. I'm home again, and wondering. Remember that place—I forget what it's called—but the Ping-Pong place in midtown? We went there once, and you kicked my ass, remember? But, I'm thinking it's time to up my game. Next weekend, maybe, if you're not busy? Let me know."

I hang up and stare at his name on my phone. It'll be good to see him. Really good.

I move through the rest of the messages. The next one is from Dan: "Cleto told me the news. Sorry, Leo. Hope you're feeling better soon."

The rest after that are from Sarah, dating way back to Saturday night: "I'm so sorry, Klee. I love you. I wasn't thinking. Please forgive me. Call me when you get home."

The words make my chest hurt. They're from more than two weeks ago. Bet she didn't realize how long I'd be gone.

I scroll through the rest. They're basically the same. She's sorry. She loves me. She didn't mean to hurt me. She's worried about how I am. They're hard to read, but here's the weird thing: I believe her, too. I don't think she was trying to hurt me. Of course that doesn't change the fact that she did.

I don't respond or call back. I'm not ready. My heart still feels crushed. I'm going to need some more time.

I take out a fresh set of paints and decide to work on my remaining portfolio piece. I may just submit something close to the painting I left for Dr. Alvarez.

By dinnertime, it's coming along nicely, but I'm stir crazy. I badly want to go out for a drive. I find Mom reading in the screened-in porch off the living room. She's got the double doors open and her view of the water. A nice warm breeze is blowing in.

"The apartment sold for twice what the house up here cost . . ."

I can't believe I thought she was being selfish.

". . . a man or a mackerel, Klee?"

A snow queen, or just my mother?

I clear my throat, and she startles. But she smiles quickly, though it's more forced than natural. Not just now, but for the last two weeks, I've scared the shit out of my mother. I get that. I'm going to have to give her time to adjust, to trust that I'm all right. That I don't want to hurt myself. That it was never my intention in the first place. Better that I hurt myself than someone else, though, right?

My breath catches. *What if my father had thought the same thing? What if I was that someone else?*

But I am not my father. I see that now. And, for better or worse, neither of us is Van Gogh.

"Are you hungry?" my mother asks. "I've been trying to give you some space. But if you are, we could order up some Green Jade Chinese."

"Sure. Not yet, but soon. Maybe in a while?" I say.

I walk over and sit in the chair across from her. I think of all the hours I sat across from Sister Agnes Teresa playing games and talking about everything and nothing, and I fiddle with the ladder in my pocket. *"For when you hit those chutes . . ."* The folded Post-it note is in there, too, with her email and her cell phone number.

"Did you know," I say, though it isn't what I was expecting to say, "that they recently discovered Van Gogh may not have cut off his own ear?"

My mother's eyes shift to mine, alarmed, unsure what my point is. I'm not sure I know what it is either. Maybe I don't have a point. Maybe it's just something I want her to know.

"Dr. Alvarez told me. Some new book is out. A biography. And they think it wasn't Van Gogh at all, but rather Gauguin who did it. Accidentally. He was a fencer, Gauguin, and apparently, they got in a fight. And in a fit of rage, they think, Gauguin may have sliced off Van Gogh's ear."

"Really?" my mother asks. "So, Gauguin, not Van Gogh?"

"Right. And Van Gogh covered for him. To protect him. I guess that's what friends are for." I wink at her, then feel stupid for it. Still, she laughs a little, which is good to hear.

"Well, that's quite a twist, then," she says. "I wonder what your father would have said about that."

My father.

God, I miss him.

The thought sits there, heavy, but it doesn't take me down.

"I'm glad you brought him up," I say, and her eyes dart to mine. "I had this dream last night. It was weird, like dreams are, you know?" She nods, and picks her book back up but doesn't open it, just fidgets with the bookmark inside. "And the details, well, they didn't make too much sense. But I was in it, of course, and you were there, too. And Dad. We were a family again." Mom dabs at her eye with her ring finger. "Armond was there, too. Which was weird, because, well, I wouldn't exactly want him to be." Mom lets out this strange, guttural sound, and I add, "I met him once, I told you that, right? At a gallery downtown. I remember him . . . Dad bought a painting. Called *Icarus's Flight Plan*. It's still here, in the guest room. We could hang it."

Her eyes meet mine with fresh concern, and I bust out laughing.

"Oh," she says, relieved. "You're just joking?"

"Yeah, I kind of hate it," I say. "Always did. It's pretty hideous."

But now that I brought him up, I feel like I have to finish, because I know we can't keep pretending none of this happened. We need to talk about it, Mom and me. About Dad, and about *him*. Armond.

I need to talk about it.

"To tell you the truth, I didn't like him all that much, either. He was nice, I guess, but weird. Then again, I was little." I sigh at how long ago it was. Dad must have been living a lie for an awfully long time. "I feel bad for Armond, though. And I keep wondering. I mean, he must be missing Dad, don't you think?" Mom nods sadly, which only makes me feel worse. "But, the painting? It's so ugly. I can't believe Dad even bought it. We should take it out back and burn it," I add, hoping to lighten the mood again. "Something ceremonial, you know?"

"Klee!"

"What? We should."

My mother laughs fully, now, and so I laugh too, because, seriously, that is one butt-ugly piece of art.

Finally, my mother shakes her head at me, and wraps her arms to her chest, fighting back another round of long-held tears. "I'm glad we're having this conversation, Klee," she says. "I'm glad to have you back home."

I think of Dr. Alvarez saying that sometimes it's better to just let it all out, get it over with, and I'm about to say that to my mom, but she turns her gaze back out over the water. When she turns back again, she says, "He tried to help Armond out that way, at first, apparently. By buying paintings, being a patron. But it wasn't enough. So he started paying his rent, too. Just for the gallery, at first, but later, for his apartment . . . I found receipts, credit card statements, or else I never would have known. I suppose that's partly my fault, for letting your father handle it all, putting it all on him. Initially, he said it was only because the gallery was going to go under, it was a business decision . . ." Her voice trails off. After a moment she shrugs and continues. "Maybe that was his way to hold on to his art."

"If he had told us, if he had wanted to be with Armond, we would have found a way to deal with it, right?" I ask. "We would have understood? No matter what, I mean. If he had given us a chance, then maybe everything would have been okay?"

"Maybe," my mother says. "To be honest, Klee, I just don't know." Her eyes meet mine again. She looks vulnerable, weary. "I'd like to believe that, yes. It wouldn't have been easy, but, we sure would have tried. Yes," she says, more firmly, "we would have found a way."

"We would have still loved him," I say. "That's all I mean. That part would have been easy. We would have wanted him to be here, on earth. Alive. Happy."

"Yes. Yes. Of course." Mom blows her nose. "But, all we can do now is go forward."

"Yeah," I say, standing. "I just wanted to say that, I guess. And that I'm sorry. Sorry for not knowing. Sorry for thinking you were the one . . ." My voice breaks. I can't say any more about that part yet. "I'm glad you got your water view," I offer.

She waves me off like I'm silly, like she's had more than enough out of me for now. "Let's be clear, Klee. That's not something that should have ever fallen on you."

"Well, still—I'm going to do better from now on," I say, not knowing exactly what that means. And how will I do anything when I'm leaving in a few short months for school? I hope to be, anyway. But what if she needs me here? What if she wants me to stay? Or what if I don't get in? I've fucked things up so much. My final portfolio piece is long overdue. I need to walk and think. I need a few minutes to clear my head.

"I was thinking of going for a drive," I say, glancing outside. "Get out for a bit before it gets dark. Just for an hour or so." My mother's face shifts, contorts with alarm. "It's okay," I reassure her. "Dr. Alvarez said no restrictions, that we need to be as normal as we can." I laugh a little. "Presuming we can be normal at all." My mother forces a smile. "Not far," I add. "Just a drive up River Road? I'll be back in an hour. Promise."

"Klee . . ."

"It's okay, Mom. Really. One hundred percent for sure."

"One hour, not more, and you come right back, yes?" I nod. "Bring your phone and answer it, or I send out the troops."

"Fair enough," I say.

I make my way up our long driveway toward the road. It feels good to be in motion, and strangely good to be on my own. In a few short months, if all goes well, I'll load the car up with all my worldly crap and head off to college in Boston. School of Fine Arts. My father's alma mater.

I turn onto Old Basin Road and head in the direction of River's Edge, the first place that Sarah took me. Our very own place to fool around.

Am I sorry for everything with her, or only the bad parts?

Will I ever get over loving her?

The back roads are quiet like they always are up here. Thankfully, I pass no one I recognize, only a few sporadic cars zipping by. When I reach the unpaved road that leads to our spot, I turn in, heart pounding, and drive up toward the empty clearing, and the guardrail.

I just want to be here and remember. One last time what it felt like to be with her.

I lock up and start down to the water. At the edge of the river, I gather a handful of stones. One after another, I skip them in. Some go six whole skips before sinking down. Something else good my father taught me.

"An old man walks along a riverbank until he comes to four pools," Dad says. "At the first pool stands a young boy. He's throwing a handful of stones.

" 'Hello, what are you doing?' the old man asks the boy.

" 'I am scaring birds,' the boy replies."

I giggle.

"What's so funny?" Dad asks.

"I just think it's funny he's scaring the birds."

"Ah, I see," Dad says. "Well, the boy must be very good at it, because there are no birds whatsoever near the pool. So, the old man walks on and comes to a second pool, where another young boy is skipping rocks.

" 'Hello, what is it that you are doing?' the old man asks the boy.

" 'I'm seeing how many skips I can make,' the boy replies. And the boy is very good at it because his rock skips ten times."

"Ten is so many," I say. "Are you sure he did ten? The most I've gotten is five."

"You have to keep trying," Dad says. "Shall I finish?"

"Yes."

"The old man walks on."

"He comes to the third pool?" I say.

"Yes, a third pool, where a young boy is tossing pebbles into the pond. 'Hello, what is it that you are doing?' the old man asks of this boy, too. 'I am just making ripples,' the boy replies. And, the boy is obviously successful, because the ripples spread outward in ever expanding circles, covering the entire surface of the pool."

"Is that good or bad," I ask, "that his ripples go out so far?"

"It's neither," Dad says, after thinking for a moment. "It just is."

"Okay."

"So, the old man walks on and comes to the fourth pool. A fourth and final pool, where he, as a young boy, used to throw stones, skip rocks, and toss pebbles. He stops there and reflects, and, after a while, the three young boys, bored with their own games, come join him.

" 'Hello, what is it that you are doing?' they ask of the old man.

" 'I am watching the pond,' he answers.

"The boys say, 'You are obviously very successful,' and so they stay with him, and they sit and watch the pond together."

"That's it?" I ask. "The end?"

"The end," my father says. "That's all there is."

I glance at my phone. I've been gone half an hour, so I start back up to the car. I need to keep my promise to my mother.

Between my father and me, how will she ever stop worrying?

As I round the bend to my car, I see a figure on the guardrail. Thin, round shouldered. Long hair.

Did my mother tell her?

My chest tightens, and my heart beats so hard I'm afraid it might break through my chest.

For a minute, I stop walking. It's like my legs won't move. I think about heading back down to the water. But I need to get to my car. I need to be home within the hour.

I jam my hands in my pockets and keep going, feeling the ladder from Sister Agnes Teresa.

"For when you hit those chutes . . ."

Hey," she calls, when I get close enough.

"Hey."

Sarah.

I keep my hand on the ladder, moving my fingers up the rungs with my own steps, one after another, stopping, finally, a safe enough distance from the guardrail.

"With wisdom and bravery . . ."

"When did you get back?"

"This afternoon," I say. "I was going to call you soon. Did my mother tell you I was home?"

She shakes her head. "No."

"How did you know I'd come up here?"

She shrugs. "It's a small-ass town, Alden, you know that. People talk. Pretty much everyone knows everything."

She's being kind. I'm predictable. I'm needy. She knew to come looking here for me.

My hand wants to reflexively move to my ear, but I keep it in my pocket and think of Dr. Alvarez, of her promise that, one day, none of this will seem so important and big.

This moment is only a postage stamp.

Still, it feels insurmountably huge.

Sarah stretches a bare foot out in my direction. She points her toes. Her flip-flops sit there on the ground.

"Warm enough for those, then?" I ask. She smiles sadly and tries to reach her pointed toes out toward me, like a peace offering. Forgiveness, maybe. Friend to friend.

I don't feel it, though. Not yet. Maybe not ever. I just need to get through the next few days.

"Are you mad that I came?" Her voice breaks a little. She pulls her foot back, sensing.

"Not mad at you," I say. "Not really. Just . . . at everything. But, mostly at myself."

"Well, you shouldn't be . . . I wouldn't blame you if you hated me," she says. I don't answer. I can't make any promises right now. "I'm so sorry, Klee . . ."

But I can't hear it, not yet, not now, so I hold up a hand, and for the next few minutes, neither of us says anything.

Eventually, I take the remaining few steps to where she sits.

"So, are you coming back to school?"

"I guess so," I say. "Yeah. What choice do I have? I need to graduate, right?"

She laughs softly. "Yeah, I guess you do. Pretty much."

She turns her gaze up to me now. Her eyes cut through me, searching, like they did that first day in Tarantoli's. For something I can't give her now. For something I never could. Or maybe it's the other way around.

"I feel awful, Klee. Just awful," she says. "I'm glad you're going to be okay."

I nod, and stare at my cell phone. The time glares up at me. Forty-five minutes I've been gone. And ten minutes, at least, to get home.

"Give me a second," I say. "I have to call my mom."

"Okay."

I walk out of earshot and call home. The whole time, I can feel Sarah watching. After I let my mother know I need a few more minutes, I shove my phone back in my pocket and return to Sarah. She's still on the guardrail, but I don't join her. I need to protect myself right now.

"Anyway, I'm really sorry, Klee. I know I probably shouldn't have come here. I know I should leave you alone. But, I feel bad, and I . . . I've been thinking a lot about it, and just really needed to explain. I do love you. I think I was trying to push you away . . ."

"Sarah, don't. Please." I shake my head, the tears welling in her eyes make mine well up, too. And, I don't want to do this. I don't want an explanation. I've thought about the reasons a hundred times.

It was both our faults. What's done is done. An explanation doesn't matter now. Maybe it won't ever. In the meantime, whatever she has to say won't change anything. I need to focus and get better. I need to get my portfolio done and handed in. And, I need to leave for Boston at the end of summer. She's been right about that all along.

I am leaving Northhollow. With or without her, in a few short months. No matter what.

So, what I want most right now is what I already have from

her: to know that she cares. And she must. Because she's already here.

"Let's talk about something else," I say, finally sitting next to her. "I have fifteen minutes before I have to head home. But only something stupid and unimportant. We need to make a pact," I say, "and, in case you forgot, you kind of suck at pacts."

She turns to me and smiles.

So, we do. We talk. Not so much about us, but about other things, like Tarantoli's class, and senior prank plans, and the soccer camp her brother wants to go to this summer. Eventually, I tell her a little about Dr. Alvarez and Sister Agnes Teresa, and even Martin and Sabrina. Not by name, though—what you do and say in the Ape Can stays confidential.

Last, I tell her some of the stuff about my mother, and that I was wrong about her. But I don't tell her about my father. It's too soon, too raw, and anyway, he's not here to tell his side of the story. So for now, it stays with us, just Mom and me, deep and safe in the abyssal zone. But one day soon, it will be time to let it out, let it float up and exist, and become part of the bright night sky.

I think about Armond, again, and worry for him. What became of him after my father died? I didn't see him at the funeral. Maybe one day down the road, when I'm sure about everything, I'll look him up and see if he's still at the gallery. Check in. Share some stories about my dad.

Maybe one day my paintings will hang on his wall. Now, wouldn't that be something?

But for now, all of that is in the future and way too big to wrap my head around. Right now I want to stay focused on smaller things.

Before I go, we talk more about the things that don't really matter at all. About teachers and new movies we want to see, and whether last spring was as rainy as this one. I think about the bowls in Dr. Alvarez's clearing, filling with rainwater, bits of life—acorns and flower petals—floating.

And, while we talk more about nothing, the tensions ease up a little between us, so that, sitting here, by her side, I don't feel particularly hurt or broken or fucked-up or angry. I just feel quiet and satisfied to be here on this planet, intact.

Satisfied to watch the edge of the sun slip away, disappearing below the gentle lull of the waterline.

And happy to watch the sky go from dusk to dark, and for the stars to come out, and the moon to rise up, illuminating the long, inky vein of the Hudson, from here all the way to the city.

Acknowledgments

I don't know where my stories come from, or, really, how I write them. They are bits of magic, wrapped in luck, wrapped in endless hours staring at a screen. They begin without outline, and often take many years to write and revise, only to be put away, and dusted off again, and only when the right person is ready to find value in them.

I am beyond grateful that *that* right person continues to be my extraordinary editor, Vicki Lame. She sees something faintly shimmering in my messy words, and believes that, pushed, I am capable of revealing them to be stars.

In addition to Vicki, I am so lucky and honored to be with St. Martin's Press and Wednesday Books, and grateful for the work you all do there to get the story from manuscript to beautiful book, from beautiful book to shelves, from shelves to readers' hands. With special thanks to Sara Goodman, Jessica Preeg (whose manuscript-love notes mean more than she will ever know), Karen Masnica, D J Smyter, Brant Janeway, Janna Dokos, Elizabeth Curione, Cynthia Merman (thank you, too, for the tiny love-note gems interspersed with your skilled copyedits), James Iacobelli (oh, my cover!!), Anna Gorovoy (thank you for the scribbles . . .), and the amazing people in academic: Peter Jansen, Talia Sherer, and Anne Spieth, who get my books into one of the most important places: schools around the country!

But even before Vicki, and St. Martin's Press and Wednesday Books, there were many sets of eyes, helpful feedback, and rungs on the proverbial ladder up to finishing and selling a good book.

To my early BETA readers who gave valuable feedback: Jeff Fielder, Terry Turner, and Wendy Watts Scalfaro; to my later BETA readers who did the same: Jordyn Dees, Eden Wirth, and Dr. Barbara Kanal; and my most steadfast BETA readers who read more times than I can count, giving me constant encouragement, honest criticism, and fresh insight each time (lather, rinse, repeat): Annmarie Kearney Wood, Jessie Grembos, Jane Small, and my mother, Ginger, who said, "make it more of a painting." I only hope it is one fraction as beautiful as the paintings she makes come to life.

To my boys, Sam and Holden, who put up with my constant questions about what young adults say and don't say, what music they listen to, and which type of guitar is which.

To my extraordinarily talented friend Nora Raleigh Baskin, who pushed me toward greater authenticity, and without whom I would not have managed, as Paul Hankins so beautifully described, to make "art come of putting a skin suit on magic."

If therapeutic magic comes in a skin suit, Dr. Barbara Kanal is that so-dressed emanation; if Dr. Alvarez is good, much of her good comes from Dr. Barbara Kanal. . . . Thank you not only for your expertise reading, but your expertise as a ladder up all these years.

Penultimately, to Jim McCarthy, who sticks with me through the roller-coaster of this biz and works harder for me than he should have to . . . Your skill, time, and insight (and theatre critiques!) are endlessly appreciated. But you still owe me a lobster lunch, and I'm waiting.

And, finally, to David, who makes it possible for me to write and live my wildest dream every day; and to my father, Stuart, David, and my boys, who all show me day after day that there are boys who grow into men who are gentle but strong, introspective, funny, caring, and kind.

31901062747110